Consequences

Also by Sasha Campbell

Confessions

Suspicions

Scandals

Published by Kensington Publishing Corporation

Consequences

Sasha Campbell

Kensington Books
http://www.kensingtonbooks.com

DAFINA BOOKS are published by

Kensington Publishing Corp.
119 West 40th Street
New York, NY 10018

All Kensington titles, imprints and distributed lines are available at special quantity discounts for bulk purchases for sales promotions, premiums, fund-raising, and educational or institutional use. Special book excerpts or customized printings can also be created to fit specific needs. For details, write or phone the office of the Kensington Special Sales Manager. Kensington Publishing Corp., 119 West 40th Street, New York, NY 10018. Attn: Special Sales Department. Phone: 1-800-221-2647.

Dafina and the Dafina logo Reg. U.S. Pat. & TM Off.

ISBN-13: 978-0-7582-6943-0
ISBN-10: 0-7582-6943-9

First trade paperback printing: April 2013

10 9 8 7 6 5 4 3 2 1

Printed in the United States of America

Acknowledgments

To Verl Williams, the First Lady at Sugar Grove Missionary Baptist, for always helping me "go back to church" when I need it. Thank you for the Bible scriptures!

To my amazing husband, Gene Saunders, Jr., for answering my numerous questions about the army and post-traumatic stress disorder. I love you, Sniffles!

To my girl Naomi Chase for taking this long ride with me. I think I just hit another one out the park!

To fellow airman, Katie R. Almus for helping me brainstorm. I really miss working with you!

I want to thank Melody Vernor Bartel for reading my work, for providing a sistah feedback, and for always writing the very first review. I truly appreciate you, girl!

And to all my readers, thank you so much for the e-mails and comments on my Facebook page. Please continue to hit me up at sasha@sasha-campbell.com.

Enjoy the ride!

1

Nikki

"Nikki?"

"Trinette? Why are you whispering?" Even though I had asked the question, I had a sneaky suspicion I wasn't going to like the answer.

"I'm out in the garage, sitting in my Mercedes."

I dropped my pen onto the desk, then leaned back in the large leather chair and closed my eyes. By the tone of my best friend's voice, I knew this conversation was going to be a long one. "Trinette, why are you sitting out in your car?" The sooner we got to the point, the better. Talking to her sometimes was like pulling teeth.

" 'Cause I didn't want to take a chance of Leon hearing what I'm about to tell you," she whispered.

I groaned into the mouthpiece. "Hell, I'm not sure I want to hear this myself. What did you do now?"

Don't you know she had the nerve to sound offended?

"Me? Why does it always have to be me?" she argued.

I gave an impatient sigh. Sometimes she can be so damn dramatic. I had enough problems of my own and really didn't have time for her bullshit. "Trinette, c'mon, just get to it."

"Okay . . . okay . . . but you've gotta promise not to get mad," she pleaded.

I shook my head, then glanced over at the clock. It was almost six o'clock. I still had boxes of books to inventory and a million other things to do before heading to the radio station tonight.

"Netta, I am five seconds from hanging up on you. Five . . . four . . . three . . ."

"Okay, okay!" she blurted in a rush of words. "I think I'm pregnant."

It took several seconds before her announcement registered. Trust me, anyone who knew Trinette Meyers-Montgomery would understand my surprise.

"*Ohmygoodness* . . . that's wonderful! And about damn time!" I laughed because I never, and I mean never, expected this day to happen. "I'm finally going to be Aunt Nikki. What'd Leon say? I know he's happy!" There was a long pause and I knew then the shoe was about to drop.

"Um . . . I'm not sure if this baby's Leon's."

"What?" There was no way I heard her right. "Trinette, please tell me you haven't been doing what I think you've been doing?" Especially since she'd promised to never do it again.

"Nikki . . . I've been having an affair."

2

Trinette

I knew I was going to regret calling Nikki. Trust me, she may be my girl, but she's not one to talk. Don't judge Ms. Netta, not when you have skeletons in your own closet. And Nichole Sharice Truth definitely had secrets that she better hope were never revealed.

But despite her being a hypocrite, she's my best friend—hell, my only friend—and I needed someone to talk to about my latest dilemma.

Ever since I moved to Richmond with my husband of ten years, I have been trying to make new friends, but women were too critical and catty. I know because I'm one of them. I am clearly a dime piece, and no offense, but women have always felt threatened by me. Especially since I've always had a thing for stealing someone else's man. Anyway, since I didn't have anywhere else to turn, I had no choice but to call Nikki, who lives in St. Louis. It was times like this that I wished I still lived close by.

"Trinette, *ohmygoodness!* How could you?"

See, didn't I tell you she was going to judge me? I could hear the disappointment in her voice. Hell, she had no idea how guilty I already felt about this situation because I didn't set out to sleep around on my husband . . . again. It just sort of happened.

Before I moved to Richmond, I fucked around on a regular basis. Once, twice, three times a week, it didn't even matter. It wasn't even about the money, because my husband had plenty of that. It was the thrill of the chase and knowing I could get away with it. That is, until Leon got sick of my shit and asked for a divorce. Trust me, I wasn't used to being dumped and it hit hard. I was so devastated I begged him to take me back and vowed I would be forever faithful.

We renewed our vows and everything was going so well until a year ago when I started having an itch that I needed another man to scratch. I love my husband, really I do, but sex hasn't always been the best between us. Meaning, on most nights, he's gotten his long before I get mine; then I'm sneaking off to the bathroom to finish the job with my vibrator.

No, don't get me wrong. Despite the sex, Leon's a good man who has spoiled me rotten to the point that nothing is good enough unless it's the best. And I think that is the only reason why I have stayed with him as long as I have—because he allows me to be me.

When I attended college, it was with one plan, and that was to find myself a husband. The second I saw Leon pulling into the parking lot in a new car, I knew I was going to be his wife. What I hadn't realized was that he was a financial genius who had been recruited by several major banks. For a girl from the projects, I was mesmerized and so caught up in the life he could offer me that there was no way I could say no when he asked me to marry him. Even though I knew deep down in my heart I didn't love him the way a man truly deserved to be loved, because Ms. Netta didn't have time for the "L" word. I was more interested in being provided for. And it ain't been easy. For so many years all people did was take and I never received. But with Leon, it was my time to get everything I felt I deserved.

I settled in as the corporate wife and satisfied my husband's needs. I provided Leon with a home he was proud to return to every night and a bed where I rocked his mothafuckin' world. In exchange, he gave me a hefty allowance that most women could only dream of having.

But over the last year, I realized that money just wasn't everything. Can you believe it? Me? Trinette Meyers-Montgomery saying money isn't everything. Well, it's true. At thirty-three, I finally discovered that no amount of money would fill that empty void in my heart. Something was truly missing in my marriage and I wanted something more. And when I met Jrue Jarmon, I finally figured it out. I needed to love somebody.

Don't get me wrong. After Leon and I renewed our vows, I had every intention of finally being committed to our marriage. That's saying a lot for a woman who'd been messing around on her husband since before the ink had dried on our marriage license.

I used to think something was wrong with me when it came to men and relationships. I had even started blaming it on my Uncle Sonny, who had climbed in my bed at age twelve, robbed me of my virginity, and continued raping me until I was sixteen. For years, every time I crawled into bed with a man and made him pay for some ass in cash, I blamed him and my crackhead mama, Darlene, for making me the woman I had become.

Leon saved me from a life that I never wanted to look back upon, and part of me stayed with him as long as I have because I felt I owed him. I tried to make it work. Lord knows I did, but I craved something more than my husband. Leon is a brilliant man with simple needs who never could challenge me sexually. A lot of that has to do with the fact that I'm a beast in and out of the bedroom.

"What do you mean, it sorta happened?"

Sometimes Nikki's worse than having a mama. "What I mean is . . . I'm in love."

Nikki started laughing in my ear. "Netta, puh-leeze! The Tin Man's gotta have a heart to fall in love."

I don't know why she thought I was heartless. Sure, I've used people along the way and stepped on the backs of anyone who stood in the path of me getting what I wanted, but I am far from cold.

"Nikki, I'm being serious. I'm in love."

I heard a heavy sigh and I knew she was probably rubbing her forehead. Hell, I know I stressed my girl out with some of the crazy shit I do, but she had no choice but to listen, because I didn't have anyone else I could talk to.

"So who is this guy?" she finally asked.

I closed my eyes, suddenly feeling so ashamed as I said, "My boss."

"Oh, God, Netta! This is getting worse. And you think you're pregnant by your boss? Have you really lost your damn mind?"

"I think I have. For the first time in my life I've met a man who touches me in more ways than just sex, and it feels so good." I was shaking from simply expressing my feelings. "Nikki, listen . . . I love Jrue."

"Jrue?" She gave a rude snort. "Is he rich?"

I already knew what she was getting at. "Yes, but it has nothing to do with his family's money."

"Mmm-hmm." She didn't at all sound convinced. I told you Nikki is always quick to judge me.

She thinks since she's the host of the popular radio talk show *Truth Hurts*, where she gives relationship advice to thousands of listeners, that made her an expert. I am the one with degrees in counseling and social work.

"Netta, girl, what you're feeling is lust, not love," she said, trying to diagnose me.

"How the hell you gonna tell me what I'm feeling? I know what love is! I can't sleep. I can't think of nothing but him and having him hold me in his arms. Hell, I can't get enough of the way his skin smells."

"What?" Nikki gasped, then chuckled. "The way his skin smells. Are you serious? You got it that bad?"

See, I knew it was going to be hard for her to believe me.

I was afraid to answer. Should I deny how I feel or just keep admitting my feelings? Expressing myself was something I had never been good at doing, but I was so desperate I was willing to give it a try.

"Yes, dammit! That's what I'm trying to tell you. I am so in love with this man that my head hurts!" I still couldn't believe I had let my guard down and let someone get in, but I had. Now I couldn't go a minute without thinking about that fine-ass man sliding between my thighs.

"Oh, Trinette! This is a big mess. I can't believe you weren't using condoms!" Okay, so she was back to treating me like a kid again.

I shifted uncomfortably on the front seat of my car. "For your information, we *did* use condoms. They just broke once . . . or twice." That's what I get for buying that *barely there* brand.

Nikki breathed heavily and mumbled something under her breath that I couldn't make out, and that was probably a good thing because I was three seconds away from going off.

"So when will you know for sure if you're pregnant?"

"My period's already a week late. You know how I feel about taking an at-home pregnancy test, so I'm going into the clinic on my way to work tomorrow." The last time I trusted one of those over-the-counter tests, it gave me a false positive. I had spent almost a week hiding out in my dorm room, wondering who the daddy was, before I'd finally made an appointment down at the free clinic and discovered all that anxiety had been for nothing. After that I never trusted self-testing again.

Nikki gave another heavy sigh. "I just pray that you're not

pregnant. It's really going to complicate things if you are. Especially when we both know how badly Leon's been wanting a baby."

It was one of the reasons why Leon had agreed to give our marriage one last try. Because I had promised to get off the birth control and finally have a baby. Me? Ms. Netta pregnant? You gotta be crazy. I admit, I thought I was too selfish to be a mother because everything always has to be about me. With a child, I would become second, and that wasn't even an option. So I kept taking my birth control pills that Leon knew nothing about. However, once I started having an affair with Jrue, I started losing my focus and got so wrapped up emotionally I was forgetting appointments and, most importantly, to take my birth control pills.

"I know, Nikki. Don't you know I've been sitting out in this car thinking about how I've made a mess of my life? A baby complicates things."

"Ya think! Goodness." She groaned into the phone. "So what are you going to do *if* you're pregnant?"

I answered without hesitation, "I'm going to get an abortion." Silently I pleaded for her to understand. Nikki was quiet and I knew why. She doesn't believe in abortions. She gave birth to her first child even when she and her husband had barely been able to take care of themselves. "Nikki, I don't have a choice."

"Look, why don't we cross that bridge when you get there? I . . . I just hate to see you make a hasty decision before you have a chance to think it through."

"What's there to think about? I can't have this baby!" I screamed, then panicked when I realized I was talking loud enough for Leon to have accidently heard me. Dammit. There was no way in hell I wanted him to know or even suspect that I was pregnant. "I just can't and I won't," I added in a low voice.

Instead of arguing with me, Nikki did like she always does and changed the subject. "So what's the deal with you and this Jrue? How does he feel about you?"

I smiled at the mention of his name and felt my juices flowing below. Goodness. He had that type of effect on me. "He told me he loves me."

There was silence and I could just see Nikki at her desk shaking her damn head, sending those honey-brown dread-locks flying in every direction.

"You know I don't approve of half the shit you do, but if you're certain that you're in love, then . . . I'm sure together we can come up with a solution."

"Hey, at least that's something," I replied with a soft laugh.

"So, then, what's the plan? Is this guy pressuring you to divorce Leon so that the two of you can be together?"

I glanced over at the door to make sure it was still closed, then leaned in close and whispered into the phone, "Well . . . there *is* one more thing I forgot to tell."

"And what's that?" Nikki groaned.

I wet my lips and mumbled, "Jrue's married."

3

Nikki

"It's ten o'clock and you're listening to Ms. Nikki Truth, the host of the most talked about radio show in the Midwest, *Truth Hurts*. As my listeners know, I don't believe in holding your hand. If you want my advice, then you better have the balls to accept the truth . . . even if it hurts. Caller, you're on the air."

"Hi, Ms. Nikki. My name is Delicious."

"Good evening, Delicious. With a name like that, your story is bound to be good," I said with a soft chuckle, trying to set the mood.

"My problem is my man doesn't satisfy me. Don't get me wrong, he's fine as hell, educated, and got a good job, but the sex isn't good."

"Haven't you heard the saying, you gotta teach a man how to satisfy you?"

"I've tried that. Like I said, I have a good man and he goes out of his way to cater to all of my needs, but sex isn't one of them."

"Okay, then, if he's willing to do whatever it takes to satisfy you, then what's the problem?"

There was a slight pause. *"He ain't working with much."*

I tried to keep the grin from my voice. "Okay, I can see where that would be a problem."

"It's a big problem. At first I tried to listen to all that mess about

it ain't the size of the ship but the motion. Well, how can you get motion if you can't feel anything? All he does is poke me with his pencil."

I laughed, trying to lighten the situation. "Have you tried talking to him about it?"

"And hurt his feelings? No way. He thinks we're a perfect fit because he slides right on in. That man has no idea the reason why he slides in is because he's no wider than my thumb."

I didn't know what it was, but lately I'd been giving a helluva lot of advice on sex. Trust me, I was no expert. "Well, you're going to have to decide if you love that man enough to live with his shortcomings. No pun intended."

"I love him with all my heart. He is so good to me. Gets up every Sunday and together we go to church. God couldn't have given me a better man, but I'm left feeling unsatisfied, and I don't know what to do."

"I think before you end up doing something that you might regret, you need to talk to him."

"Well . . . see that's the problem. I already slept with someone else."

I leaned in closer to the microphone. "Ooh, now we were getting to the juicy part! Please continue."

"Well, one of the guys at work had been trying to get with me for years, and last week a bunch of us went out for drinks and afterward I went with him to his apartment."

"And . . ." I urged for dramatic effect.

"Ohmygoodness! Sex was off the charts! That man made my toes curl!"

"Good sex will do that to ya." I laughed.

"It was so good I met him at his house today for lunch. I can't stay away, and it's not even the guy. He's broke, with five kids by four different women. He's nothing I would ever date."

"But he's satisfying your needs," I added.

"Good Lord, yes! That man has made me realize what I have

been missing all these years. Now I find myself comparing my man to him, who, I have to say, is packing a baseball bat between his legs! Hell, the other night I was afraid my man was going to fall in behind him."

I covered my mouth to keep from laughing and stared through the glass at my producer, Tristan, who was also having a hard time holding it together.

"Delicious, let me give you a piece of advice. If you truly love this man, you gotta be honest with him and tell him the truth. You're never going to find that hundred percent with any man, yet there are just some things you can't live without. For you, maybe sex is one of those things."

"Thanks."

"Good luck." I ended the call. "The phone lines are lit up; let's take some calls and see what my listeners have to say. Caller, you're on the air."

"Good evening, Ms. Nikki. This is Cortez. I have to say I can't understand women."

I chuckled. "You are not alone, Cortez."

"I'm serious. Women say they want a good man and when they get one, they still ain't happy."

"I think that's where the debate of what constitutes a good man comes into play."

"That man is a good provider. If it walks like a duck and it talks like a duck, then it's a duck. Hell, I work long hours at Burger Heaven, flipping burgers over that hot grill. I bring home my entire check, and yet my girl still ain't happy. She wants me to strive for something better. Why? I've been working there almost eight years and have a golden spatula to prove it."

"No offense, Cortez, but women want men who are not only hard workers, but who are striving for something more."

"I am striving for more. After ten years, I shall be promoted to shift supervisor." He had the nerve to have an attitude. I guess I would, too, if I made my living flipping burgers.

"Then get ready for two more years of unhappiness. Next caller." I ended the call and pressed the next blinking red light.

"Ms. Nikki, this is Mimi. I just wanted to say, Delicious, girl, go buy some toys, it beats having a no-good man any day."

I chuckled. "I know that's right. Thanks for calling. You hear that. Delicious, maybe you should try adding toys to your relationship. Caller, you're on the air."

"Ms. Nikki, Delicious needs to dump that pencil dick! It doesn't matter how hard she squeezes her pelvic muscles, she's never going to feel anything down there. Trust me, I had one. I ain't never felt shit, so I was shocked when my doctor told me I was pregnant."

I had to laugh at that one.

"Thanks for calling. Next caller."

I took a few more calls and before long it was time to sign off for the night. "This is Nikki Truth at Hot 97 WJPC signing off. Remember to tell the truth even if it hurts. Good night."

Ron Isley came onto the air. I took my headset off and leaned back in the seat. Another good night and I was pleased. At least something in my life was going right.

Within minutes the door opened and my dear friend and producer Tristan Bell came into my office. "Well, girlfriend, another *fabulous* night!" he said with a dramatic pose.

I grinned at him as he batted his long fake eyelashes. He was such a diva with perfect nutty brown skin and black shoulder-length weave that bounced with every move. I'd known Tristan since I started working at the radio station, so we've been friends for almost eight years. After Trinette left St. Louis and joined her husband in Richmond, Tristan and I had become besties; that is, as long as Trinette doesn't know anything about it. That chick is territorial when it comes to our friendship; although most of the time our relationship was one sided, which meant she only called when she needed something. Just thinking about our phone conversation still had me shaking my head.

I think there are some women who are meant to be tied down to one man and then there are women like Trinette, who are meant to be free to do whatever she wants whenever she wants with every Tom, Dick, and Barry as long as he's got enough money to keep her in the lifestyle to which she's grown accustomed. Don't get me wrong, I love that girl like a sister, but she is definitely a piece of work.

Tristan's high-pitched voice broke into my thoughts. "Some friends and I are having a get-together at my place this weekend. You and Donovan are invited."

I gave Tristan a hard look. "Now, you know Donovan ain't coming to a barbecue with you and all your flaming friends." I wasn't trying to be mean, just keeping it real. Hell, it took my husband long enough just to get used to being around Tristan. It wasn't that Donovan didn't like gay men. He was just like any other black straight man, ready to go off if you even hinted at the possibility.

Tristan sucked his teeth, then wiggled into the room making a fashion statement. Of course he looked great in Baby Phat jeans, a black blouse, and black rhinestone studded pumps. "I really want you to meet this *fiiine* dude I'm seeing."

"Another one," I said with a chuckle. Between Tristan and Trinette's social calendars, I couldn't seem to keep up.

He took a seat on the comfortable old couch beside my desk and crossed his long legs. "Uh-uh. This one . . . there's something special about him. No, listen, Nikki! I'm serious. The second I spotted him walking into Straight Shooters, I knew I wanted my lips all over that gorgeous body."

I swung around on my seat, laughing. Tristan always did have a way of lifting my spirits. Lord knows I needed any distraction I could get. Otherwise, I'd find myself thinking about the problems I had at home.

"So I guess you took him home."

His dark eyes widened. "No, we went to this little coffee shop on the east side and spent most of the night talking."

That was definitely a first. Usually they went to some motel getting their freak on. "So is this guy gay or on the down low?" I asked, tossing him a curious look.

"If you're asking if he's married, then the answer is yes. But he's planning to leave her. I'm hoping a little loving will help persuade him sooner." He ran his tongue across his glossy lips suggestively.

"You are so nasty."

He gave me a knowing look and smiled. "I know."

I was still laughing when my eyes traveled over to the clock. "Speaking of nasty . . . I better get home to my husband."

"Must be nice to have in-house dick. Some of us aren't as fortunate," Tristan added with a playful eye roll.

"I wouldn't say all that," I murmured, especially since we hadn't made love in over a week.

Tristan must have seen something on my face for him to lean forward and ask, "Are things getting any better?"

I hated talking bad about my marriage, especially at this point everything should have been perfect, so I simply shrugged. "Barely, but I'm taking it one day at a time."

"Just give him time," he reassured me. "It's only been a few months."

I nodded. "Thanks."

Tristan rose. "And kiss Aiden for me."

I smiled at the mention of my two-year-old son. "I will."

After he left, I gathered up my things and slipped my purse onto my shoulder, and we walked out to the parking lot together.

"If you decide to come this weekend, let me know. My Big Daddy is planning to stop through."

My brow rose. "Really? Wow! Maybe he *is* planning to come out the closet."

He grinned broadly. "I told ya! Smooches!" He gave me a two-finger wave, then strut his long legs over to his Impala like he was moving down a runway. Like I said, Tristan was such a diva.

I climbed into my Lexus and headed toward home. While I listened to Marsha Ambrosius's CD, I said a silent prayer. *"Please let tonight be a good night."* I wasn't asking for much. I just wanted things back the way they used to be.

Donovan Truth was serving in the National Guard and had done two deployments: one to Iraq and the second to Afghanistan. It had been rough for us, considering when he'd left for Iraq our marriage had been on the rocks. After the death of our first child, Mimi, we just couldn't seem to get our relationship back on track, so his deployment had been like a blessing because it had given us the distance we needed. Luckily, when he came home, we were able to save our marriage, and within a month I discovered I was pregnant with our second child. That had been a time for us to start over new. Then a year after Aiden was born, Donovan's unit was being deployed again. It had been three months since his return from Afghanistan, but it was still evident that the second twelve-month deployment had taken a toll on Donovan. When my husband came home, he wasn't the same man who had left.

I know that, as a military wife, I have to be supportive of my husband and help him through the tough times, but sometimes it's more than I can bear. The mood swings, the distance, sometimes it's like he's still gone. I just don't know what to do anymore except pray and take it one day at a time.

I pulled into the garage beside his Cadillac Escalade. It was his gift to himself after two deployments. Who needed a gas guzzler in this economy, yet I just nodded and said nothing.

I stepped into the house and Rudy, my spoiled schnauzer,

greeted me at the door. "Hey, stinky butt. How's Mama's baby?" I cooed while I showed him some love. That little boy had been with us since he was a puppy and was a part of our family.

I looked across the room and saw the light on in the family room. I gave Rudy a treat, then hung my purse on a chair in the kitchen and stepped into the family room, located at the rear of the house. Donovan was relaxing on the couch, watching the basketball game.

"Whassup, baby," he said as soon as he spotted me stepping through the doorway and signaled for me to come over.

I breathed a sigh of relief, then smiled, sauntered over, and lowered across his lap. "Hey, handsome." We kissed and I could taste the tequila on Donovan's breath. Ever since his return, he'd been drinking way too much. I bit my tongue and decided not to say anything. For one night, I just wanted everything to at least *feel* normal. "Where's Aiden?"

Donovan planted another wet kiss to my lips before answering. "After his bath he was out like a light." He kissed me some more. "How was the show tonight?" I was surprised. Asking about my radio show was something he rarely did anymore.

I smiled. "It was good. Women talked about how they loved their men, yet they weren't satisfying them in bed."

He winked. "Glad you don't have that problem."

"How do you know I don't?" I purred playfully.

"Because your man knows how to put it down."

I started laughing and thought Donovan would join in, but instead his eyes darkened as he locked his gaze with mine.

"Oh, so you got jokes. Then I guess your man needs to show you." In one fluid motion, he lifted me into his arms and his mouth covered mine hungrily. One thing about my husband, he was one helluva kisser. My arms circled his neck and I leaned forward and felt the strong pumping of his heart as he carried me upstairs to our bedroom. Already I could feel myself getting moist. Donovan was right. He knew how to put it down in the bedroom, and I was more than anxious to feel him sliding inside of me.

When we got into the room, he lowered me slowly to my feet. He raised his arms over his head while I pulled off his shirt and tossed it. Damn, I loved looking at his gorgeous body. My husband was redbone, five-ten with a medium build and a chest and arms that were the result of spending hours pumping iron at the gym. My eyes followed the narrow trail of dark hair over the ripples in his stomach. Donovan dropped his jeans to the floor and stepped forward.

"You want some of this, don't you?"

"You know I do, so quit playing," I teased.

"How do you want it?" he asked, then reached up and released every button of my blouse.

"I want it long and hard," I said, tossing the fabric onto the floor.

"I think I can handle that." He grinned, flashing that smile I loved so much. My man had been blessed with perfect teeth.

"I missed you, Don. Now please make love to your horny wife before she explodes."

"Well, we definitely can't be having that. Last thing I want is for your friends to think your man ain't on his job."

"Then get wit it, sexy," I said playfully.

"At your service, madam." His erection thrust against my belly and I got all hot and bothered at the thought of my husband making love to me again.

Reaching behind me, I unclasped my bra and tossed that sucker across the room, then waited while my husband slid my black lace panties over my hips and down to my ankles.

"Hold up. Don't move."

Standing in front of him, I watched his eyes as they took their time traveling the length of my body.

"Dayum! How did I get to be so lucky?"

I giggled and kicked the panties away. "I guess it was your lucky day," I cooed.

Donovan snaked a hand around my waist, pulling me against the length of his hard body. I drew in a sharp breath while he left a trail of kisses along my neck and cheek.

"I'm the lucky one," I said.

Reaching down, I cupped my magic stick, stroking the length, and was already getting excited thinking about having all those inches pounding between my thighs. Before he was deployed, we'd had sex almost every day and dammit, I wanted those days back.

"I think someone misses me," I purred as I stroked the tip of his dick with my thumb until Donovan sucked in a hiss.

"Hell yeah, I missed you." One of his hands rounded my ass while the other eased my fingers from around his penis. "Yo, you better quit before it's over before we even get started." Laughing, he backed me slowly toward the bed. "Lie down, baby," he ordered.

He didn't need to tell me twice. I slid up on the bed and exhaled as his warm, hard body covered mine. Donovan stared down at me. "I haven't been taking care of my wife's needs. But all that's about to change."

God, I hoped so.

His fingers traveled downward and didn't stop until he reached my slippery wet folds, where he slid two fingers inside.

"Yes." Moaning, I arched off the bed.

"You like that?" he urged.

I shuddered. "Yesss, you know I do." Any attentive husband knew what it took to please his wife. Don pulled his fingers out to the fingertip and then pushed again, touching my G-spot. I was beyond ready and started rocking my hips, meeting his strokes. "Don . . . now . . . please hurry," I whined, and was seconds away from exploding when Donovan slid down on the bed, positioning his head between my thighs.

"Hold up, Nikki. First I need to eat that pussy." Pressing his mouth to my sensitive lips made me cry out with pleasure. Then he licked and sucked, getting his eat on until I thought I would lose my mind. "You taste so good." He stroked me up, down, and around, using his tongue and teeth with this move that jerked my hips up off the mattress. And when he sucked at my swollen clit, I was squirming on the bed and moaning hysterically.

"Oooh . . . baby!" And then I came hard enough that I felt like I was having a seizure. My entire body shuddered until his tongue took that final stroke across my clit. I was delirious with need by the time Don moved up on the bed and spread my thighs wide.

"You missed Daddy?" he asked.

"Yes, Mama missed you," I panted. My body was weak with need. "Now, please. I *need* you inside of me." With one push my baby drove inside and I cried out in shock, then exhaled and drew him deeper.

"Nikki . . . oooh, baby," he groaned, then began thrusting, pounding his length into me. I cried out his name and raised my legs back toward my shoulders, wanting to feel all of him, driving deeper. Each thrust wasn't enough until an entire week of pent-up frustration burst free.

"Don! Yesss . . . *yesss!*" I cried out with incredible force.

"That's it," Donovan groaned as I squeezed my walls tightly around his dick. Then he began to move faster, and the muscles along his back tensed. "Aughhh!" he cried out as he came, then collapsed on top of me.

I smiled and trailed soft, wet kisses along his shoulder. How I loved him. This was the man I had loved since junior high. We took it slow. I didn't give him my virginity until our sophomore year, and I never regretted it. As soon as we graduated high school, we got married and I never looked back.

"I love you, Nikki."

I sighed and closed my eyes. "And I love you."

And then I prayed that things could stay that way. Although at the back of my mind, I already knew that before things finally got better, it was going to get a lot worse.

I just had no idea how bad.

4

Trinette

I pulled into the parking lot and was pleased to see staff parking spaces were available close to the building. Trust me, *that* was a good thing. I didn't know what it was with kids, but the students attending the community college where I worked as a program coordinator were either too stupid to read the RESERVED parking signs or just didn't give a damn, because most times they were taking up staff parking. My parking. Trust and believe, Ms. Netta had no problem calling security and demanding that he put tickets on all their damn cars.

I climbed out of my CLK500 Mercedes, then straightened my gray Gucci skirt, making sure there wasn't a wrinkle in place. I spent a great deal of money making sure I looked good, and rumpled was unacceptable. Satisfied I looked fabulous as ever, I sashayed toward the building.

Students were hurrying off to class, but I saw the way they were looking at me out of the corners of their eyes. Hey, what can I say? I'm a bona fide dime piece.

As I drew closer to the building, I could feel my temperature rising. It wasn't because it was April and the forecast was seventy degrees. Nope. I felt like that at just the thought of seeing Jrue again. I didn't know what it was about that fine brotha, but he was like potato chips. One was never enough. I couldn't wait to feel his arms wrapped around me and those juicy, thick lips pressed against mine.

"Good morning, Trinette."

I swept my fabulous weave over one shoulder and gave the security guard, Herschel, a nipple-clenching smile. "How's it going, handsome?" He was nothing to look at with his high-water slacks and round belly, but if I wanted him to keep dishing out parking tickets when I needed, then I had to be willing to throw him a bone every now and then.

I moved into the building and immediately my eyes were drawn to the clock up on the wall. I was thirty minutes late—not that I was really that concerned. After all, I was sexing the boss. Besides, I had something important to do this morning. In a couple of hours, I would have answers and could get past my ridiculous *situation* and enjoy a fabulous weekend.

Pregnant? Me? There was no way in hell I was having a baby. The Lord knew who to bless with babies, and that woman wasn't me. I was selfish and spoiled. Some things were just meant to be, and that wasn't one of those things. Besides, I'd been having cramps all morning and was certain my period was going to start before Sunday.

As soon as I stepped into the Career Pathways office, I was met by the smell of our administrative assistant Josie's cheap perfume. I started to think that chick bathed in that shit.

"Good morning," I said as I swung my hips down the hall, giving my best Miss America wave. Sometimes I can't believe how beautiful I really am.

I worked as a program coordinator for the Great Expectations program at John Tyler Community College. I helped children who've grown up in foster care gain access to higher education and transition successfully from the foster care system to living independently. I took care of their tuition, purchased their books, and even helped the single moms find daycare if needed. It was a rewarding opportunity, and I still couldn't believe how lucky I was to have been blessed with such an amazing job. But the icing on the cake was the director of the Career Pathways department, Jrue Jarmon.

I unlocked the door and stepped into my small office, then slid behind my desk. From the other end of the hall I could hear Jrue on the phone, and that man had my heart pounding hard beneath my breasts. Quickly, I reached into my middle desk drawer for a handheld mirror and made sure my makeup and hair were still perfect, and wasn't at all surprised to find that they were.

By the time I had my computer booted and tuned in to *The Steve Harvey Morning Show*, I heard the clicking of high heels coming down the hall. Zakiya popped up at my door.

"What's up, girl?"

I looked up and took a moment to assess her attire, and had to give her a nod of approval for the animal print wrap dress she was rocking. Even her weave looked good. Zee was a pretty woman. Not as cute as me, but definitely on point. No offense, but I'm a caramel deluxe, so it takes a lot to compare to a size sixteen beauty like myself.

Since I'd started working at the college, Zakiya and I had become close as I could ever come to being friends with a chick besides Nikki. Nikki and I grew up together and are like sisters. But Zakiya was cool people. We shopped and hung out at the clubs together on occasion. She wasn't Nikki, but she'd do.

"Good morning, Trinette. Dory was by this morning looking for you."

Dory was part of the Great Expectations program. She had spent years in foster care after being sexually abused by her father. Her mother had turned a blind eye just like mine had when I was her age. One of the reasons why I had majored in social work was because I wanted to make a difference for these kids, and it was hard not to feel sorry for each and every one of them. I knew what they had gone through. I felt their pain, and that's what made me so passionate about my job.

"Did she say what she wanted?"

Zakiya shook her head and I loved the way her weave swung along her shoulders. Yep, she definitely had spent money on some good-quality hair.

"She showed up with little Quita. She was running all over the place. I thought Jrue was going to have a fit when she ran into his office. That man knows absolutely nothing about kids." She laughed.

Just the mention of Jrue and kids made my stomach do a nervous roll. He didn't have any and neither did I, and as far as I knew that's the way we both wanted it. I nodded. "I'll give her a call."

I was hoping Zee would have gone on down the hall to her own office, because I knew for a fact she had plenty of work to do. She monitored the Dual-Enrollment program, which were high-school students taking free college courses for credits. Jrue had mentioned during one of our lovemaking sessions that he was still waiting on this month's status report. But instead of leaving, she stepped farther into the room.

"So what you got planned for the weekend?"

I grinned. "Leon and I are going to see Kevin Hart this weekend."

Her eyes lit up at the mention of the stand-up comedian's name. "Ooh, girl! I wanted to see that show, but there were no good seats left."

That's because her husband wasn't the CFO of one of the most powerful banks in America like mine. Leon had connections, so there were always tickets to concerts and sporting events. Nothing but the best for me, and Leon made sure I got it. *Always.* The lifestyle he provided was the main reason why our relationship had lasted as long as it had. The other was I truly did love my husband in my own unique way.

We were talking about how funny Kevin Hart had been in *Think Like a Man* when Jrue appeared in my doorway. Oh, that man is gorgeous, with his dark chocolate skin, goatee, and midnight black eyes.

"Good morning, Trinette."

I leaned back in the chair and greeted him with a smile. "Good morning, Jrue."

I noticed the way Zakiya was staring at my man like she wanted to lick him up and down like a Popsicle. He definitely had that effect on women. Luckily, I was the only woman he had eyes for.

"Could I have a moment with you to discuss something private?" he asked and looked so serious I sat up straight on the chair.

"Uh . . . sure." I glanced over at Zakiya, hoping she caught the hint and was glad she had.

"I'll see you at lunch," Zakiya mumbled before she walked out of my office and closed the door behind her with a click.

Jrue stared at me as if he were a starving man and I was the main course. He reached over, turned the lock, and then walked toward my desk. "Hey, sexy." He stopped in front of me.

"Hello yourself." Smiling, I flipped my hair away from my face and tilted my chin to greet his succulent mouth. As soon as our lips met, a warm feeling flooded my body. It was an emotion that was so new to me. I'm not going to lie. It felt so good. I was so crazy about this dude that I didn't know where my head was most times. The second his tongue slipped between my lips, my coochie started throbbing. I just loved the way Jrue kissed me. He made me feel loved and special. When he finally broke the kiss, he stared down at me with those beautiful, dark eyes of his. I just loved black men.

"I missed you. I was starting to wonder if you were coming in this morning."

I sighed, then nodded my head. "I had a . . . I was just running late this morning."

"I'm glad you could make it." He kissed me gently once more.

I grinned up at him. "So am I."

Jrue took my hand, then lifted me onto the end of my desk and stood between my parted thighs. "I woke up this morning with a hard dick."

"Really? Then you shoulda asked your wife to take care of you," I said with a playful eye roll.

He stepped closer, reaching for me. "I don't want my wife . . . I want you."

I smirked. Of course he did.

He didn't even wait for a response. His fingers dipped beneath the hem of my skirt and grazed my throbbing kitty-cat. Cocky ass.

"What are you doing?" I asked like I didn't already know. He had an insatiable habit of scheduling private meetings in my office.

"What do you think?" Jrue murmured, then leaned forward and claimed my mouth in a kiss so filled with hunger I had to hold on to keep from falling. Oh, how I loved this man.

"I missed you last night," he mentioned between kisses.

I leaned back. "I guess you should've canceled dinner with your wife." I rolled my eyes and was still pissed at him for canceling on me. We had been meeting at the Holiday Inn in Colonial Heights every Thursday evening for the last six months. His wife had the nerve to drag my man to a fundraiser with her. Sometimes I wondered who was wearing the pants in that relationship.

"I'll make it up to you . . . I promise." Jrue's skillful hands roamed over my luscious curves before finally settling on top of my ass, where he gripped and squeezed, making sure I knew how hard his dick was.

Hell yeah, I noticed.

"Nasty ass," I whispered. I got a kick out of our little game. "That's all that's ever on your mind." That wasn't completely true, but it felt good saying it.

Jrue lifted a hand and caressed the side of my face. "Baby, you have that kinda effect on me."

"Is that so?" I said, gazing up adoringly into his eyes.

"Yes, that's so," he confirmed.

My nipples were hard, not to mention heat was settling between my thighs. His tongue eased into my mouth and I met his confident strokes. I moaned, then leaned forward, pressing my pelvis against his, desperate to feel every inch of him. And my man had plenty.

Jrue's hands clutched at my hips, holding me to him. It was his way of letting me know without a doubt what he wanted from me. "I need some pussy," he hissed.

"Is that so?" I whispered. Who was I to deny him what he wanted? Especially when I wanted him as well. With Jrue I had found my sexual equal.

Jrue sucked and licked at my throat. My breasts swelled and my nipples puckered. "Play with my titties," I commanded. Naturally, my man aimed to please and grabbed the twins.

I had to struggle to keep my voice down to a soft moan, which wasn't easy to do, considering how good Jrue made me feel. I already had a suspicion the other women in the office knew what was going on. I saw the looks and the way they rolled their eyes every time Jrue said he needed to talk to me *in private*. Jealous hos.

One of his hands continued to play with my breasts while the other left my hips and smoothed its way down under my skirt again. As soon as I felt his warm touch, I shuddered with excitement.

"What's wrong?" he asked barely above a whisper.

"Nothing. Nothing at all," I breathed. Except that touching my inner thigh was not enough. I wanted those long fingers to climb higher, where I needed to feel him most.

As if he could read my mind, Jrue growled against my throat. His fingers slid upward and the closer he got, the tighter my muscles clenched. I braced myself and the second he stroked my clit, my eyelids flew open with a gasp. The intense look on his face was almost my undoing. Lust was blazing in his dark eyes while his hand cupped my coochie possessively.

"Jrue," I warned.

"What's wrong? You want me to stop?" he asked as he slipped a finger under the elastic band at my crotch and stroked.

"Yes . . . no." I licked my lips, trying to stifle a moan. I couldn't think straight when he touched me like that. "You're starting something."

He arched a brow at me. "That's the plan." He separated my lips and stroked my swollen clit while he spoke. "You're wet. Seems to me I'm not the only one who's horny."

"Yes, God, yes," I whimpered. Jrue always did have a way with words.

"Then let's get this party started. Turn around," he ordered.

His words were music to my ears. I loved doggy-style.

I swung around and Jrue lightly pushed at the center of my back, drawing me down until I was flat against the desk. Without hesitation, he lifted my skirt over my hips. "Damn," he hissed softly.

I smiled and could just imagine how I looked leaning over the desk, with my phat caramel ass in the air, thighs slightly parted, and his gaze devouring me from my ass down to my brand-new pair of Manolos. Did I mention how much I enjoyed fucking in designer pumps?

"Spread your legs."

I assumed the position. It wasn't the first time we had made love in my office.

He chuckled lightly. "Now, push that ass back and hold on to the desk."

He didn't have to tell me twice. I heard a zipper and his slacks fell to the floor. In a matter of seconds he had a condom on. Jrue moved between my thighs, gripping my ass just the way I liked it, and spread me wide. He slowly eased inside a little at a time, and I thought I was going to die from the pleasure.

"Oooh yes," I moaned as he slid farther, then pulled out slightly before pushing forward again. Dammit, he was teasing me, reminding me who was in control. Jrue knew just how to make sure my body craved him.

I squirmed. "I want to feel all of it, dammit!" I said, urging him to pound my ass. Finally, he pushed all the way in. Nothing had ever felt so good. Using the desk as leverage, I rocked my body back, matching his steady rhythm.

Jrue held on to my hips and penetrated hard and deep. With my mouth closed, I moaned, trying to hold it in, when what I wanted to do was scream at the top of my lungs how good this man was making me feel.

"Ooooh, shit, you feel good!" Jrue groaned and steadied his strokes.

Reaching around, his thumb massaged my clit again. And when he pulled out and slammed back in again, I cried out his name. "JJJJJrue!"

"Shhh," he whispered and began to move faster, driving even deeper. "Don't forget . . . the walls . . . are thin," he reminded me between pumps.

Fuck it. Let them listen.

Within seconds, Jrue was sexing me harder and burying himself so deep I wasn't sure how much longer I could hold on. "Come for me, Trinette," he coaxed, and that was all the encouragement I needed. My inner walls squeezed his length as a long and powerful climax tore through my body. I clamped my teeth into my lower lip, suppressing Jrue's name, and screamed inside. Jrue continued to pound and shortly after I heard a loud moan; then his body slumped on top of me.

"Do you think anyone heard us?" I managed between breaths.

"I don't give a damn," Jrue growled, and pressed his lips to my ear. "Nothing is gonna stop me from making love to you."

I wanted to say his wife had last night, but decided to leave it alone.

"How about on Sunday we drive down to Charlottesville and have dinner?"

What he really meant was Ms. Netta was on the menu.

"It's gonna cost you," I warned.

Grinning, he nodded. "I think I can afford it."

Yes, he could. His grandfather, a real-estate tycoon, was loaded and had left him millions.

We fixed our clothes; then he kissed me once more and returned to his office. I reached for the can of air freshener from under my desk and quickly sprayed the room before I opened the door. No one would think twice about the heavy scent since I always liked my office to smell good. Just like me.

The phone on my desk rang, indicating it was time for me to get my ass back to work. I grabbed the phone and sang, "Great Expectations, Trinette Montgomery speaking."

An even, merry voice came over the phone. "Good afternoon, Trinette. This is Natasha, Dr. Parks' nurse."

As soon as she identified herself, I sat up straight on the chair. "Oh, yes. I've been waiting for your call." My heart was pounding so hard I could barely get the words out.

"I just wanted to call and congratulate you. Your test came back positive. You're pregnant."

5

Nikki

I pushed the cart to the front of the store. My assistant, Karen, had been busy checking out customers all morning, so I had no problem pitching in when time permitted. The one thing I loved about owning my own bookstore was seeing all of the new books as they came in from the distributor.

I was in the African-American section adding a few new authors to the shelves, as well as some of the more popular ones. I noticed two copies of Naomi Chase's latest book that were supposed to be on reserve behind the desk had accidently gotten in the wrong pile. Ever since that author came blazing into the literary world, her books were hard for me to keep in my store.

Some of my customers complained that I segregated black books, but I did it for a reason. I wanted to make sure that African-American authors had a chance. How else can you introduce readers to new authors if their books are thrown on the shelves with all the others? As soon as you walked into my store, the colorful books were proudly displayed with eye-catching banners, poster-size cover displays, and more. The large section was proof that AA books were popular and our folks really do read, but I'm not going to lie. I kept the section close to the front of the store where Karen could keep a watchful eye on anyone who was browsing the aisle. No offense, but the popular authors, Carl Weber, Mary B. Morrison, and Zane, their books always seemed to come up short in my inventory and I just wasn't having any more of that. It's a shame that black folks would rather borrow and steal a book before spending money, yet we had no problem getting our hair and nails done on a regular basis. All I can do is shake my damn head. Sometime our priorities aren't where they should be. Hell, I would know. I had been that same person back in the day.

I spent most of the late afternoon rearranging books on the shelf to showcase a new author who was coming into the store next weekend for a book signing. I also had a dozen on display in the storefront window. Like I said, I believed in supporting authors.

I was down on my knees when I remembered I still needed to get the podium and microphone from the storeroom and set them up. Wednesdays were open mic night, and by seven o'clock the couches in back would be filled with students from the University of Missouri–St. Louis and from the local area for poetry, singing, and spoken word. Mia, a student, facilitated the event, while two others assisted with serving coffees and teas. After Aiden was born, I had hired a part-time evening manager to run the store and allow me more time with my family. Terrence Miller, a business major, was a godsend. He usually relieved me by seven.

The phone rang and I rose from my knees and walked up to the desk just as Karen was saying good-bye to a customer with two little children. I grabbed the phone before whoever was on the other line hung up.

"Book Ends, how may I help you?"

"Nikki Truth, please."

My brow bunched because I knew that voice. "This is Nikki."

"Hey, Nikki . . . this is Ann. I hate to bother you, but we're about to close and Aiden still hasn't been picked up."

"What?" I glanced over at the clock on the wall. It was almost six. Where the hell was Donovan? "Ann, I'm so sorry. Let me see if I can reach my husband. Otherwise, I'm on my way to get him."

"Okay, ummm . . ." She paused and I didn't miss the hesitation. "I've been meaning to talk to you. I know this isn't any of my business, but yesterday when your husband came by to pick up Aiden, I smelled liquor on his breath."

I didn't even respond because in all honesty I didn't know what to say. I knew Donovan had been drinking more than normal, but I hadn't realized he was starting so early.

"Really?" I said, then gasped for dramatic effect. "Thanks for telling me. I'm on my way." I hung up because I just didn't want to hear anything else about my husband or his behavior. I was confident it was nothing he and I couldn't work out ourselves.

"Karen, I need to go and pick up Aiden from daycare. As soon as Dominique comes in to relieve you, could you please set up the mic before you go?" Dominique was my part-time cashier.

She looked at me and nodded. Hell, it wasn't like it was the first time she'd had to cover the store while I jetted off. "Sure, no problem. Is something wrong?"

We had been working together long enough that I guess she could tell when something wasn't right with me. But I just couldn't bring myself to tell anyone yet what was going on in my house. Big Mama had always said keep your problems between you and your husband. It was times like this I missed her so much. She had been the only person I had ever been able to talk to. Sure, I had a mother, but she and I had never been close like me and my grandmother, who had passed away over three years ago.

I shook my head. "No, everything's fine. I guess Donovan forgot he's supposed to pick up Aiden." I couldn't even look at her as I spoke, because it was all a lie. Lying was something I had been doing a lot of lately. I moved back to my office, grabbed my purse, and as I headed to my car I called Donovan on his cell phone and got no answer.

An hour later, I carried a sleepy Aiden into the house and up to his room. He was such a good little boy and beautiful, too, with dark mahogany skin like me and dimples that could melt a lady's heart. I slipped him under the covers and kissed his cheek, then went in search of my husband. I found him in our bed, asleep.

"Donovan!" I called out to him. When I got no answer, I leaned over the bed and tapped him on the shoulder. The second I made contact, his eyelids flew open and he jumped up, screamed, and rolled out of the bed onto the floor. He scared me so bad, I jerked back and bumped my head on the wall. "Dammit!"

He was in such a panic it took Donovan a few seconds before he remembered where he was. "Why the hell you sneak up on me?" he shouted.

I was rubbing the back of my head. Damn, that hurt. "I didn't sneak up on you. I called your name."

He kicked away the sheet that was tangled around his legs. "Then you should have called louder." Donovan then rose and noticed me holding my head and immediately his expression softened. "Are you hurt?" He walked over and took a closer look, clearly concerned. One thing about my husband, he would never raise his hands to a woman.

I shook my head and lied. "No, I'm fine."

He kissed my cheek and stood in front of me. I took a moment to take a good look at him, standing there in nothing but boxer briefs. My husband had a body, so it was truly a beautiful sight. However, I suddenly noticed he was starting to lose weight, so the briefs didn't hug his butt the way they used to and he knew how much I loved gripping that ass. There were also the dark bags under his eyes, and he had two-day growth at his chin. Where the hell was the gorgeous man who had held me in his arms and made love to me less than a week ago?

"Help me to understand . . . what are you doing in bed? Did you even go into the barbershop today?" I asked.

Donovan scrubbed a hand across his face and shook his head. "I didn't feel like it."

I wanted to scream at his ass to snap out of it. He hadn't felt like it in over a week and it was starting to annoy the hell out of me. I guess what I wanted was for the man who had left for Afghanistan fifteen months ago to come walking through that door, not this alien invasion who was impersonating him.

I took a deep breath, then stepped closer to Donovan and gave him a huge hug and was pleased not to smell the stink of stale alcohol. "Baby, you've gotta snap out of it."

"Snap out of what?" he shouted, then backed away from my grasp. "I just got back, Nikki. Damn! Give yo man some time to adjust to being at home. You expect everything to just be the way it was. Well, guess what? It ain't. I need time to get used to being home."

I looked into his eyes, hoping he could see evidence of how worried I was about him. "It's already been three months. How much longer is it going to take? I'm trying to be patient. Really, I am, but Aiden and I need you." Lord knows I was trying to be a loving and supportive wife, but this was getting to be a bit much.

Donovan closed his eyes and rubbed his face with his hands. I know he was tired of having this same discussion. Well, guess what? So was I. I wanted my husband back. He had been my rock. The old Donovan had always had my back and his goal, first and foremost, was to make sure his wife was happy. Before he'd been deployed we'd made love almost every night and had an insatiable appetite for each other, but now it was hit and miss. I ain't gotta have it all the time, but can I get it at least consistently? Last night, I reached over and grabbed what I wanted and he had pushed my hand away. What man does that?

I lowered onto the bed and forced myself to take a deep breath before I ended up saying something I'd later regret. "You forgot to pick Aiden up from daycare."

He swung around and I saw the look of confusion before my words suddenly registered. "Oh, damn! Baby, I'm sorry. I guess I should have set an alarm or something."

Seriously? Was that all he had to say? He should have set a damn alarm. I raised a finger, ready to light into his ass, then thought better of it. Arguing was clearly a waste of precious time that I did not have. Thanks to him.

"I've gotta get back to the bookstore. Are you going to be able to watch Aiden until I get back?"

"Why the fuck you ask me that? Of course I can watch my son." He shook his head and sucked his teeth, but I didn't care.

"I'm just asking," I said with attitude. "By the way . . . one of the daycare assistants mentioned she smelled alcohol on your breath yesterday." I raised a perfectly arched eyebrow and searched his face for some kind of reaction.

"Which one? The chick with the wide forehead?" Donovan rolled his eyes. "Probably because she tried slipping me her phone number and I turned her skinny ass down."

I didn't know what to make of what he said. Part of me really wanted to believe it was just a jealous chick hating on my happiness, but deep down I knew it was more than that. "Listen, Don, I don't know what the hell is going on with you and I'm trying to be patient, but that's *my* baby sleeping down the hall, and I'll be damned before I let anything happen to another one of my kids."

His eyes widened, letting me know that he knew what, or in this case, whom I was referring to. "You think I don't know that," he stressed. "I can't believe you gonna sit up here and think I would do anything to harm my son." He had the nerve to try and look like his feelings were hurt, but I wasn't bullshitting. There was no way I would allow anything to happen to Aiden.

"That might be the case," I snarled with attitude. "But until things get better with you, the *only* person who'll be taking Aiden to and from daycare will be me."

Donovan turned his dark eyes to me and gave me an evil look, but must have seen the fear in mine and backed down. I just wasn't about to take that chance and allow anything to happen to my only child.

As I took a seat on the bed, my mind flashed back to when I had first opened my bookstore. I had just finished working a double shift and was in the backyard lying on a recliner while my daughter, Mimi, played with her toys. I had dozed off and apparently the gate hadn't been properly secured. Mimi had only been two years old when she had run out into the street and was hit by a car. Losing her had ripped a hole in my heart and my marriage that had taken years to repair. Just thinking about that time in my life caused my hands to shake. I'm sorry, but there was no way I could ever endure that pain again.

Donovan came around to the side of the bed, took a seat beside me, and studied my face, probably still trying to figure out if I was serious. Did I stutter? Hell yeah, I was serious.

He hesitated, then said, "Nikki, I'm really sorry. I didn't sleep good last night. I went to the gym this morning and then tried to watch a little television and the eyelids got heavy. Like I said, I didn't plan on oversleeping . . . it just happened. I'm sorry, baby, really I am." Donovan grabbed me and pulled me close, and I felt my cold attitude starting to thaw. I desperately wanted to believe him. "Trust me, baby. It won't ever happen again."

I was starting to feel bad for doubting him. Easing back slightly, I gave him a weak smile. "I know it won't."

Then he French-kissed me and I wrapped my arms tightly around him and prayed that for once he was right.

6

Trinette

"Hey, Netta, baby. For some reason . . . your breasts seem bigger."

I jerked upright on the bed and gazed at my husband lying beside me. His eyes were paying way too much attention to my 44DDs. "Leon, puh-leeze. That's from you sucking on my damn titties so much," I spat, then hurried into the adjoining bathroom and shut the door behind me. Thank goodness I was a quick thinker.

I moved over to the mirror and gazed at my naked body. He was right. My breasts were rounder and fuller. Damn! The last thing I wanted was for him to start noticing my body changing, especially since I was scheduled to have an abortion the following Monday.

Ever since the nurse called and dropped the Mac bomb on my life, I have been losing my mind while trying to figure out how the hell I had gotten myself into this mess. Having a baby was the last thing in the world I ever wanted. So why? I asked. Why me? Especially since I was sleeping with two different men. Hell, sometimes in the same night. So there was no way to know *whose* baby I was carrying until after I gave birth and trust me, that wasn't going to happen. Besides, I worked too hard to look this good to let it all go to shit. I know too many women who've never gotten their bodies back after giving birth, and I just couldn't imagine losing my perfect curves.

Turning to the side, I stared down at my stomach, making sure my stomach was still smooth and flat, and was glad to see that it still was. The only evidence was my swelling breasts.

Leon knocked at the door. "Hey, baby, you wanna take a shower together?"

I rolled my eyes. He can be so worrisome at times. I just gave him some, now he wanted to spend the rest of the weekend in each other's arms. I was supposed to meet Jrue at two o'clock in Williamsburg for lunch and, more importantly, dessert.

"No, sweetie, because we'll never get out and I don't want to get my hair wet," I whined like a little girl, just the way he likes. "I told you I wanted to spend the afternoon at the outlet mall. You wanna go with me?" I asked, although I already knew the answer.

Leon was quick to object. "No, I'm going to kick back and watch the basketball game."

I grinned. I am so damn sneaky.

Within minutes I was showered and spreading *Beauty* body lotion all over me. Jrue loved that scent on me. And who am I not to give my man what he wanted?

I stepped into the master suite, then looked around the room and grinned. We'd been living in our home on Cary Street for over a year and I still couldn't believe how beautiful it was. The master bedroom was a dream all by itself, with more than 2,000 square feet, large picture windows, a cathedral ceiling, and French doors that led into a master bath that was better than any spa I've ever been to with a Jacuzzi tub big enough for me and Leon. I moved across cinnamon-colored carpet where stone columns led into a spacious sitting room where Leon spent hours watching the game from a 55-inch flat screen that was mounted to the wall. He had gone downstairs, probably to find something to eat, and I was glad to have the bedroom all to myself. Leon loved watching me walk around the room naked, but after a while he'd be ready for round three, and I was trying to save some of my energy for Jrue.

I stepped into my walk-in closet. For my birthday, Leon had a contractor come in and build me all kinds of neat shelves and racks perfect for all my clothes and accessories. One thing no one could ever say was that my husband did not love my dirty drawers.

I brought a hand to my hip as I browsed the assortment of clothes in my closet. It was a shopaholic's dream. Most of the items still had price tags hanging on them from my favorite stores such as Neiman Marcus, Saks Fifth Avenue, and Macy's. Thanks to Nikki, I even occasionally scanned the shelves at T.J. Maxx, but I'm very selective about what I buy there, and even then I have to get there the same day the trucks arrived before everything was picked all over. There's nothing worse than trying on a dress after several other women had it on. Just seeing the deodorant stains gave me the creeps.

I finally decided on a pair of skinny denim jeans, a ruffle red blouse that showcased the twins in the best way possible, and fire-engine red heels. I even wore lipstick to match. A sistah's gotta keep it cute.

I grabbed a colorful leather purse and took one final look in the mirror. I had wrapped my hair so my weave draped perfectly around my shoulders. I sauntered down the double staircase into a marble foyer with a large crystal chandelier hanging overhead.

I found Leon in the kitchen making himself something for breakfast. He knew when he married me I hadn't known a damn thing about cooking. After ten years, nothing had changed.

"Hmmm, something smells good," I commented as I moved into the beautifully decorated kitchen. It had stainless-steel appliances, dark oak cabinets, and chocolate granite countertops. Leon was standing in front of a large island with a spatula in hand. He took his cooking skills seriously. The moment he saw me strutting into the room, he grinned like he was looking at a runway model or, in my case, a plus-sized diva.

I grabbed a slice of bacon and took a bite. "What kinda waffles are those . . . pecan?" I loved his cooking. He didn't mind experimenting and trying new things.

"You know it, baby," he said with that goofy grin of his. To most women, my husband probably wasn't much to look at. He was about five-nine, thin, dark skinned with a receding hairline that seemed to get thinner every time he brushed his head. But he had the gentlest brown eyes and an outgoing personality that people were drawn to. Not to mention, he had a financial mind that was so sharp it made him the genius that he was.

"You want me to make you one?" he asked, because my husband was thoughtful like that. That's why we made a good team. He loved to cook. I loved to eat.

I shook my head. Otherwise, I'd never get out the door. "No, I'm not hungry. I'll just eat a granola bar on the drive down. I gotta keep a watch on this figure."

He was staring at my titties so hard, Leon looked like he was a second away from drooling. "I'm watching and that figure looks mighty good from over here."

He drew me close and I leaned in and made sure my breasts brushed his bare chest. I then French-kissed him until I felt an erection jerking beneath his sweatpants.

"Damn, you keep that up you won't be going anywhere except back to bed," he warned with a playful chuckle. I'd been married to Leon long enough to know he was serious. He loved making love to me. He just had a problem holding out long enough for me to get mine. It's a curse. I seem to have that effect on most men.

I eased back and smiled. "If I stay home in bed, then I won't be able to pick up something extra special to model for you tonight."

That got his attention. Leon's eyes got wide with interest. "Something like what?"

Grinning, I pulled away. "I guess you'll have to wait until tonight to see what little something something I come up with. I might even find a pair of pumps to match."

Leon drew in a slow breath. "Do I need to get a stack of dollar bills ready?"

I paused long enough to bat my eyelashes at him. "You might want to make it two stacks. Tonight I plan to drop it like it's hot." I cooed and then dipped down, winding my hips seductively, giving my husband a quick demonstration. "Speaking of tonight's entertainment . . . can I have some extra money?" I asked in a whiny voice.

"No problem," he said, and reminded me of one of those bobblehead dolls. "I'll transfer five hundred dollars into your account just as soon as I get done making breakfast." He walked over and flipped the waffle iron and I gazed down at the golden brown cake.

"Thank you, baby." I kissed his lips and gave him a little tongue, hoping he'd decide to transfer a little extra. My husband was rich but stingy at times. He said he didn't get rich by letting his wife spend all our money. I guess there was some truth in that. My money was my money, but his money—Leon actually gave me an allowance, and a hefty one at that. It's just with the lifestyle I was accustomed to, it was never enough. So in order to pull Leon's purse strings, I had to serve up a little extra Ms. Netta from time to time.

"Baby, I won't be too late. Zakiya's planning to meet me after church and we'll probably have dinner while we're in Williamsburg."

He nodded. "See ya tonight." He kissed me one last time.

"Absolutely," I purred.

I grabbed another slice of bacon and was walking through the foyer when my head started spinning. I reached out for the bannister and cried out to Leon; then I felt myself falling and everything went black.

I don't know how long I was out before I finally opened my eyes and found myself in a strange room. I sat up straight and realized I was in a hospital bed. What the hell?

"Oh, thank you, Jesus! You're finally awake!" Leon cried, then sprang from a tacky-looking chair in the corner with a sigh of relief.

"What happened?" I asked while I glanced down at the slender watch next to the hospital bracelet on my arm and noticed it was almost five-thirty. Had I really been out that long?

"You fainted, and scared the hell out of me. I carried you to my car and drove you straight to St. Mary's." He stroked my hair affectionately, then lowered his lips to my forehead. "I don't know if I've ever been that scared before in my life."

I heard a light knock at the door and then a woman wearing blue scrubs with a stethoscope around her neck burst into the room. "Well, I'm glad to see the patient is finally awake!" she said with a sincere grin. "How are you feeling?"

"Tired. Thirsty," I mumbled. I quickly looked around the room for a mirror and was pissed there wasn't one. There was no telling what kind of hot mess I looked like.

"Dr. Bey, what did the test say? What's wrong with my wife?" Leon insisted and squeezed my hand.

"Uh . . . Dr.—" Before I could stop her from doing what I was certain she was about to do, Dr. Bey said the last thing I ever wanted my husband to hear.

"Congratulations. You're pregnant."

Leon's eyes traveled from me to her. "What . . . did you just say my wife is pregnant?"

Bitch.

Leon stumbled over to the chair and took several deep breaths. Clearly, he was stunned to hear the words he'd been waiting a decade to hear. Words I never wanted him to hear.

"Whoo-hoo!" he shouted, and scared the crap out of me. Leon sprang from the chair, hurried around the bed, and hugged me close. I quickly put on a fake smile.

"Pregnant, huh? I had no idea," I lied.

That thirtysomething–looking brunette smiled like she had just told me I had won the lottery. What I wanted to do was reach across that bed and slap the crap out of her for telling my business. Did she ever think that maybe I didn't want him to know? Some people can be so inconsiderate at times.

She and Leon were talking while I lay there feeling sorry for myself. Why in the world did things like this always happen to me?

What I could never get Leon to understand was I never had any intention of being someone's mommy. He wanted a wife and a mother to his children, but I was just too cute to be contained.

". . . She'll need to make an appointment to see an obstetrician. In the meantime, I want to start her on some prenatal vitamins."

Prenatal vitamins? After that I really didn't hear a word she said. This was like a bad dream or some shit. I was supposed to be in Williamsburg at the Hampton Inn with my legs in the air and Jrue on top of me, not lying in a damn hospital bed with an IV in my arm. Speaking of Jrue . . . I'm sure he was worried sick wondering where the hell I was. Thank goodness I left my phone off when I was at home. The last thing I needed was for Leon to have picked it up and accidently read some of the nasty text messages Jrue and I sent each other.

As soon as Dr. Bey left the room, Leon took a seat on the bed beside me, grinning like a damn fool. "Netta, I can't believe it! We're finally going to have a baby."

I shook my head, still in a daze because this was not at all supposed to happen. "Yeah, I can't believe it either." Especially since I still planned to get rid of the baby next Monday. Someway, somehow, I would just have to fake a miscarriage or some shit. Then when I screamed at Leon that I was bleeding and he rushed me off to the hospital, I would have to threaten the doctor who examined me that if she breathed a word of what I had done, I'd sue her and the whole damn hospital. I remembered reading something about doctor–patient confidentiality.

"How about we go to Virginia Beach next weekend? I want to spend some time pampering my wife," Leon suggested. "We can stay at the condo."

"Pampering, huh?" I guess I could just enjoy the next week with Leon believing he's about to become a father. Nothing wrong with milking it for everything that it's worth. Then the following Monday I'd still sneak to the clinic in Norfolk and terminate the pregnancy.

Trust me. There was no way in hell I would change my mind. The sooner it was over, the better.

7

Nikki

"Something sure smells good."

I glanced over my shoulder at Donovan. I had just removed a piping-hot pan of lasagna from the oven. "Dinner should be ready in a few minutes."

"I can't wait 'cause a brotha is starving." He stepped over, kissed my lips, and I savored the feel of my man's mouth on me. "While that cools I'm gonna take Aiden out on the porch and let him play with his ball."

"That sounds like a good idea." I nodded.

"Come on, Aiden," Donovan called into the other room.

"Okay, Daddy!" Aiden yelled as he made a mad dash toward the door with Rudy at his heels.

After I heard the door shut, I popped some garlic bread in the oven and caught myself humming. The past week had been amazing. Donovan was back at the barbershop taking appointments and hanging out with his boys. And did I mention the sex? *Ohmygoodness!* The brotha was satisfying his wife on a regular basis, and in fact, he had been putting in a little extra. Just last night he sucked my toes until I had tears in my eyes! Nope, I don't have any complaints at all.

But I'm not going to lie. There have been moments when I saw him staring off in space. And also he's still drinking a little more than I liked, but at least he's making an effort to transition himself back into the real world and make things feel as normal as possible at home with his family, and that's all anyone can ask for.

The house phone rang and I walked over and grabbed it. I didn't even bother to look down at the caller ID, but whoever was on the other end was bawling.

"Hello?"

"N-Nikki!"

"Netta, is that you?" My pulse started racing like crazy. I've known her a long time and I have rarely ever heard Trinette cry.

"Nikki . . . w-what am I going to do?"

She had me so scared I had to take a moment to catch my breath. I walked over to the kitchen table and took a seat. "Calm down and tell me what's wrong."

"I really *am* pregnant!"

"Dammit, Netta. Don't you ever scare me like that again!" I snapped. "Don't you know you had me thinking something bad had happened?"

"Nikki, I'm sorry. I didn't mean to scare you. I'm just so confused right now. I feel like I'm going to lose my mind." She then blew her nose in my ear.

"Trinette Montgomery is pregnant. Ain't that some shit." Even though she had already suspected she might be pregnant, just hearing her confirm her suspicions was a shocker. Trinette and pregnancy were just two words I never expected to hear in the same sentence. "Are congratulations in order?" I asked.

"Hell no!" she screamed into the phone. "What's there to be happy about? Other than you, nobody knew I was pregnant and I planned to keep it that way. Then before I could have the abortion, I fainted and Leon found out the truth. I should sue that hospital for telling my damn business."

I was feeling brain overload. "Wait a minute . . . you scheduled an abortion?"

"Yes, of course. I told you I would. I mean . . . come on. What do I look like carrying a baby for nine months?"

Yeah, she did have a point. "So what are you going to do now that Leon knows?"

"Well . . . I had planned on still getting that abortion, b—"

"Hold up!" I shook my head. "Even after Leon found out the truth?" I told you that girl's crazy.

"Would you just listen?" she hissed.

I blew out a long breath. "I'm listening."

"Before you rudely interrupted, I was saying I had gone to get the abortion and I was lying on that table with my legs spread, then realized I just couldn't go through with it."

"What? You mean to tell me my best friend, the Tin Man, *really* does have a heart?" Oh, hallelujah! Trust me. It was a shocker, because the only person Trinette has ever cared about was herself.

"I know, right. But it's all their fault. At the clinic, they make you wait so damn long before it's your turn that you get to thinking, and I started thinking about my mama and how she had all five of us when what she should have done was aborted a couple of my brothers." She gave a lackluster laugh. "Anyway, I just couldn't bring myself to do it. It was like I suddenly got scared that God was going to strike me down."

"Netta, I didn't even know you knew who God was?"

"Come on, Nikki. I'm serious! I was on that table and started shaking; then the next thing I knew, I was running out that room like Flo Jo and grabbing my clothes."

I couldn't help it, I started laughing. "Good for you. You know how I feel about abortions."

Trinette blew a frustrated breath in the phone. "I know, I know, but now what am I going to do? Leon *thinks* I'm carrying his baby."

"Are you?" Because inquiring minds wanted to know.

"I don't know," she groaned. "I seriously don't know. My gut says this baby belongs to Jrue. Hell, the way that dude was stroking me deep, he was shooting damn near more bullets than Leon."

That girl was forever giving me too much information. "Does Jrue know you're pregnant?"

"Hell no, and I want to keep it that way, but I don't know how I'm going to get around it. Eventually I'll start showing and then the truth will come out for sure."

I shook my head because only Trinette could get herself in a mess like this. I told her that at some point her past would catch up with her, but as always she thought she was unstoppable.

"I just can't believe this is happening to me," she wailed.

I rose and started setting the table for dinner while she talked about all the reasons why a baby was not something she needed in her life. I have to admit that for once Trinette was right. She doesn't need a baby, because her ass was way too selfish. To be honest, I feel sorry for Leon. He's a good man and all he has ever done was loved that girl with everything he's had, yet all she does is run over him. Ain't nothing worse to me than a weak man, and Netta is definitely Leon's kryptonite.

"Trinette, it could be a lot worse. At least Leon is excited over the news."

"Yeah, but . . . what if the baby isn't his?" she asked, and I could hear the fear in her voice.

"Do you think he would even know the difference?" Goodness, I couldn't even believe I had said that.

After a long pause, Trinette started laughing. "You're right. That baby could come out looking like Shemar Moore and Leon would swear up and down the child got his good looks from him."

I laughed right along with her and was glad to see her coming out of her shell. Nothing was worse than a depressed Trinette. I remembered that one time Leon had found himself some balls and ended their relationship. I had never seen

Trinette so broken up over that man. Especially after the way she had been treating him, messing around with everything with three legs and a lucrative bank account. Eventually she had come to her senses and begged Leon to take her back. If he had asked me, I would have told him to make her ass sweat for a while, but not Leon. The second she promised to be a faithful wife and sit down and have some babies, he took her back with open arms. Trinette had been faithful for a year and a half and then look what happened.

"*Ohmygoodness!* Nikki, you're so right. I don't even know why I'm tripping. Leon loves me too much to question anything! He'll fall in love with my child and would do anything in the world for me. I'm definitely having him hire a full-time nanny to help take care of this baby."

I rolled my eyes. Now that's the Netta I know.

"What did the doctor say about your kidney?" A couple of years ago Trinette had done an unselfish act of donating one of hers to her mother.

"She said something about my kidney not being directly involved with the reproductive system, but there's still a chance that a full term pregnancy may cause a strain on my remaining kidney."

"Oh no! That doesn't sound good."

Trinette blew out a dismissive breath. "I'll be fine. Dr. Brown said she'll keep a close eye on it. But since I'm in such good health she didn't seem overly concerned."

I had to smile at the suddenly positive attitude. "Well, then that's one less thing we have to worry about."

I heard laughter on the porch and remembered my husband was waiting anxiously to eat. "Look, I better let you go so I can get dinner on the table. I'm happy for you, Netta. Just hang in there and I'll talk to you tomorrow." I hung up the phone and grabbed the tossed salad from the refrigerator and carried it over to the table. Once everything was ready, I stepped out onto the porch and was surprised to see Lorenzo

Wade standing there. He and Donovan owned the barbershop A Cut Above the Rest. He looked spooked when he saw me.

"Hey, Nikki."

I took in his freshly creased jeans, wifebeater, and clean white Air Force Ones. He was a tall, cocky dude with peanut butter brown skin, short dark hair, and a beard that he kept fresh. Lorenzo and Donovan had been friends since high school. I could only stomach his cocky attitude in small doses. But if he's the reason why my husband was laughing, something I hadn't heard in a while, then I guess I would learn to tolerate Lorenzo just a little more.

"What's going on? You here for dinner? I made plenty." I even gave him a half smile. That fool looked dumbfounded.

"Uh . . ." His voice trailed off as he glanced nervously over his shoulder at Donovan, who was sitting on one of my wicker chairs, playing ball with Aiden.

"Nah . . . baby. Lorenzo just stopped through for a sec to holla at me."

Something was going on. Donovan was looking everywhere but at me. Lorenzo, I noticed, kept glancing down at the corner. I followed the direction of his eyes and at the end of the block I saw a familiar white car with tinted windows pull to a complete stop. Lorenzo saw it, too, and started grinning like a damn fool.

"Yo, Donovan, I'm gonna run up the street for a second. I'll be back." He tried to sound as convincing as possible, but I knew better and he knew it, too, that's why he dropped his head and hurried off my porch and down the sidewalk.

I felt my eyebrow inching up. "What's he up to?"

Donovan met my gaze with a blank stare, then handed Aiden to me. "If Tammy calls, he's over here having dinner with us."

"Say what?" I said with attitude. "So now we're covering for folks?"

I leaned over the edge of the porch so I could see past my

neighbor's large tree. Lorenzo made it down to the corner and hopped into the passenger's seat. As the car drove slowly past my house, I felt like my jaw hit the ground.

"What the . . . ?" I wouldn't have believed it if I hadn't seen it with my own eyes. Did those two know his wife was crazy?

I turned and followed Donovan and Rudy into the house and lowered Aiden to his feet. Instantly, he raced over to his toys. "Do you know whose car he just got in?" I asked, and with good reason.

My husband headed into the kitchen shaking his head. "Nah, he's seeing some chick and asked me to cover. All I know is she's picking him up on the corner."

A smile curled the corners of my mouth as I walked into the kitchen and washed my hands. Lorenzo wasn't meeting some chick. That white Impala with the tinted windows belonged to Tristan.

8

Trinette

For the past two weeks I have been trying to think of a way to end my relationship with Jrue. Yet every time he touched me, and I felt all eight inches of that chocolate goodness sliding inside of my body, for the life of me I could barely find the strength to even whisper his name. I knew I had to end the affair and focus on my husband and the baby, but part of me wanted to hold out until the last possible second. Mainly because, dammit, it wasn't fair. I had finally found a man who made me feel like the woman I knew I could be. He is the man I had been waiting all my life for, and what happened, I can't even have him. I swear to you someone up above is truly testing me.

"Hey, Trinette."

I glanced up from my computer to see one of the students enrolled in my program standing right outside my door.

"Come on in," I urged. Dory shuffled in with her head hung low, wearing boot-cut jeans and an oversized T-shirt. "How are classes going this semester?" There were only four weeks left in the semester.

She shrugged. "I think I'm going to have to withdraw before the grade counts."

"Why's that?" I signaled for her to take the seat across from me.

Dory's eyes shifted nervously. "My mother and I haven't been getting along. She moved another one of her boyfriends into the house and I don't feel comfortable with him being around my daughter all day when I'm not there."

I understood better than she'd ever know. My mother had moved her brother into the house when I was twelve. Back then she was so strung out on crack she had no idea he had been raping me in the next room. Uncle Sonny abused me for four years until I finally had the guts to try to bite his dick off. He never touched me again, but the pain of all those years of my mother not being there for me had scarred me bad. Over the last three years Mama and I had worked to restore our relationship and get past that dark period of my life, but it hadn't been easy.

"What I need to be doing is tryna get a job so I can get a place of my own," Dory continued.

I nodded because I clearly understood where she was coming from. "There's a program out there that may be able to help you get a housing allowance, but you have to be a full-time student."

Her eyes lit up. "Really? I have no problem with staying in school as long as my baby is safe."

I smiled at her. She was such a beautiful girl; no one that young should have so much pain to bear. "Let me make a few phone calls this afternoon and see what I can work out. In the meantime, you make sure you study so you can keep your GPA up."

Dory nodded and looked pleased by my answer; then I hurried her off so she wouldn't be late for class.

I wished someone had cared about me when I was young. Instead, I raised my brothers and grew up fast. I learned to survive by any means necessary.

I heard a light knock at the door and looked up to see Jrue standing there.

"Hey, sexy." He licked his lips and had my body watering for a lot more than just lunch. "You ready to go?"

I took a moment to take in how good he was looking today in charcoal gray slacks and a black shirt with the top button left loose. The fabric strained across his shoulders and emphasized every muscle on his magnificent body. Every time I looked at Jrue my heart turned over in my chest. I loved that man so much it hurt.

I rose from my desk and was reaching for my purse when I got hit by a wave of nausea. "Oh, God! Excuse me," I said in a panicked whisper. I then shoved my purse in his hands and raced down the hall and practically knocked Josie, the administrative assistant, over as she was coming out of the bathroom. I made it into the stall in just enough time to puke my guts out. Morning sickness. I'd been feeling it all week. By the time I stepped out of the stall, Zakiya and Josie were standing near at the sink.

"You okay?" Zakiya asked. I could see the suspicion in her eyes. Women were so damn nosy. Eventually everyone would know I was pregnant, but it would be on my terms, not theirs.

I gave a dismissive wave. "I'm fine. I've been feeling nauseated ever since I ate that Chinese food last night." I moved around them to the sink, rinsed out my mouth, and gargled the tap water. They stood silently watching me.

"You sure? I mean this isn't the first time this week we've heard you puking in the bathroom," Zakiya said, waiting with a hand at her hip. Josie just sucked her teeth, sighed, and stared at me.

There was no way I was giving these two something to gossip about, especially since I still hadn't told Jrue. "I've got a bug that I can't seem to shake. I'll be fine." I stood my ground.

I reached for a paper towel, wiped my mouth and hands, and left those two nosy bitches standing in the bathroom.

Sorry, but Ms. Netta is not about to be this afternoon's topic of discussion.

Jrue was waiting outside my office with this worried look on his face. "You okay?"

"Yes, I'm fine." Nodding, I took my purse from his hand and followed him out to his Jaguar. He helped me into the car, then walked around to his side and got in. I started talking nonstop about this ring I had seen at Jared's that I was dying to have. I didn't realize I was the only one holding the conversation until we pulled into Applebee's parking lot and I realized Jrue hadn't bothered to turn the car off.

"What's wrong?" I asked, because I suddenly got a bad feeling.

He took a deep breath, then swung around on the leather seat. "What's really going on with you?"

I had no choice but to play dumb. "W-What do you mean?" I stammered.

"I mean . . . I love you, Trinette. I want to spend my life with you. So why are you lying to me?"

I dropped my gaze. Was I really that transparent? "What makes you think I'm lying to you?"

"Because when you tossed me your purse, it fell onto the floor and I saw the prenatal vitamins."

Damn. I was busted. *So much for the cocktail ring.*

"Are you pregnant?"

My heart did a nosedive. Goodness, how did I get myself in these messes? And I was really looking forward to us spending the summer together.

"Yes . . . I'm pregnant. I just didn't know how to tell you," I pouted and batted my eyelashes at him.

"Oh, my God," he said, and blew out this long breath and started laughing. "I can't believe this shit!"

It was going to be worse than I thought. I averted my gaze, looking everywhere but at his face. "I'm sorry. I didn't mean to deceive you."

"Deceive me?" He cupped my chin so I had no choice but to look him in the face. "Trinette, you just made me the happiest man. You're carrying my baby." A proud grin curled his lips.

My mouth hung open. "Y-Your baby?"

He had the cutest smile. "Of course it's mine. You told me Leon was impotent, so unless you've been making love to someone else, that seed growing inside you is mine."

I quickly shook my head. "Nope, you're the only one."

He started shouting with joy. I couldn't believe the way he was behaving like he had just landed another huge grant for the department.

"You're not angry?"

His eyebrows shot up. "Angry? Why would I be angry?"

He was dumber than I thought. "Because we're both married and I'm carrying your child?"

He knew I was right, but that wasn't what he wanted to hear. "Listen . . . my wife can't have children. We've been trying for years and it just ain't happening. You are about to give me the one thing I had always wanted, an heir. Someone to pass on the family name. You're giving me the one thing she never could, and that means a lot to me."

This was turning out better than I thought imaginable. "But Leon thinks this baby is his. I don't know how because he can't ever stay hard enough for anything to happen, but he feels confident that he did enough." Ooh, I was so good with the lying.

"Then let him keep thinking that. In the meantime, I want you to take care of my baby growing inside of you, because I promise you that child will never want for anything." He pressed his palm against my stomach and kept on grinning. "As soon as the time is right, I want us to be together."

I couldn't believe how shit was working out for me. Here I was all set to lose him, and instead we were going to be closer than ever. Men could be some stupid something. But it was their stupidity that made me the smart woman I am today.

Maybe now he would finally leave Charlotte. She is a breast cancer survivor, and Jrue refused to ask her for a divorce until he was absolutely certain her cancer was still in remission. Looks like it was time to hurry that shit up.

"Why don't we have lunch and then we can run over to Jared's and look at that ring you were wanting?" Jrue suggested. "Emeralds, right?"

"Really?" Now I was excited too.

"Absolutely." He leaned over and kissed my lips. "Anything for the mother of my child."

I was starting to like the way that sounded.

9

Nikki

"Is there something you need to be telling me?"

Tristan sauntered into my office batting his eyelashes. There was nothing innocent about him. "Something like what?" He was looking everywhere but at me.

I leaned across the desk. "That you've been messing around with Lorenzo?"

One of his eyebrows went up and his mouth kind of hung open. "*Ohmygoodness!* How did you know?"

I rolled my eyes. "How do you think? For the last two weeks I've seen your car parked at the end of my block."

Tristan did one of those dramatic performances where he cupped his mouth and paced around the room mumbling, "Ohmygoodness!" like Sheneneh from *Martin*.

"Nikki, I'm not lying. I had no idea he worked at the shop with Donovan until he asked me to meet him. I knew the address sounded familiar. It wasn't until I pulled onto your street that I finally put it together. Girl, I was floored! You just don't know how badly I've been wanting to say something to you, but Lorenzo swore me to secrecy," he added, then flopped down in the chair beside me and crossed his legs.

I still couldn't believe Lorenzo was on the down low, considering he was always talking loud in the shop about getting with some female. Now I knew what he had meant by "tapping that ass." I sat back in my chair with a hard look and folded my arms. "You need to be careful with that one, because his wife, Tammy, is crazy jealous."

Tristan leaned close. "You know her?"

Yeah, I knew her, and we could have been friends if she wasn't so damn stuck on herself. She was high-yellow, rocking a short natural, wide hips, and a pair of double Cs. She was cute, but truly had low self-esteem the way she called and checked on her man all day long. I told Donovan I didn't know how he dealt with her worrisome ass, popping up at the shop and demanding to know who Lorenzo's clients were.

"Hell yeah, I know her, and the two of you are headed for disaster. She's always in the shop clowning Lorenzo in front of all the customers. I'm surprised she hasn't caught the two of you together." Tammy was such a bitch, part of me felt Lorenzo deserved better, and if he was happy, then who was I to rain on his parade? "You know how I feel about your involvements with married men."

I looked at Tristan with a disgusted look. I love him more than I love my own sister, but I've already told him on several occasions how I feel about him messing with someone's husband. Men want to mess with each other? That's their prerogative, just as long as they had enough respect for the woman he had to go home to. "Please tell me you're using a condom."

Tristan lowered his head, then lifted it and met my hard stare. I wanted to make sure he knew I was serious. "Of course we used condoms. You know I always practice safe sex. Don't worry. Lorenzo knows exactly what to tell his wife and has everything worked out," he said with a little too much confidence.

"That's fine, but just keep me out of it. I'm serious. I don't want to be in the middle of that shit. Because if Donovan knew . . ."

His eyes widened. "Please don't tell him!"

I gave a dismissive wave. "You don't have to worry about that from me." Besides, I seriously doubted Lorenzo wanted anyone to know either. "I still can't believe Don's partner is gay."

Tristan's eyebrow lifted. "I've told you before it's always the man you least suspect that's undercover. Although with all this lusciousness over here, I can understand why it's hard for a man to resist." He gave me a shit-eating grin. "I'm crazy about him."

I was half listening because I still had a hard time picturing Lorenzo with Tristan.

"He's leaving her."

I had to slide a little closer just to make sure I had heard him right. "Who's leaving whom?" I needed clarification.

Tristan grinned. "Lorenzo's leaving Tammy as soon as he pays off a few bills."

He was looking full of himself today. I didn't have the heart to tell him there was no way Tammy would allow that to happen. She was one of those types of women who had saved her virginity for that one man. And after giving birth to three of his babies and building a life together, there was no way she was letting her husband go. She told me before that her parents had been married for fifty years and she planned to do the same.

"Pump your brakes and slow it down," I warned, because Tristan had a nasty habit of moving way too fast when it came to relationships and usually ended up getting hurt. "You really need to tread lightly with this one. I'm serious."

"Oohh-kay, chica. I hear you." He sucked his teeth, rolled his eyes, and gave me that look like he wished I'd just be happy for him. I sighed. I knew I needed to talk some sense into Tristan's head, but with that big glossy grin and that faraway look in his eyes, like the time he had met Janet Jackson in the elevator, I knew now was not the time.

After another drama-filled radio show, Tristan and I got

our things and headed out into the parking lot together. The weather in May was my favorite time of the year.

"You wanna go shopping this weekend?" Tristan suggested while he scrolled through his text messages.

"Oooh! That sounds like fun. We haven't done that in forever." I stopped walking, then looked up at him, grinning. "Just as long as we go to the Cheesecake Factory."

"You're on." He gave me a high five.

"And you have to show me where you bought those shoes." I pointed down at the pumps on his feet.

"You like? Lorenzo bought them for me last weekend at the flea market. Oooh, Nikki! These Mexicans had a bad pair of leather boots that I gotta have."

I was still trying to digest Lorenzo going out in public with Tristan to the flea market. Maybe I didn't know that man as well as I thought. Or maybe Tristan was making more of the relationship than it really was. Like I said, I just hated to see him get hurt again. He is a good person with a funny, flaming personality, and if anyone deserved someone special in his life, it is Tristan.

I noticed Tristan kept looking over my shoulder.

"What's wrong? Damn, don't tell me Tammy's out in the lot waiting for you?" I teased.

He rolled his eyes. "Girl, no, but, uh . . . isn't that Donovan's SUV over there?"

My head whipped around; then I felt my heart do a little flip. Sure enough, at the end of the lot was a gray Escalade. I made out enough of his license plate to know it was him. The question was what the hell was he doing here? His headlights were dim, yet I could make out his image in the front seat.

"Uhhh . . . Tristan, I'll see you tomorrow."

"You sure?" Even after I nodded, he looked skeptical at leaving me. "Aw'ight, but you be careful."

My cheeks were hot and I was so embarrassed. I forced a smile, then walked across the lot and over to my husband's vehicle. He was sitting behind the wheel, seat reclined, and the engine running. "What are you doing here?" I asked, keeping my voice neutral.

Donovan tossed me a blank look. "What? I can't come and check on my wife?" he said like I should feel guilty about something. I couldn't believe that he was just sitting in the parking lot like there was nothing wrong with him popping up at my job after midnight.

My eyes strayed to the back seat where Aiden was sound asleep in his car seat. "Why isn't Aiden in bed?"

"Why you tripping?" He looked at me like he couldn't understand what I was angry about. "I told you I came to check on you."

I was stunned. "Check on me for what?" Lord knows, I wasn't sure how much more of this behavior I could take.

"What were you and Tristan talking about?" he demanded, and looked like he wanted to kill somebody. That person being me. Seriously, what the hell was going on with my husband?

"We were talking about going shopping and out to eat this Saturday while Aiden's with Mama," I said all nonchalant like there was nothing weird about my husband sitting in a parked car questioning my whereabouts.

His eyes locked with mine. "You sure that faggot isn't covering for you?"

"What?" I heaved a sigh. I hated when he used that word.

"I think you're tryna leave me." He sounded disgusted.

"What?" I was trying to be patient because my heart hurt for this man, but he was starting to trip. "Nobody's trying to leave you."

Donovan looked at me through narrowed eyes, letting his suspicions get the better of him, and actually looked insulted. "Tell me the truth, Nikki. You're tryna leave me, aren't you?" Some of his anger disappeared, but not all of it. I wasn't sure where all this insecurity was coming from, but it was getting old.

"No, baby. I'm not trying to leave you." I shook my head, then leaned inside the window and kissed him on the lips with all the love I could muster, yet the second his tongue slipped inside my mouth, I felt the hair at the back of my neck stand up. I drew back and screamed, "What the fuck! Have you been drinking?" Now it was my turn to get mad. Donovan got ready to deny it, but I cut him off. "Uh-uh. I'll be damned if you're going to jeopardize my son's life with your bullshit!" I had every right to be irritated. Like I said before, I already lost one child. I'd be damned before I lose another.

He punched the steering wheel and had the nerve to act offended. "Damn, Nikki. Get off these nuts! I've only had a couple of beers."

"And that's a couple too many. Get the fuck outta the vehicle!" I demanded, and didn't even wait for him to get out. I swung open the door and practically yanked his ass off the seat. Donovan looked like he wanted to slap me. I knew he wouldn't, but it didn't change the way he looked.

"Man, you're tripping!"

I had a hand at the hip and my finger all up in his face. "No, you're tripping if you think I'm going to let you drive around drunk with my son in the car!" My voice broke and I had this huge lump in my throat. Our life wasn't supposed to be like this. My daughter had been taken way too early and now my husband . . . My marriage was heading toward disaster, and that little boy in the back seat was right smack in the middle of it all.

I had to take a deep breath and count to five before I went clean the fuck off. "Something has got to change, because I can't keep living like this. The drinking, mood swings, and the accusations. All that has got to stop!" I hollered loud enough for the entire block to hear. There were a couple employees of

WJPC coming out of the building. They stopped and were staring at us. "What the hell are y'all looking at?" I screamed. Luckily they had sense enough to keep it moving.

Donovan stared at me dumbfounded for several seconds like he couldn't believe I had flipped out. Trust and believe, I'm from the hood and can get down and dirty with the best of them, but clowning my husband out in public was not one of them. Big Mama raised me better than that.

By the time a car peeled out of the parking lot, I had finally got my breathing slowed down. Donovan sighed and dragged a frustrated hand across his face. I was so mad at him the last thing I wanted to hear was his excuses. "Baby—"

I threw my hands up in the air. "Go ahead and get in on the passenger's side. You can bring me to get my car in the morning." I was too through with him. While he dragged his feet around to the other side, I got in behind the wheel. As soon as I looked back at my little angel who was sleeping peacefully, I got angry all over again. Thank goodness Aiden was too young to know what was going on. Donovan climbed in and shut the door, then turned on the seat. The fire was gone from his eyes and his gaze held so much pain I wanted to cry.

"Listen, baby, I—"

I held up a hand, cutting him off. "Save it for in the morning after you sleep it off. Right now I'm too pissed off to listen to shit you gotta say." I put the SUV in Drive and headed home. I wasn't sure how much longer I could go on because I was emotionally exhausted. Yet I had a strong feeling that this was just the beginning.

10

Trinette

The second we pulled into the circular driveway in front of the double doors of a two-story brick home, my best friend hurried down the steps to greet us.

"Hey, Netta!" she cried.

Smiling, I stepped out of the car and removed the sunglasses from my eyes. "Whassup, Nikki!"

My best friend, Nichole Truth, was a beautiful woman with dark mahogany skin, itty bitty breasts, and wide hips. Ever since giving birth to Aiden she'd packed on a few extra pounds around the middle, but she was still cute as hell. Nikki had been rocking locks for years, and they looked like they had been recently cut and barely brushed her shoulders. It was good to see that even though I wasn't around, my girl was still keeping it cute. I threw my arms around her and squeezed tightly. She had no idea how happy I was to see her.

Before I moved to Virginia, we used to see each other practically every day. I lived in St. Louis most of my life and loved that my girl had only been a car ride away with a bottle of Moscato chilling in the refrigerator.

"What took y'all so long?" Nikki asked as I released her.

I rolled my eyes so she'd know I was clearly annoyed. "Girl, we got delayed in Atlanta. I hate that airport."

"Well, I'm just glad you finally made it." She looked down at my belly and started grinning. I guess she never expected to see the day Trinette Montgomery lost her waistline. She ain't the only one. Neither did I. "Look at that belly. I still can't believe you're pregnant."

"Yeah, me and you both," I mumbled. I was dying to say more, but my husband was climbing out of the car.

Leon looked over the top at the two of us and grinned. "What's up, Nikki?"

"What's going on, *Daddy*?"

He started cheesing all proud. Fatherhood had made him a happy man and Mama an even happier woman. I was already four months' pregnant and haven't had to want for anything.

Nikki hurried around the rental car and wrapped her arms around Leon. They had always been close. "I'm so glad to see you two!" she squealed. I don't think I've seen her that happy in a long time. She was practically grinning from ear to ear.

"Where's Don?" Leon asked.

I noticed the frown on Nikki's lips when he mentioned her husband's name. "He's in the bathroom getting dressed." She then smiled and changed the subject. "Grab your bags and come on inside. Don was waiting until you got here before he threw a few steaks on the grill."

Leon rubbed his belly. "Mmm. I can't wait. I'm starved."

"Then follow me inside. I just made some potato salad." Nikki came around and hugged me again, then gazed into the back seat. "Goodness, Netta, how long are you planning to stay?" she teased when she saw I had two rolling Louis Vuitton suitcases and a tote bag.

"You know how I do. I can never make up my mind what I want to wear, so I brought extra just in case." Did she really think after all these years I was going to change?

Nikki shook her head the way my mother used to do. "Just

wait until you have a baby on one hip and a diaper bag on your shoulder."

"Whatever." I shuddered at the idea. That's what a nanny was for. "Don't worry about our bags. Leon and I decided to stay at the Hampton Inn up the street."

Her head whipped around and she looked clearly offended. "What? Y'all too good to stay at our house?"

Leon held up his hands. "No, it's nothing like that. I just want to spend the entire weekend making love to my wife and running around the room naked."

Nikki scrunched up her nose, then laughed. "Okay, that is too much information. I guess I can understand y'all wanting to get your freak on while you still can."

I kept my comments to myself. Lately, sex with Leon had improved. He found my changing body such a turn-on. Every time he saw me naked, he commented on how big my breasts were getting; then he wanted to squeeze and suck on them and the next thing I knew, we were sexing it up for the next hour. I felt so guilty about my relationship with Jrue and the paternity of my unborn child that I just let him have it whenever and how often he wanted it. I mean, come on. It's the least I could do.

"Where's my godson?" I asked as we stepped into her house.

"Girl, he's taking a nap. And don't you go waking him up either. He's teething and been cranky all morning."

"I can't wait to see that little rugrat." Ms. Netta loved kids just as long as they belonged to someone else.

I glanced around the house admiring her large foyer and the spacious living room beside it. Nikki had a nice big house. Not as nice as mine, but definitely a far cry better than that little house she'd sold last year. They were now living in West County in a two-story house with four bedrooms and three baths. I guess years of hard work were finally starting to pay off. Definitely not something I knew anything about. Hard work was Leon's responsibility, not mine.

I followed her into the kitchen and almost screamed out loud when I saw Donovan leaning over the sink. *What the hell?* The last time I had seen him was six months ago when Nikki had organized a surprise welcome home party. Leon and I flew in for the celebration. Damn. Since then he had lost so much weight his jeans were hanging off his hips, and not in a good way. His face looked sunken in, and for him to be a barber, that nappy stuff on his head was a hot mess.

"What's up, Netta?" he greeted me with a bear hug. One sniff and there was no mistaking the tequila on his breath. Trust me, I would know. It used to be my drink of choice, and my pregnant ass has been fienin' for a shot of Patron.

"Hey, Don," I muttered, then eased out of his grasp and looked him in the eye. "How have you been?"

He gave me this sad-looking smile and I noticed the dark circles underneath his eyes. "I can't complain," he said with a chuckle that I've loved for over twenty years.

I looked over at Nikki and noticed the scowl across her face. I figured he'd done something to piss her off. Okay, what's really going on?

Leon stepped into the kitchen and Donovan's face lit up like fireworks on the Fourth of July. "Whassup, boy!" He hurried over and the two hugged and gave dap.

I knew it was rude, but I couldn't stop looking at Donovan. This was the man I used to be jealous about. He had once been so sexy. Now the finest dude from the hood looked like he had just gotten out of rehab. I remembered when I used to have the biggest crush on Donovan in elementary school, yet the only woman he had ever wanted was Nikki.

"Nikki, baby . . . Grab that bottle of Cuervo from under the sink."

She sucked her teeth. "Don . . . isn't it a little early to be drinking?"

At first his eyes flashed with anger like he was about to explode, but then he gave that silly smirk of his. "It's never too early to celebrate with my man." Ignoring her, Donovan walked around the island, reached under the sink, and removed a half-empty bottle of tequila. I noticed the worried look in Nikki's eyes.

"My man, let's have a drink and toast the new baby!" Don was already reaching into the cabinet removing two small glasses. "Netta, girl! When's that baby due?" he asked.

"Not soon enough," I mumbled, and tried to pretend I was tickled, for Leon's sake. "Nikki, what you got to eat? I'm starving." I glanced over at her. She was still staring at her husband. I was starting to think that maybe she and Donovan had a fight before our arrival. "Nikki, concentrate!" I snapped my finger in front of her face and she startled. "Food . . . please . . . your godchild's hungry."

"Oh, damn, right." She gave a nervous laugh. "Snacks coming right up." She grabbed a bag of potato chips, poured them into a large bowl, and put them in front of me, then grabbed a jar of French onion dip from the pantry. It wasn't what I had in mind, but I guess it would do until dinner.

I walked over to a barstool and took a seat. The four of us hung out in the kitchen talking and laughing, although with every passing second Nikki looked more upset than she had when we first stepped into the room. She stood off to the side with a weird look on her face, laughing off cue and barely contributing to the conversation even when the subject returned to my baby.

"Nikki, you okay?"

She nodded her head. "Sure, girl, I'm fine." Liar. "I just can't get over you being pregnant." Okay, maybe that part was true because hell, I hadn't gotten over it either.

Leon was walking across the kitchen with his skinny chest stuck out. "Yeah, we're getting pretty excited about the baby. I think Netta's bought out the entire store."

This time when Nikki's head whipped around her smile had returned. "Oooh! Did you find out the sex of the baby?"

I shook my head. "No . . . not yet."

Leon moved beside me and gave me a loud wet one on the cheek. "We were thinking about keeping it a surprise, aren't we, baby?"

I stuffed another chip in my mouth to keep from answering. I guess that was true. It would be a surprise. I would find out the sex *and* the baby's daddy all in the same day. Now how fucked up was that?

I was chewing on chips and watching Donovan as he passed Leon a glass. "Man, you better enjoy your sleep while you still can, because it's all about to change, dawg!" He started laughing real loud, then brought the glass to his lips and downed its contents, then reached for the bottle and poured himself another. Nikki was mumbling something under her breath that I couldn't make out.

I know Nikki had said that Donovan had been acting strange since he had gotten home, but I had no idea it had gotten this bad. I had planned to take her in the other room and find out just what the hell was going on, but for now, I needed to find something to eat other than potato chips.

11

Nikki

We were in my car, heading to the grocery store for pickles and barbecue sauce, when Trinette asked, "What's going on with Donovan?"

Leave it to Trinette to get straight to the point. Her eyes were locked on mine as she waited. I focused on the road while I tried to think about my answer. "He's just trying to adjust."

"Adjust? Girl, since when is Don an alcoholic?"

Already, I was starting to regret her coming up to spend the Fourth of July weekend with us. I knew he had issues, but it wasn't that bad. "He's still having some troubles adjusting to being back at home."

"Some? Girl, your husband is a freaking lush. I ain't ever seen him drink like that before. I hate to say it, but he reminds me of his father."

I knew what she was saying was true. Don's father had been an alcoholic who abused his kids until they all had found a way to escape. Donovan said it was because Brown had never gotten over his wife, Donovan's mother, being murdered in an alley on her way home from work. I always believed his illness ran deeper than that. The way he used to beat Donovan until he broke skin and then put him out of the house for days, there had to be some serious mental issues brewing. At one time, Donovan refused to drink because he was afraid he would end up just like Brown. Yet after Mimi was killed, he started drinking. However, it had never been this much.

I tried to make excuses, even blamed it on the war; but no matter how I spun it, my husband drank way too much. He was depressed and I read that alcohol only made it worse. I didn't know what to do and had almost been tempted to call Trinette and cancel the trip, but I was so lonely and missed my girl so much that I couldn't do it.

"He's going through a lot, Netta," I said all nonchalant.

"You told me that, but I had no idea it was this bad."

I stopped my car at the light and took a deep breath.

"Nikki, really, what's going on? Come on, it's me . . . Netta . . . you're talking to. Something is seriously wrong with Don."

She was right. Everything she said was correct. I shook my head, then the tears started running down my face, and then I was bawling.

"Oh, damn! Pull over there." Trinette was patting my back and pointing to the curb ahead. I waited until the light changed, then went through the intersection and brought the car to a stop. "Now talk to me," she demanded.

"I don't know where to begin except to say that everything in my life is falling apart. I wake up every morning and never know what to expect. Some days he's that sweet, loving man who I married, and other days he's moody and cussing and accusing me of trying to leave him for another man. I just don't know how much more I can take."

"He sounds like Jekyll and Hyde."

Trinette wagged her eyebrows and I gave a sad chuckle. Well, at least she was still good for a laugh. "You're stupid! But you're right, that's exactly how he acts. I've been trying to be patient, but, Netta . . ." I started shaking my head. "I'm ready to pack up Aiden and move in with my mother for a little while."

Her hazel eyes got large with surprise. "Girl, now you know I have no patience when it comes to a man, so I'm the worst person to ask for advice. But you know I love me some Donovan, and the two of you have been through so much together. Have you tried going to church?"

My head whipped around. "Church? Since when do you go to church?" I asked between sniffs. Don't tell me my best friend is losing her mind as well.

She waved her hand at me. "Uh-uh. I don't go to church, but Mama's always talking about putting your problems in the Lord's hand, and whenever I try that it actually works."

I sniffed and took a moment to think about what she said. I would have never guessed in a million years that Trinette would encourage me to go back to church. I used to attend quite regularly when Big Mama was still alive. Donovan and I had even started going again after his first deployment and really got involved, but once Aiden was born and he was deployed, I just could never find the time. Now that he was back, church was no longer a part of our lives. Maybe Trinette was on to something.

"That's a good idea. How about we all go on Sunday?" I suggested.

Her eyes widened and I was sure she was going to decline when she shocked me and nodded her head. "Girl, the things I do for my friends."

"What friends? Last I checked I was the only friend you got." I laughed.

"You know it." She reached across the seat and gave me a much needed hug. "I got an idea. Why don't we surprise Mama and attend service at her church?"

I knew her too well. That was Trinette's way of spending time with her family, that way she didn't have to make any special trips.

"Sure, that sounds good to me." I smiled and wiped my eyes. I was actually feeling a lot better. I don't know why I hadn't thought of it, but church was exactly what we needed to get our lives back on track.

I put the car back in Drive and eased into the flow of traffic. We were supposed to be going to the grocery store, but the second I hit the corner, Trinette started squirming on the seat.

"Ooh, Nikki! Pull in there."

I grinned over at my friend and made a quick right into T.J. Maxx's parking lot. "What you planning to do? Buy another suitcase full of clothes?"

She shrugged. "I just want to see what treasure I can find." That's my girl. She can never resist the urge to shop. Trinette has always been that way. Even while we were growing up she'd had filet mignon taste and hamburger money, but she never let it stop her from living like a diva. And then once she hit college, there was no stopping her. She learned how to make men spend their money on her all the way down to the expensive soap that she lathered on her body. Men had spoiled her and then Leon, and now she expected it to continue. I just hoped she realized that once that baby is born, her needs will become second to her child's.

I pulled the car into the parking lot and killed the engine.

"Hey . . ." Trinette began, and I turned and looked at that rare serious look on her face. "Even though I think church might be a good start, I really think your husband needs some help."

I looked down at the steering wheel. I just couldn't take her feeling sorry for me. I had married my high-school sweetheart. Our marriage was supposed to have been perfect. "I know you're probably right. I'm just trying to be patient and let him do things on his own terms."

She shook her head. "Uh-uh. That shit went out the window the second he stepped foot back in that house. I know you believe in that love, honor, and obey crap, but you've got to put you and Aiden first." She tossed her hands in the air. "All that drinking and crazy talk, girl . . . you're better than me. I would have left that crazy mothafucka a long time ago!"

I finally looked up at her and rolled my eyes. "That's because you don't take your marriage vows seriously and I do."

"True, but that's not what I mean." She leaned back on the seat with her hands on her belly. "My uncle, the one who used to rape me? Well, he was one of those crazy-ass Vietnam vets. He'd be up at all hours of the night sleepwalking and screaming like he thought he was still on the frontline."

I couldn't even set my lips to tell her Donovan was doing the same thing. Thank goodness Leon insisted on them staying at a hotel three blocks away. The last thing I wanted was for the two of them to see how bad it really had gotten. "How bad was it?"

"Like hell. I remember I used to feel sorry for his ass. Then one night he climbed under the covers calling me Connie, his wife who had left him. And that's when he first raped me. At first I thought he still thought I was his wife, but then he started moaning 'Netta' in my ear and I knew that crazy bastard knew what he was doing."

I couldn't believe how calm she sounded, because it had taken years before Netta had told me about her uncle raping her. I never could understand how a woman could leave her own daughter alone with another man, family or not. For years I hated her mother just like she had. But Big Mama raised me to forgive and forget. Once Darlene went to drug rehab, then started attending church and gave her life over to God, I forgave her and encouraged Netta to do the same. I was glad that she had been making some effort.

"What I'm trying to say is don't just try to sweep this under the rug. If Don needs help, then you need to make sure he gets it. I'd hate to get a call in the middle of the night saying something happened to either of y'all."

"Thanks, girl. I appreciate that." I really loved those rare moments when Trinette proved that she cared about someone other than herself.

"All right, now let's go see what treasure we can find."

I figured shopping was a good way to shut her up at least for a little bit while I had a chance to think about Don's behavior and come up with a way to keep him under control for the entire weekend.

Trinette grinned and her eyes lit up the way they always do when it comes to spending money. Netta used to spend years shopping for designer clothing and accessories at all those high-end stores until I dragged her ass into a T.J. Maxx and proved to her she could buy the exact same item for a fraction of the price. What I didn't realize was that I had unleashed a monster.

We were filling up the second shopping cart with stuff for Trinette when I decided things were getting out of hand. "Netta, why are you buying a swimsuit? You're not going to be able to wear any of these things until next summer."

"So what? At least I'll have them when I get my body back."

I pursed my lips with disgust. She was back to thinking about herself again. "Come on, I want to find something for the baby." I didn't even wait for a reply and pushed the cart over to the infants' section. Trinette was trying to come off as uninterested, but I knew better. She could act like she didn't like kids, but I remembered the way she had behaved the day Aiden was born. She had flown down and spent three days kissing and hugging her godson. Not many people knew this, but beneath all that ice she really did have a good heart.

Trinette spotted a tiny designer dress and removed it from the rack to get a closer look. "Oh, this is so cute!"

I gave her a weird look. "Yeah, but you don't even know what you're having."

"I feel it in my heart that this is a girl. She's going to be a little lady just like her mother."

"You mean a slut," I mumbled under my breath and started laughing when Netta slapped me upside my head. "You know I love you, though."

Smiling, she rubbed her stomach. "This little girl is going to be spoiled just like her mother."

"Ain't that the truth?" I gave her a long look. "How are you getting used to being pregnant?" I asked, because I knew it was a major adjustment. Just wait until she sees the stretch marks. Boy, I would love to be a fly on her wall.

She picked up a baby blanket and smiled at me. "I guess I'm coming around. Jrue is excited about the baby. And Leon's excited, and when they're happy, Netta gets to shop."

That wasn't at all what I meant. "And how do you feel about that?"

She sighed and tossed the blanket into the cart along with matching socks and bonnet. "I guess I had no choice but to get used to the idea. Every day I look in the mirror and I can see my body changing. As long as it's not too much, I think I'll be able to deal with it. Cocoa butter and I are now best friends."

She is so silly. I chuckled. "Just wait until your feet start swelling." She cut her eyes in my direction and I really started laughing. "Seriously, though. What have you decided to do about Jrue?"

Trinette moved over to a rocking chair and took a seat. "I wake up every morning and ask myself how in the world is this happening to me? I am in love with a man. Me? Netta? In love?" She shook her head. "I want nothing more than to spend my life with Jrue." Trinette blushed, something I was not used to seeing.

"Damn, girl. If you're still feeling like that, then maybe you really are in love."

She cut her eyes at me. "Bitch, what have I been tryna tell you all this time?"

"Yeah, but I had to see it for myself and the eyes don't lie."

She gave me a sad smile and started rocking back and forth

in that chair. "If this baby's Jrue's, then I can just walk away and start my new life with him. If it's Leon's . . . I don't know what I'm going to do. That man wants this baby so bad. I'm also afraid of what he might do if he finds out it's not his."

She wasn't lying. Leon might be quiet and let Trinette run over him, but after their last breakup I had finally gotten a chance to see another side to him. That man was not one to be messed with. He forgave her once and they renewed their vows with a pledge to make their reaffirmed marriage work. I was afraid that if he found out Trinette had been having an affair, he just might snap.

I couldn't keep my fears to myself. "I'm just worried all this is going to blow up in your face."

She waved her hand in dismissal. "I'm not worried about that." Trinette rose from the chair and walked over to finger a beautiful christening gown. "I just wish I had gotten rid of this baby while I had the chance."

My head snapped back. "You don't mean that."

She nodded and met my wide stare. "Yes, I do. I believe in staying in control. I can't do that pregnant. Right now I have absolutely no control over how all this is going to turn out. And I don't like that feeling."

For once I had to admit she was right. Lord knows I don't believe in abortions, but maybe this was one time when it would have been considered necessary, because when that baby is finally born, someone is going to get hurt. "Maybe you're right."

"Damn right. But in the meantime, I'll just milk it for all it's worth," she said, and that devious smile returned to her lips. I knew deep down she was worried. Acting like she was still large and in charge was Netta's way of making it all better. "I told Jrue I was coming down here to visit with my best friend and he dropped two grand in my checking account this morning. Told me to be safe. I've got precious cargo onboard."

I sucked my teeth. "He sounds like another lame ass."

She tossed her head back with laughter. "You know that's how I like them. But seriously, though . . . Jrue is different." I heard Usher's "Climax" and Trinette reached into her purse and looked down at her cell phone and grinned. "Speak of the devil." She brought the phone to her ear and walked toward the register.

I shook my head. Some things never change.

We made it back to the house just as Donovan was carrying in the steaks.

"Mmmm, something smells good," Trinette said, and put the bag with the barbecue sauce on the counter.

Donovan lowered the meat onto the stove, then eyed me suspiciously. "Took y'all long enough. What you do . . . go see your other man?"

I laughed and tried to play it off. "Dude, whatever."

Donovan didn't see anything funny. "Man, I told you she was trying to leave me for another mothafucka. That's what they do. When you're away fighting a war, your wife's out there straddling some other nigga's lap."

"No, he didn't," Trinette breathed under her breath.

I looked at her out the corner of my eye and then at Leon, who looked clearly embarrassed.

"Nah, not all women. Don, man, you got one of the good ones," he said, trying to simmer the tension.

My husband looked unconvinced and tipped his glass. "You can only trust them as far as you can see them. Hell, you should know that firsthand." He laughed at his joke.

I could see Trinette was ready to go off. Unfortunately, she knew it was true and Donovan knew it too. I quickly hurried to diffuse the bomb that was clearly ticking in the kitchen.

"Why don't we go out onto the patio and eat? I don't know about you, but I'm starving." I hooked my arm through Trinette's and pulled her along with me.

"You know I was about to snap," she hissed.

"I know. That's why I grabbed you." I pleaded with her to understand, and luckily she rolled her eyes and blew out a long breath.

She helped me set the table and before long we were all outside eating and laughing and having a good time. Don was even stroking my thigh under the table and giving me that look that said tonight it was on and popping, and my body radiated with heat. Of course that warm fuzzy feeling only lasted until Donovan's next drink.

"Netta, motherhood definitely complements you well."

She grinned. "Thanks, Don. We are really looking forward to having our first child."

Smiling, Donovan leaned back in his chair and glanced around the table. "Well, Leon, at least you don't have to worry if you're the father of her child."

"What the . . ." Trinette started to cuss him, but Leon touched her arms and shook his head. I knew it wasn't easy. Trinette struggled to keep her composure, although she looked ready to jump her pregnant ass across that patio table and strangle him. And probably would have if Aiden wasn't sitting on her lap.

"Seriously, man, how did you forgive your wife for messing around? How'd you manage to stay together?" he queried.

The table grew quiet.

"Don, I don't even know why you had to even go there," I snarled.

"Hey, I'm just having a conversation," he said with a smirk. "I was hoping my boy can enlighten me so when I find out what's really going on around here, I will know how to handle the situation." He tossed his glass back, then rose. "Anybody else want a drink?"

"No, and neither do you," I said with a warning glance. I wasn't going to keep playing this bullshit game with him. All this arguing and accusing me of doing shit behind his back had to stop.

And just like that it was like his head spun around like the girl from *The Exorcist* and the sweet Donovan returned.

"Yo, Leon, I'm sorry about that. That was completely out of line. How about we have another toast to congratulate you on the baby?"

Trinette kept that sour look on her face, but Leon's smile returned. As usual, he didn't bother to take Donovan's behavior personal. "Now that's something I can toast to."

"Let me go get the bottle." Donovan rose and then as if it were an afterthought, leaned down and kissed me hard on the mouth. "I love you, Nikki," he said, and I saw so much fear in his eyes I gasped. I had never seen that before. My husband had always been the strongest man I had ever known, and now he almost looked like a scared child. As he moved into the kitchen, tears filled my eyes.

Leon pressed a gentle hand to my arm. "Hey, you okay?"

I shrugged because I really didn't know anymore.

"Hell nah!" Netta exclaimed. Quickly, she handed Aiden to Leon, then leaned so far across the table her belly was practically on top. "Listen to me, Nikki, and listen good. Get that man some help before I break my foot off in his ass!"

She was right. I needed to find some way to save my husband's life.

12

Trinette

"I never knew I could be so happy . . . And I never knew I'd be so se-
cure . . ."

I was up out of my seat with the rest of the congregation as
the soloist rocked the room. There were thirty people in the
choir stand, an organist, and a choir director who was just as
good as, if not better than, Kirk Franklin.

My mama had been an active member of Sugarland Baptist
Church since recovering from a drug addiction eight years
ago. The congregation was large, yet it seemed everybody
knew everybody and all their business, so who was I to judge?

Mama was sitting in the pew in front of me and she
glanced over her shoulder for the umpteenth time. Pride was
all over her face as she clapped her hands and swayed her narrow hips. Two years ago after I had gotten past the anger of my
mother being a crackhead and all the consequences of her ne-
glect, I had donated to her one of my kidneys. Since then we'd
been slowly building a relationship. I don't think we'll ever be
joined at the hip, but it felt good knowing that I finally had my
mother back in my life.

"LET THE SAINTS SAY AMEN . . . I SAID, LET THE
SAINTS SAY AMEN!!"

"Amen!" I shouted.

The minister rose and walked across the pulpit. Everybody lowered onto their seat and got ready for a powerful sermon. Something about being in church had me feeling all good inside. I laced my fingers with Leon's. He turned his head and grinned, and I smiled back at him.

Nikki and Donovan were sitting to my left. She leaned over and whispered near my ear, "At least the church hasn't burned down yet."

"You ain't neva lied," I giggled softly. I had worried about that myself. We both knew good and well I hadn't stepped foot in a church in years. Leon squeezed my hand and mouthed, "Be quiet." Smiling, I straightened up on the pew and was actually looking forward to what Reverend Williams had to say.

"Saints . . . something has been weighing heavily on my heart." He paused and dragged a handkerchief across his forehead. "Some of y'all may know someone who's doing this and then again, that someone may be you. I'm talking about sliding under the sheets at night and slipping out the back door before the sun rises. Y'all know what I'm talking about. Can somebody help me?"

"Amen!" the congregation shouted from around the room.

"I know I'm not speaking from experience, but when a man and woman say 'I do' to each other, they're not saying 'I do' to all the others."

"Preach, Rev!"

"Amen!"

"Today's sermon comes from Proverbs 6:32. '*But whoso committeth adultery with a woman lacketh understanding.*' "

Oh shit—oops—I meant, oh shoot. My heart leaped nervously and I glanced up at the ceiling, expecting the building to finally come tumbling down. Nikki tapped me on the leg and I looked up and caught her ass trying not to laugh. There was nothing funny about the situation. I kid you not, Reverend Williams was looking directly at me as he preached about the sin of climbing in another man's bed.

"I have been told that we are having a problem here in the church that is starting to cause conflict amongst our members. That at Bible study there was an incident that we need to address before it goes any further, because God don't like ugly in His house!"

"Preach!"

"The root of ugliness in God's house is the devil's work. I don't want to talk long on this subject because I know I'm stepping on some toes here. But this is God's house and His house is sacred!"

"Mmm-hmm."

"Amen!"

I felt myself trying to scrunch down low on the seat. Why was he staring directly at me? Leon brought my hand to his lips, kissed it, and I started feeling guilty as hell.

"I'd like to begin my message with a word of prayer. Can I have all the deacons and deaconesses come down to the front of the church. Everyone else in the pews please hold hands as we pray."

I glanced around and watched everyone else rise and realized I had better join in.

"Bow your heads, saints. Heavenly Father . . . I want to come to you in your glory and honor and ask that you look over our church and our church members . . . touch the ones that need it and cleanse their bodies and souls, and bring Jesus Christ in their lives. Because only he can do what we cannot do, and that is save souls."

Oh, God. I was a sinner. My heart was pounding so hard, I felt like I was hyperventilating.

Why me, Lord? Why did I have to fall in love with a man who wasn't my husband? It was crazy, yet I couldn't deny it. Sure, I've been a slut all my life. Bed hopping and taking men's money had been my favorite pastime. Yet in the ten years Leon and I have been married, I never thought twice about messing around on him because I didn't feel that level of respect and commitment the reverend was preaching about. Then bam! I meet Jrue and I was ready to be faithful to one man. The wrong man. I know it was adultery, but it never felt like such a nasty word until now while I'm standing beside my husband, fingers laced together, in church.

We finally lowered back to our seat and the pastor's powerful voice boomed off the church walls. I think I flinched a couple of times. All around me, everybody was listening intently to his sermon. Leon draped an arm across my shoulders, drawing me close. Even Donovan was nodding his head and getting all wrapped up in the Word. Mama was in front of me dabbing her eyes with a tissue, probably remembering all the husbands whose dicks she had sucked while turning tricks. I cringed at the thought, because I truly was no better than her. I couldn't even count all the men I have slept with. I figured as long as I used a condom, I never had to see them again. The longer I sat there, the guiltier I felt, until finally I couldn't sit still a moment longer.

"I need to go to the bathroom," I whispered to Leon, then tiptoed past Nikki out of the pew and down the aisle. For some reason, I suddenly started to feel hot and decided that I needed to go and get some air. I hurried over to the other side of the church and went into the bathroom and splashed water onto my face and took several deep breaths. Goodness, what the hell was wrong with me? I was reaching for a paper towel when Nikki walked through the door.

"Netta, you okay?"

I blew out a long breath. "Girl, I had to get out of there. All that talk about fornication and sleeping with someone's husband, I felt like the walls were closing in on me!"

Her eyes sparkled with laughter. "I wonder why?"

"It was just more than I could handle. That's why I don't
like coming to church, because I always walk away feeling so
guilty."

Nikki moved in front of the mirror and gave a rude snort.
"Then maybe that's an indication that it's time to change."

Damn. She was as bad as Reverend Williams.

"I know I'm not living my life right and I need to get it
together, but everybody does things on their own terms. But
really I felt like the preacher was talking directly to me."
Goodness, I definitely needed a drink right about now. Too
bad I couldn't have one.

Nikki was primping in the mirror and laughing at the
same time. "You reap what you sow," she said between chuck-
les.

Oh, no she didn't. "Uh-huh, and those without sin may
cast the first stone."

Her head whipped around so fast it was a wonder it didn't
snap from her neck.

"Don't act like I'm the only one who's committed adultery," I hissed. I know I was being mean, but I hate when others try to judge me.

"Whatever," Nikki mumbled under her breath, but I could
see the fear in her eyes. She practically jumped six inches off
the ground when the door swung in and Mama stepped into
the bathroom.

"Nikki, honey, your husband is at the altar on his knees,
turning his life over to God!"

Her eyes were wide and wild before she took several deep
breaths and Mama's words sunk in. "What? Praise the Lord!"
She bolted out of the bathroom. I would have been right behind her if Mama wasn't blocking the door.

"Netta, honey, what's going on? Is something wrong with
my grandbaby?"

I grinned down at Mama. She looked so pretty. Her face

was fuller. Her natural hair was cut in a low fade. She was wearing a beautiful blue suit I had gotten her for Mother's Day. Ever since the kidney transplant she had been living a healthy drug-free life, and I was proud of her.

"Mama, I'm fine. I was just feeling a little light-headed," I lied and waved my hand like it was no big deal.

"Uh-huh. The minister was hitting home with his sermon this morning, wasn't he?" She gave me that knowing look that only a mother had permission to give.

"Yeah, it was definitely deep."

She stepped closer and gave me a suspicious look. "You're not doing anything you're not supposed to be doing, are you?"

I don't know why everyone thinks they know me so well. "Of course not. What would make you think that?" I denied.

"Because you're a Meyers, and I know how Meyers women think," she replied, then walked over and turned the lock on the door. Immediately I knew it was going to be something I didn't want to hear.

"When you were at my house this morning, I noticed the way you kept looking at your cell phone, texting and grinning. Now, Leon is a good man, Netta, and good men are difficult to find, and even harder to keep." I started to turn away, but Mama grabbed my arm. "Listen to what I'm telling you, Netta . . . whatever or whomever it is, it ain't good, so leave it alone," she warned. I hated to see the worry I had caused on her face. Was I that obvious?

"If I haven't been able to give you anything, please let me just give you that bit of advice. Like Reverend Williams said, you gotta pray about it."

"I hear you, Mama." I hugged her close. She was all up in my business, yet part of me was glad that I finally had her around to nag me the way Nikki's mama had always done for her. I had every intention of finally getting my life right and being dedicated to one man. And I planned to do just that just as soon as this baby was born and Jrue left his wife.

I decided it was time to change the subject. "C'mon, Mama. Let's get back inside. I want to personally witness Donovan's day of resurrection."

Who knows? Maybe today might be the start in the right direction for both of us. I hoped so. At least for Nikki's sake.

13

Nikki

I was shelving books in the romance section when I noticed Rae walking into the bookstore. I couldn't stand that chick. Her husband and Don were in the same unit, and both had been deployed to Iraq and Afghanistan. Rae was the head of the FRG, Family Readiness Group, and took her responsibilities way too seriously. Somehow she was always in someone else's business and knew who was sleeping with whom while her husband was deployed. I'm just glad she never found out about my brief affair while Don was in Iraq.

Usually I blew her ass off when she dropped into my store, because it was mostly to brag about something new her husband had bought. Today I was actually glad to see her.

She waved a hand merrily in the air. "Good afternoon, Nikki." As she sauntered over to me, I took a moment to check her out. Rae was a full-figured sistah with the prettiest dark chocolate skin. She wore her natural hair in an Afro puff that actually made her look years younger. I used to think she was so pretty, that was, until she opened her loud mouth. She was wearing black slacks and tall pumps while her titties threatened to pop out of a tight purple blouse.

"Hey, Rae. It's good seeing you." I got up from my knees and dusted off my jeans. I didn't miss the look of disapproval on her face. Ms. Prissy probably didn't even wash dishes at home.

"I came in to find a cookbook with sinful desserts. Carl and I are having a get-together this weekend with a few *friends* and I want to impress them with my cooking. Not that that isn't easy to do." She smiled.

"Sure, let me show you where they're at." I signaled for her to follow me to the back far left of the store. Trust me. I hadn't missed the way she had emphasized the word *friends*. I guess she was making it clear I wasn't one of them. Not that I cared. The last place I wanted to be was at one of her stupid get-togethers. I've been down that boring road one too many times.

"How's Carl doing?" I asked, making small talk.

Rae suddenly stopped, turned, and looked at me like I had a lot of nerve asking her about her man. "He's fine, why?"

"Let me ask you something." I paused and took a moment to collect my thoughts. "Since he's been home, does he seem different to you at all?"

Her eyes drooped down to her hands before returning to me. "A little, but that's expected, considering . . ."

I shook my head because I totally disagreed with her assessment. "Yes, I understand that, but something just seems a little off about my husband." I was lying when I used the word *little*. Ever since Netta came down and visited last month, we'd been attending church regularly and Donovan was making more of an effort to go into work, but the mood swings were still there, and if I was even ten minutes late he'd start the bullshit about me messing around again.

"Something seems off?" Her head jerked back like I had just punched her. "I can't believe you would even set your lips to say something like that."

I shot her a sour look. "Why'd you say that?"

Rae shook her head, looking like she was disappointed at me. "Because we can't begin to understand what those men went through over there. Their camp was the subject of a mortar attack. Lives were lost right before their eyes."

"I know all that, but it's been months since they came home and several of the other wives I have talked to seemed to be having similar problems."

"What?" Her face crumbled and she looked upset. "I'm the FRG leader. Why hasn't anyone talked to me about this?"

"I'm talking to you now." I couldn't help the attitude, but like I said, I really can't stand this chick. "I need you to talk to the unit about having a therapist come in next drill weekend. I'm serious. I think the unit should be doing something to help these soldiers adapt, because my husband isn't." I felt like I was pleading with her to understand.

Rae didn't at all look moved by my request. "Well, that's a shame, because Carl is doing just fine considering all that he's gone through. I think what you need to be doing instead of talking about your husband behind his back is try showing him more support."

No, she didn't go there with me. "Hell, I have been supportive. For the last six months I have been more than patient, but I'm certain my husband is suffering from PTSD."

That chick had the nerve to laugh at my comment. "There you go, self-diagnosing the man! Wasn't he evaluated by his unit?"

I nodded.

"And what did they determine?" she asked, then crossed her arms and frowned.

"They said he was fit for duty, but—"

She rudely cut me off. "Then there you have it. Just give the man time to adjust. Trust me, there's nothing wrong that a little time and TLC won't cure." She then patted me on the head like I was a damn puppy. "Now . . . where is that cookbook you wanted to show me?"

★   ★   ★

This is Nikki Truth and you're listening to *Truth Hurts* on 97 WJPC. Tonight I'm going to read an e-mail that I received from a listener.

> Dear Nikki,
> My fiancé is in the military and after two deployments he just isn't the same man I fell in love with. I know that I'll never understand what he's been through. I've tried to be supportive, but the nightmares, depression, and mood swings are getting to be more than I can handle. As we are getting closer to the date of our wedding, I'm not so sure if I can still go through with it. What should I do?
> Signed,
> Prisoner of War

"Well, Prisoner of War. That is a tough question. Being the wife of an army soldier as well, I honestly know what you're going through, and it takes a strong woman to be a military wife. We have to be able to hold things together while our husbands are deployed and be able to pull things together when he returns. We are the backbone, and those men rely on our love and our strength to persevere. As my pastor said last Sunday, the Lord doesn't give us any more than he knows we can handle. Well, listeners, there you have it. Our men and women are sacrificing their lives for this country and coming back traumatized." I paused long enough to bring the microphone closer to my mouth. "From what I've read in the e-mail, I have a strong feeling her fiancé has PTSD, and the first thing she needs to do is try and get that man some help." It felt good to finally say that. After months of denial and hoping that time would heal all wounds, I'd finally realized it was going to take much more than prayer to cure what ailed Donovan.

"For my listeners who are not familiar with the term, post-traumatic stress disorder, or PTSD, is an emotional illness classified as an anxiety disorder and usually occurs as a result of a life-threatening experience such as the wars our American soldiers are fighting in. Once they've returned home, these men and women continue to re-experience the traumatic event in some way such as flashbacks and dreams. They're drinking, can't sleep, and are basically having a hard time adapting to life back at home." Lord knows, I know. "I am a strong advocate that prayer helps, but this is one sickness that requires so much more. POW, get that man some help," I emphasized, saying aloud something I had known all along. "But what about the rest of my listeners? How many others of you are going through the same things, and for those who are not, if it were you, would you stick by them or not, regardless of how bad things get? I'm going to open up the phone lines and see what my listeners have to say."

I looked up and caught Tristan giving me a suspicious look. I guess he knew I was lying. I shook my head. Now was not the time to be judging me. The only prisoner of war was me, but I had to know if I was the only one out there who was dealing with post-traumatic stress disorder. After Rae had left the store, I called the unit and left a message with Donovan's first sergeant to call me back. I still had yet to hear from him. I don't care what anybody says, six months home is long enough. My husband was definitely suffering from PTSD, and he needed help.

Tristan held up two fingers and I glanced down at the phone lines and pressed the flashing button.

"Caller, you're on the air."

"Hi, Ms. Nikki. This is Danny."

"Good evening, Danny."

"I just had to call in. That woman should be ashamed calling herself a POW, because she doesn't know the first thing about what her man has gone through. People around them being killed and hurt. Hell, that's enough to make any of us go insane."

"You're right." Especially about going insane. "Thanks for calling. Caller, you're on the air."

"Ms. Nikki, she needs to run while she can! I was married to one of those psychos. He came home and I woke up to a gun pointed at my head. I refused to play Russian roulette with my life, so I left that crazy mothafucka."

Tristan was going to have to do a lot of bleeping tonight. "I know that's right," I said and gave a soft chuckle, trying to bring the mood down a notch. "Hopefully he got better over time?" I asked more for myself.

"Last I heard he was locked up at some mental hospital being tube-fed."

I groaned inward. "Wow! Thanks for calling." I pressed the next flashing button.

"Good evening, Ms. Nikki. This is Carlita."

"Whassup, Carlita, girl!" I shouted. She was one of my regular listeners. "What's your take on tonight's topic?"

"POW needs to walk away, because if she's already doubting her commitment to that man, then that tells me she isn't ready."

"Okay now."

"When a woman pledges through sickness and health, they have to be ready to take those vows seriously. It's been tough. My husband's been home from Iraq almost a year, but yet it's like I'm living with a stranger."

I know that feeling.

"But we've been going to church and I've been praying and I know God is going to take care of him."

The more calls that came in, the guiltier I felt for wishing I could be anywhere but with Donovan. I had touched on a controversial issue that had callers debating back and forth. Normally I got a kick out of the antics, but not tonight. The mood was way too serious because what was happening in my home and in other houses around the country was no laughing matter. By the time the show was over, I was calling the house. It had gotten to the point I liked to be prepared for *which* Donovan was at home waiting for me.

"Hey, baby." Donovan answered after the first ring in a voice that was way too cheerful that I immediately assumed he must have been drunk. "How was the show tonight?"

"It was good." And for once I was glad he rarely listened to the radio. "Aiden sleep?"

"Yep, me and my man sat on the couch, ate popcorn, and watched *Madagascar* until he passed out. Have to admit that cartoon was kinda cute." He laughed and I felt myself starting to relax. "Now I'm waiting for my big baby to come home so I can show her how much I missed her."

"I can't wait to get home. I want to show you just what I plan to do to you." Those rare moments when he was in the right state of mind, sex was good. And tonight I needed him to put out the fire he had started between my thighs.

"I'll see you in a few. Hey . . . I love you."

I exhaled a sigh of relief. "I love you too." I blew a few kisses and was hanging up the phone when Tristan came swiveling in.

"Hey, girlfriend . . . do you need to talk?" He pulled a chair up beside me. His concern was so genuine.

I shook my head. "No, I'm okay."

He turned to me and commented casually, "Doesn't sound like you are." Tristan was so damn observant. But I guess *real* friends are.

"I'm trying to hold it together, at least for Aiden's sake." As I spoke, I felt my bottom lip quiver.

"Donovan's a good man and he's lucky to have a woman

like you. I wasn't going to say anything . . . but even when I picked you up that day we went shopping . . . I could tell that something was off about him."

"It is." I paused and blew out a long breath just to keep myself from crying. The second Tristan had pulled into the driveway, Donovan went flying out of the house and peered all in his car to make sure I didn't have some man scrunched down low in the back seat. "Tristan, I feel like I'm walking around in a revolving door. I just don't know what to do anymore. One day my husband is acting like a crazy alcoholic, the next day he's sweet as apple pie, then he's a space cadet or the paranoid jealous husband."

Tristan's hand flew over his mouth in shock. "Nikki, girlfriend, I had no idea things were that bad!"

I shrugged my shoulder, struggling to keep from crying. I'd been doing a lot of that lately. "It's worse, but he's my husband and I love him. Last week I got him to agree to see the minister for marriage counseling. He seems willing to make things work, yet he refuses to admit that anything is *really* wrong with him. Tristan, I feel like I am losing my mind."

"We can't have that," he teased. I know he was trying to make me feel better.

"Nope, it's been long enough. Tonight I'm going to suggest that he see a therapist, because I really think he is suffering from post-traumatic stress disorder. It's just hard when he's just in so much denial."

He gave me a long, hard stare. "I really wish there was something I could do to help you out."

"You can." I forced a smile. "Talk about something else. How are you and you-know-who doing?"

Tristan looked more than happy to change the subject. Who could blame him? At the mention of Lorenzo his face lit up. "We're doing really good. That man practically lives at my apartment when I'm not at the station. We're talking about me opening my own boutique."

"What?" I was still having such a hard time envisioning the two of them together.

Smiling, Tristan nodded his head. "You know I've always wanted to open my own business and with my sense of style, I really think I could make a success of it."

I definitely had to agree. "You know how much I love going shopping with you. And you definitely know how to coordinate outfits."

"Well, you know what they say . . ." He gave a dramatic sweep of his hand. "Every girl needs a gay man as a best friend."

"Someone to gossip with and definitely to take along shopping," I added with a chuckle. "I think it's a fabulous idea!"

"I know, right." He was glowing with excitement. "Anyway, Lorenzo plans on showing me how to get my business off the ground."

"Wow! It sounds to me like Lorenzo is really good for you. What's up with him and Tammy?" Tristan gave me one of his saucy grins and I could tell he was dying to tell me something. "What?"

He looked to his left, then right, and said, "He told her last week he wanted a divorce."

I was floored. "What?"

Tristan nodded. "Lorenzo said sister girl went off calling him all out of his name! But that heifer refuses to leave 'cause you know it's Lorenzo's house, so he said he'll just do things the legal way."

I shook my head. "Too much drama for me, but at least you seem happy." I couldn't resist a smirk.

"Yeah, girl. Happier than I have felt in a long time. I really feel that Lorenzo is the one. That man makes me so happy and treats me like a queen. I've never had a man be so good to me before. Look." He leaned closer so I could see the diamond studs in his ears.

"Dang! You got it like that?" It had to be at least two carats.

His grin broadened. "I told you. What we have is special."

"I sure hope so." At least for Tristan's sake.

We talked a few more minutes; then I grabbed my things and hurried home to see if something special was still waiting for me at home, or if Mr. Hyde had returned.

14

Trinette

"Netta, come quick!"

I tossed aside the baby magazine I had been reading and hurried up the stairs as fast as I could manage, considering I was six months' pregnant.

"Where you at?" I called, hoping he hadn't fallen, because there was no way my big ass could help him.

"I'm back here!" he called, and I followed the direction of his voice to the bonus room. My heart was pounding and I was nervous what I might find. I turned the knob, stepped into the room, and gasped. "Surprise, baby." Leon stepped to the side grinning ear to ear.

I couldn't believe it. What had once used to be my work-out room had been transformed into a high-end nursery. The room was a soft yellow, and a blue sky and clouds covered the ceiling that looked so real it was like the room now had sky-lights.

"Leon, it's beautiful. How did you manage all this without me knowing?"

"Easy. I had the wallpaper man come in while you were at work. Then I hired an interior decorator to design the room." He looked pretty pleased at himself and he had every right to be. I walked around admiring the large wooden rocker near the window; there was a tall dresser drawer, a changing table, and a large crib covered with beautiful stuffed animals. I rubbed my stomach and for a split second I wished it was Leon's baby I was carrying. It's such a damn shame. I loved Jrue and looked forward to spending my life with him, yet a part of me wanted to give Leon what he had always wanted, a son.

"This room is so beautiful."

He grinned. "I was hoping you felt that way."

"I do." I leaned over and wrapped my arms around him. Leon pressed his mouth against mine. I parted my lips and allowed his tongue inside.

"I still can't believe we're having a baby." He eased his head back, stared at me, and for a second I thought he was about to cry. He was so excited about the baby. And again I felt guilty, because all my husband had ever wanted was a family.

"Well, it's true, sweetheart. We're finally going to have a baby. You just be ready to hire me a personal trainer when this is all over because I'll be damned if I don't get my body back."

Chuckling, Leon drew me close. "Netta, after this you can have anything in the world you want."

That was exactly what I liked to hear.

His lips traveled to my cheeks, then lips. "All this talk about having a baby has me horny as hell. Why don't you come over to this rocking chair and straddle your man's lap?"

The last thing I wanted was to have sex, but I know not to bite the hand that feeds me. Besides, when Leon is feeling good and happy, he is generous as hell.

He unbuckled his jeans and they dropped to the floor; then he lowered his boxers and took a seat. I removed my maternity pants doing a little striptease just the way I knew he liked it. My panties followed.

"C'mere, baby." Grabbing my hands, Leon dragged me down on top of him. For several seconds our eyes locked while his fingers stroked my face. "You have made me the happiest man in the world. How could I be so lucky?"

I laughed. "I guess you just happened to be in the parking lot at the right time." We had met while attending college. I was walking across the lot to class when Leon had pulled in driving a brand-new Toyota Camry. As soon as he climbed out, he had my full attention.

He groaned. "Oh, what a day that was." I had ended up straddling his lap on the front seat the way I was doing him now.

Leon reached down between my thighs and discovered I was wet. "Leon." I moaned his name and spread my legs, welcoming his touch. "That feels good."

"I know something that feels better." He lifted me up until I felt the head of his erection nudging my kitty-cat. Then with one glorious push he found his rightful place and I exhaled at the feeling of him being inside me again.

"Shit!" he hissed.

Leon drew back, then plunged, pumping his hips and had the chair rocking. I just prayed that for once he could hold on long enough for me to get mine. Eyes closed, I gyrated my hips and cried out his name, loving the way he felt, but it still wasn't enough.

"That's it, baby . . . ride your dick."

I loved the way his erection felt sliding in and out of my wet kitty. I rode him long and hard, coming out to the tip and thrusting down onto him.

"Damn, that feels good," he moaned, and started rocking upward, meeting me halfway. "Yeah . . . that's it . . . ride that dick," he chanted over and over and his voice, low and aroused, had me pumping wildly over his length. I moved up and down, loving the way the head tickled my G-spot with every downward thrust. Leon reached down between us and rubbed my clit in quick little circles, matching the fast, heated rhythm of my thrusts. All conscious thoughts were erased as I was met by a wave of ecstasy. Leon started pumping hard and fast. The faster he moved within me, the more I wanted.

"You belong to me," he whispered against my lips and my eyelids flew open. He had never said anything like that before. Claiming what was his just wasn't something Leon did, yet I found it to be the most arousing thing he had ever said.

I looked up into his eyes as his thrusts became feverish and he ground his hips into me. As the feeling of an imminent climax built, Leon held on to my waist, slamming my body down onto his penis. Within seconds my pussy clenched and after one final thrust, I screamed as an orgasm claimed me.

"God, Netta." He kissed me, then several jerking spasms also delivered him over the edge.

My limp body collapsed against him, sending the chair rocking. I couldn't remember the last time sex had been that good between us. Maybe because I had been so busy with other things and consumed with my own life. It was something that had me wondering about all that I was planning to give up to start a new life with Jrue.

"Netta, baby, I need to talk to you about something."

I pulled back, almost afraid to hear what he was about to say. For a moment I wondered if he knew . . .

"I need to fly to Germany for a couple of weeks."

"What?" I said. Then my shoulders began to relax as I realized what he'd just said. "Oh." I felt like a bubbling fool.

"We're having problems at our overseas office and I need to go down and see why they keep having the same issues." He blew out a long, frustrated breath. "Trying to manage a team in Germany from here is a lot of hard work."

While he rattled on explaining the issue, my mind was already planning how I was going to spend the time he was away. It meant I had more time to spend with Jrue. I was so excited I had to catch myself from smiling.

Leon gave me a doubtful look as he stroked my arm. "This really isn't a good time with the baby coming and all—"

I wasn't hearing that nonsense, so I quickly cut him off. "Sweetheart, we still have three months before this baby is due. You go handle your business." Mentally, I was already picturing two weeks of Jrue and I holding each other.

"But I don't feel good about leaving my pregnant wife alone. I want to be there for your doctor's appointment."

"And you will . . . when you get back. By then I'll be seeing my OB every week."

Leon still didn't look convinced, so it was going to take a push on my part.

"I'm going to be fine. I promise if I have any issues, I'll call you." I gave him a saucy grin.

"And I'll be on the first plane back."

I kissed his lips, trying to reassure him. "I'll be fine. We have enough going on at work to keep me busy. Trust me, women used to have babies in the morning and be back out in the cotton field before sundown."

I kissed him again and then gripped his length between my fingers. I was willing to do whatever it took to get my husband on that plane. That meant Jrue and I would have plenty of time to play house and plan our future together.

15

Nikki

"*Gurrl* . . . he tried to blow my back out!"

Uh–uh. There was no way I was letting Tristan take me there. I had better things to be doing with my afternoon than listen to him giving me a play-by-play of his evening with Lorenzo. "Tristan, I don't have time to be listening to your nasty ass stories."

"You know you're lying, right?"

"No, I'm not," I laughed. "Some of us have work to do." I chatted a few more minutes before I finally got off the phone, shaking my head. Tristan was so in love. Every time I talked to him it made me think about when Donovan and I had first started dating and how inseparable we were. Reverend Williams had mentioned during one of our counseling sessions that we had to remember to find time for each other. Even though we were married, it didn't mean we couldn't still date, as long as it was with each other.

I yawned and stretched my arms over my head. I could always tell when I had been sitting in front of a computer for too long, because it made my shoulders hurt. I'd been going through the sales numbers all morning and was starting to see double. Glancing over at the clock, I realized it was almost lunchtime. As I rose from my chair to do a full body stretch, an idea came to mind. When was the last time I'd had lunch with my husband? Far too long as far as I was concerned.

I made sure Karen had the store under control, then hurried out to my car. The weather was beautiful for September, and I was rocking Dereon jeans and a royal blue shirt and gold pumps. I had just had my locks tightened on Saturday, so I let them hang loose around my shoulders. I climbed in my Lexus and drove over to Sweetie Pies restaurant for some of their collard greens, oxtails, and peach cobbler, then jumped on I-70.

The last few months had been good. Donovan and I had weekly counseling sessions with Reverend Williams and church every Sunday. He still refused to see a therapist, but at least at home his mood was calmer and he wasn't accusing me as much of messing around on him. Things were damn near normal and I was just grateful for that. I was no longer nervous about going home.

I couldn't believe how lucky I was to find a parking spot with as much traffic as there was on Page Street. Skillfully, I parallel parked my car a few doors down from the shop, then reached for the bag of takeout on the seat and climbed out the car. As I walked past the storefront window of the barbershop, I could hear loud talking all the way out onto the sidewalk.

"That mothafucka is full of shit!" I heard Lorenzo shout; then the room erupted with laughter. As usual, he needed to be the center of attention. If they only knew what I knew, their friendly neighborhood barber would suddenly be the talk of the area.

As soon as I swung the door open and stepped into the shop, all eyes were on me. I glanced around at all four workstations. Gabby was the only female who worked at A Cut Above the Rest, and it appeared she had already left for lunch.

"What's up, baby girl?" Lorenzo greeted with that signature grin of his. I could see why Tristan had fallen for his charm and pretty-boy looks. He was waving a pair of clippers over an older gentleman who was sitting in his chair.

"Hey, Lorenzo," I replied, then waved at all of the others. "What are y'all in here laughing about?" I asked with false curiosity.

"Not a damn thang." He winked. "What you got in that bag smelling all good?"

"Nothing for you."

"Oh, why you wanna hurt a brotha like that bringing that good shit up in here! You should have brought enough for all of us," he joked.

"Nah, Sweetie Pies is just for my sweet pie," I chimed in.

Grinning, he shook his head. "I guess I'm gonna have to call and have my baby bring me something down here to eat," he said with that cocky attitude of his.

I wanted so badly to ask him which "baby" he was referring to: Tammy or Tristan. Like I've said, I don't have a problem with a man being gay. What I had a problem with was a man pretending to be something he wasn't.

"Where's Donovan?"

Lorenzo tipped his head toward the back. "In his office."

I nodded, then following a two-finger wave walked toward the rear of the building. I could feel the heat of somebody's eyes on my ass. I tell you . . . men ain't shit. Without knocking, I pushed the door open and spotted Donovan sitting behind his desk with his back toward me. I stood there for several seconds, watching him staring out the window. He looked so sad my heart hurt.

"Baby?"

Startled, his head whipped around; then his expression softened with a grin when he spotted me. "Hey, you. Whatcha doing here?"

I sashayed into his office and lowered the bag to his desk. "I thought I would bring my handsome husband some lunch," I purred, then walked over and kissed his mouth.

"Your man loves those kinda surprises." He brought his lips over mine again and kissed me long and deep.

"Mmmm." I lowered onto his lap and wrapped my arms around his neck.

Donovan eased back slightly. "By the way . . . you look sexy as hell today."

I grinned up at him. "Thank you, baby."

In a matter of seconds my husband's hand crept inside my bra, not that I was complaining. Instead, I groaned loud and deep before my hand traveled down to his crotch that was nice and hard.

"You wanna eat lunch first or are you ready for dessert?" he asked with a dark, penetrating stare. The way he was licking his lips, I knew he wasn't talking about the peach cobbler.

"Let's eat first; then I've got the rest of the afternoon to enjoy my dessert," I answered.

"I'm too hungry to argue." Donovan kissed me once more, then focused his attention on lunch. "Okay, let's see what's in the bag." He reached inside. I noticed his eyes sparkling like a little kid as he removed the Styrofoam containers. "I'm surprised you were able to get in that place. Ever since Sweetie Pies' reality series started airing on television, I heard the lines have been crazy as hell."

I was pleased to see he was happy with my choice. We used to eat there a lot but hadn't been there in a while. "I got there early enough to beat the crowd."

"I see." He opened up the container and stared down at oxtails and rice. "Oh, yeah! My baby knows exactly what I like. I'm about to tear this up. Then I'm going to tear that ass up," he added with a playful wink.

I loved when he talked dirty to me. "Then I guess we better hurry up and eat."

I slid off his lap and took a seat on the edge of the desk and reached for my own lunch. While we ate we had small talk like normal married couples. Discussing household bills and Aiden until I remembered what we had learned in our counseling sessions that the importance of "dating" your husband was to talk about each other.

"Don . . . I was thinking . . ." I hesitated, not sure how he may react. "How about we take a trip next month? Just you and me?"

He swallowed his food, then washed it down with a gulp of orange soda. "That sounds like a good idea. Where you wanna go?"

"I was thinking maybe a cruise?"

He stared at me doubtfully. "I don't know about being confined to a ship for that long." He looked almost frightened at the idea and that was the last thing I wanted, so I quickly suggested something else.

"Okay, then how about we just fly to Jamaica for a week?" I quickly suggested.

He chewed while he considered that option. "I like that idea."

"You do? Oh, good!" I was so happy. Just the thought of spending a week on an island alone with my husband already had my juices going.

We were talking and laughing and having a good time, and by the time we had finished eating I had this feeling that everything really was going to be okay.

"You know you're the only woman I've ever loved, right?" He pulled me by the arm and drew me closer.

I smiled at him. "And you're the only one I've ever wanted. But since we live in the 'Show Me' state, I think I can show you better than I can tell you."

"Oh, really?" he laughed.

"Absolutely. Now how about my dessert?" I purred. I always did have a weakness for chocolate.

I pushed his chair back and dropped down to my knees. "Lift up," I commanded and reached for the waistband of his jeans, signaling for him to raise his hips slightly off the seat.

"What are you doing?" he asked with a nervous laugh, although he knew damn well what was about to go down.

"Just kick back, relax, and enjoy the show." I dragged his jeans and boxers down over his waist and my husband's beautiful penis sprung free. The second I wrapped my hand around his erection, Donovan squeezed his eyes shut and moaned.

"Daddy, what's wrong?" I asked in my baby voice.

His answer was a combination of a grunt and a moan. I chuckled quietly, then leaned forward and blew my warm breath across the tip.

"*Shhhhit,*" he hissed.

I started licking, sucking, teasing, and his hips jerked off the chair. "You like that?" I asked.

"Hell yeah."

"Did I hear you say you want me to stop?" I taunted.

"Don't you even think about it," he said, then opened his eyes and I caught him staring at me. Donovan knows how much I like him to watch.

I pushed my hair away from my face so I wouldn't miss his expression. Lust and love were staring down at me and my nipples hardened. Damn, I loved that man! Our eyes were still locked when I lowered my mouth over his erection, taking him as deep as I could manage. I then wrapped my fingers around the base and began to stroke.

"Babe, you look sexy as hell sucking my dick," he hissed.

"Mmmm-hmmm, I love sucking my husband's dick," I cooed between slurps. "I love the way it tickles the back of my throat."

Together my lips and hand worked his entire length while Donovan continued to watch me, eyes glazed and soft, low sounds coming from between his lips. He held on to my head, guiding me, and rocked his hips in rhythm with my long, deep strokes. I moved up and down, again and again, and Donovan flinched and gasped. I flicked my tongue across the head and applied pressure to the large vein right near the tip. It was my husband's sensitive spot.

"*Shhhhit*, you about to make me nut!" he warned.

His words were magic to my ears. It felt good knowing I still managed to make him come after all these years. I moved faster, trying to deep throat him, and within minutes I heard a ragged cry. Donovan came and his penis pulsed inside my mouth. I sucked vigorously and swallowed every drop.

My husband collapsed against the chair, breathing heavily. "Damn, babe."

I giggled. "I take it you enjoyed dessert."

He looked down at me with half-lidded eyes. "That's my favorite."

We were smiling at each other when I heard a commotion up front that caused my brow to bunch.

"Where the hell is he?" shouted a familiar voice. Next thing I knew the door to Donovan's office flew open and he jerked upright on the chair.

"What the fuck?" He gently pushed my lips from around his dick and fumbled to zip his pants. I was already trying to come from up under the desk to find out who had the balls to come barging into my husband's office like they owned the damn place. "Yo, what the fuck you doing barging into my office?" Donovan demanded to know. As soon as his zipper was in place, he slid his chair back and rose.

"Where the hell is my husband?"

I scrambled from under the desk and looked over the top and found Lorenzo's wife, Tammy, standing in the middle of the floor with a hand at her plump waist. The second she spotted me, she dropped her hand, rolled her eyes, and walked around in a circle like she was trying to calm her nerves.

"Tammy, look . . . Lorenzo must have gone to get something to eat. He'll be back shortly, but don't come barging in my office like that again."

"Uh-huh," she said to Donovan, but she was looking straight at me. "Let me guess. Nikki, you knew all along, didn't you?"

I glanced nervously at Donovan, then back at her. "What are you talking about?" I had a pretty good idea what she was hinting at, but when it comes to an angry wife, the best thing to do was play dumb.

She started charging me, temper flaring. "You know damn well what I'm talking about. That my husband's been fucking that bitch!" she screamed and slammed her hand on the desk. I flinched.

Clearly confused, Donovan looked from me to her. "Tammy, you need to calm the fuck down. Baby, what the hell is she trippin' about?"

I wanted to snatch Tammy by her neck and shut her up. Instead, I shrugged and faked ignorance. "I'm not sure," I replied.

"Uh-uh. I can't believe you gonna stand there and act like you don't know what the fuck's going on!" Her head was swiveling around on her neck. "Donovan, your wife knows damn well what I'm talking about! Her bestie has been fucking my husband," she said bluntly.

"Besties?" He turned and faced me. "Trinette's messing with Lorenzo?"

I laughed, trying to stall as long as possible. "Baby, don't be ridiculous. She's all the way in Richmond."

"No, he's fucking her bestie . . . Tristan."

"He's what!" Donovan shouted. Then he went from looking confused to amused. "Hell nah!" He started laughing. "I know my man ain't fucking that fag." He turned to face me. "Is he, baby?"

I looked from him to her and wanted so badly to pretend I

hadn't known anything about it, but I couldn't even fake it anymore. "No, she's right."

There was no mistaking the horror on his face. "What the . . ." Donovan's voice trailed off with disbelief. "Hell nah."

As much as I wanted to cuss her out for barging into Donovan's office and ruining my perfect afternoon, I had to give Tammy her props for figuring it out. I always said it was hard to get anything past that crazy bitch.

She looked at me through narrowed eyes, still letting her anger get the best of her. "All this time he's been messing around and you knew about it. Yeah . . . okay . . . I got something for both y'all." She was rolling her neck and pointing her finger at me.

"Tammy, if you can't control where your husband sticks his dick, then that's your problem because it sure in the hell ain't none of mine." I spat because I was pissed off at her for bringing her fat ass up in here trying to act like she was running things. I propped a hand to my waist and took a step forward, itching for her to get smart with me. She had a whole lotta nerve showing up at the shop and starting shit.

"You know you wrong for this," she mumbled under her breath, then shook her head and walked out of Donovan's office.

I didn't know what to say, so I just turned around and waited for my husband to say something. Of course it didn't take long.

Donovan shot me a look. "I knew he was messing around on Tammy, but . . ." He shook his head. "All this time . . . I can't believe you knew Lorenzo was fucking that fag and you didn't say nothing." He sat down in the chair with a look of disgust.

I sighed. "What was I supposed to say . . . hey, baby, guess what . . . Lorenzo is screwing Tristan." I walked over and tried to kiss his lips, but Donovan turned his head so I caught his cheek.

His eyes flashed with anger like he was about to explode. "I can't believe this shit. All this sneaking around going on behind my back!" He sprung from the chair and stormed across the room. "I knew I wasn't crazy."

"Who's sneaking? What's going on with Tristan and Lorenzo doesn't have anything to do with us. If your boy wanted you to know he was sexing Tristan, then he would have told you. But for obvious reasons he wanted to keep their relationship a secret."

He glared over me. "Yeah, but you could have at least given me a heads-up."

I tossed my hands in the air with frustration. Maybe I should have told him, yet I took my friendships seriously and besides, that was one love triangle I didn't want to be in the middle of because I knew how crazy Tammy acted when it came to her man.

Donovan started pacing the length of the room and with each passing second I grew just as agitated.

"Talk to me," I urged.

"I don't have nothing to say," he pouted.

Out on the floor there was loud talking and then Tammy screamed so loud, it's a wonder she didn't shatter the storefront window.

"I guess Lorenzo's back."

There was a crash. "Got-dammit!" Donovan raced out onto the floor to break it up.

The second he stepped out the door, I dashed over to my purse and grabbed my cell phone and called Tristan's number. "Come on . . . answer," I mumbled, because I wanted to give him the 411. I was sure Tammy was going to come after him next. The phone just kept on ringing and as soon as his animated voice came on the line I hung up. There was no point in leaving a message because he rarely checked them.

"This is some bullshit!" I heard Don say as he came storming back into his office. I quickly stuck the phone in my back pocket. There was no telling what he would say if he knew I had tried to reach Tristan.

"What's wrong?" I asked, trying to show him just how concerned I really was.

"Nothing now. Lorenzo had to tell that crazy chick of his to get the hell up outta here with that mess. This is a place of business."

I agreed. "I know that's right."

"I can't believe that bitch broadcasted that shit for the whole floor to hear!"

Hell, I could. Tammy planned on taking Lorenzo down with her. "What did Lorenzo say? Did he deny it?"

Donovan pierced me with a look of disbelief. "What the hell you think he did?"

I had asked because I wasn't sure. Especially since the way Tristan talked, Lorenzo had already asked Tammy for a divorce. But I didn't dare say that out loud because Don would never have believed it.

"What I still can't understand is why the hell you didn't tell me he was fucking around with that fag." Donovan had fury in his eyes.

"Listen, I wish you'd stop calling him that! His name is Tristan and I'm not going to keep going over this. Tristan told me not to say anything, and I was tryna respect his privacy."

"Since when do you keep secrets from your husband?"

Women keep secrets from men all the time. I don't know why he was acting like this, especially when he never really wanted to hear the truth anyway. That's why our marriage had struggled for years, because he never wanted to talk about the problems that we were having. He'd rather keep it swept under the rug. I know that was in the past and our relationship had evolved since then, but I just couldn't help but think that this had to be his paranoia again. I sure hoped not.

"I tell you everything I think you need to know about.

Tristan and Lorenzo was none of my business. Lorenzo should have told you. Hell, he knew me and Tristan worked together and that I was bound to find out. It's not my fault he was messing around behind Tammy's back." Now I was starting to get pissed off. Everything was going just fine between us until that crazy chick came barging into the shop.

Donovan was quiet; then eventually he lowered back into his seat and sighed.

I spoke again, my voice softer this time. "Baby, I'm sorry for not telling you, but it wasn't my place to tell you your boy was on the DL."

Donovan looked up at me and after a few seconds he started grinning. "You're right. But damn! Lorenzo a fag? You know how many times that nigga's seen my dick?" His eyes widened.

"Mmmm-hmmm, and I'm sure he liked what he saw just as much as I do," I said, then started laughing.

Donovan shook his head and tried to keep a straight face. "Damn, I don't know how I'm going to be able to look at him the same after this shit."

I walked behind his chair and wrapped my arms around his neck. "Ain't nothing changed."

"The hell it ain't!" he barked.

I leaned in close and ran my tongue along his ear just the way he liked it. "Baby, we got our own problems. Let Tammy and Lorenzo work that shit out on their own."

"Yeah, my bad. You're right." He gave me that boyish grin that I adored. "C'mere and give your husband a kiss." He grabbed my arm and brought me around the chair and back onto his lap. "I'm sorry for trippin', but, baby, you gotta understand, it's a man thang."

"I get it. Trust me, I do."

He dragged me close against him and brought his mouth down over mine. As soon as he kissed me, staying angry was the furthest thing from my mind. I just wished I could find a way to keep us this happy, because I was growing tired of walking on eggshells all the time.

POW! POW!

"What the—"

Before I could wrap my mind around the sound, Donovan sprung from his chair, practically knocking me on my ass.

"What the hell?"

"Take cover!" he demanded. Then I watched in slow motion as he reached inside his desk drawer and pulled out his gun—the one he kept in a lockbox on the top shelf of our bedroom closet.

"Donovan, what the hell are you doing with that gun?"

POW! POW!

Two more shots came from the front of the shop and there was screaming and the sound of broken glass.

"Donovan, don't go in there! Someone is shooting!" I shouted. But he ignored me and dashed out onto the floor. I hurried after him and into the shop, and what I saw caused me to stall. Glass was everywhere and all of the clients had dropped to the floor. Donovan raced over to the window, gun pointed. "Donovan, don't!" I screamed.

"I told you to stay back!" he yelled as he moved around the room like he was on reconnaissance in some damn combat zone. A gun? Seriously? Later he had some serious explaining to do.

I heard sirens in the background. "Is everyone okay?" I asked, glancing around. Folks nodded as they rose to their feet. I was moving over to place a comforting hand to my husband's shoulder when I noticed a man lying on the floor beside one of the barber chairs, not moving. It was Lorenzo.

I walked over. "Hey, get up," I said, tapping his shoulder with my foot. There was no movement. My heart started pounding like crazy. Something was definitely wrong with him. One of the other barbers also noticed.

"Yo, Lorenzo. Get yo ass up!"

There was still no answer. "Baby, come over here a minute," I murmured. My stomach fluttered with nervousness.

Donovan walked over and tapped his boy on the shoulder and when he didn't get a response, he leaned down and rolled him over onto his back. I jerked back.

"Holy shit!" he hissed.

I heard a loud-pitched scream and it took all of twenty seconds before I realized the sound had come from me. This couldn't be happening. It had to be a bad dream.

Lorenzo was lying on the barbershop floor with a bullet hole in the center of his forehead.

16

Trinette

It was Thursday, my favorite day of the week.

I glanced up at the clock and it was two minutes since the last time I had checked. I guess it's true, a watched clock never moves. I just couldn't help it. I was anxious to get the hell out of the office and meet Jrue at our spot.

He left at noon for a phony meeting and I was scheduled to leave at two for an advisory meeting at Petersburg Public Schools. I planned to cancel on the way to the hotel.

I tried to focus on the applications on my desk for next semester. Several new students were interested in continuing their education at the college in the fall. They were waiting for my stamp of approval to make that happen. Did I mention how much I love my job? Most importantly, I love helping kids from broken homes strive toward a better life. It was more than I could say for my ghetto-ass cousins who've known nothing but public assistance. Trifling.

At two o'clock, I finally logged off for the day.

"See you tomorrow," Zakiya said as I stepped in front of her office. "Must be nice that you get out of here early every Thursday."

I shrugged and tried to act nonchalant. "You know I schedule all my school visits for the same day of the week."

She grinned like she knew a secret. "Yeah, but I notice Jrue always has appointments on the same day." She didn't say anything, but it was implied.

"So what are you trying to say?" I scrunched up my face and tried to appear confused, like I had no idea what she was trying to say.

"I don't know. You tell me." She leaned back in her chair and folded her arms across her large breasts.

No, she wasn't trying to go there. Why she all up in my business? "Zee, girl, puh-leeze. Jrue might be fine and all, but if you haven't noticed . . . I'm pregnant," I said and gave her a disgusted look.

She thought about what I said, then the smirk dropped from her face. "Oh yeah, damn. I hadn't thought about that."

I laughed. Women are so stupid. "That's what you get for trying to be Matlock or some shit. If Jrue is sneaking off to meet some chick, it sure the hell ain't me." Damn, I was good. Maybe I should have gone into acting instead of social work.

"My bad. Me and the girls just assumed it was you the way he's always in your office having *private* meetings."

I shrugged. "Hey, he might be feeling me, but I'm too busy focusing on this baby." I rubbed my stomach and grinned.

I waved, then walked out to my car smiling like a damn fool. Wait until I tell Jrue that he's the topic of the office gossip. I climbed into my Mercedes, then drove to the hotel in Colonial Heights.

As usual, Jrue had a key waiting for me at the front desk. I made it up to the fifth floor to room 505 and slid the key in the lock. The moment I opened the door it's a wonder I didn't go into premature labor. My jaw dropped. There were red rose petals all over the floor. I could barely see the Berber carpet the petals were so thick. The sounds of Maxwell's "Sumthin' Sumthin' " from *Love Jones* flooded the room while the sweet smell of vanilla was in the air. I felt tears in my eyes as I stepped around the corner and found Jrue sitting in the chair. He looked sexy as hell, leaning back against the cushions, legs wide, wearing nothing but a pair of silk boxers.

"Hey, baby." He grinned.

"Hi, sexy." I dropped my purse down on the nightstand and smiled. The bed was also covered in rose petals, but what had my attention was that beautiful pink box with the large bow that was right smack at the center of the bed. I wanted to rush over and open it, but I decided to pretend like I hadn't even noticed. After all, this was his show and I didn't want to spoil it for him. "What's all this?" I asked with a sweep of my hand.

"Just wanted to show my baby how special she really is to me."

He had transformed our spot into something special. I don't know if I ever loved that man more. He had always been thoughtful and considerate and doing things to surprise me, but never anything like this.

"I can't believe you did all this for me!" I was grinning like a damn fool because seeing all the trouble he had gone through made me feel so good. As I gazed around the room I even spotted a box of chocolates from The Candy Factory on the small table beside him. "Are those chocolate-covered strawberries?" I gasped. Jrue knew how much I craved them.

He nodded. "Absolutely. Only the best for you. Now come over here and give your man some love."

I swayed my hips playfully as I moved over to the chair. As soon as I was close enough, Jrue reached out and pulled me down onto his lap.

"How are you and my son feeling this afternoon?" he asked, and gently caressed my stomach.

"Me and your *daughter* are fine now that we're here with you." I laughed because we'd been debating for the last few weeks about the sex of the baby. He wanted a little basketball player and, of course, if I had to do it, I required a little diva like myself.

Jrue leaned in close and we French-kissed for what felt like forever but still wasn't long enough. Jrue then reached over and opened the box of strawberries and brought one to my mouth. I bit down and moaned as I chewed. It was so sweet and delicious. Just like the man holding me in his arms.

"I can't believe you went to all this trouble. The roses . . . the music . . . even the scented candles. I didn't know you could be so romantic."

He offered me another bite of the strawberry. "Trinette, this is just a taste of what life is going to be like once we're finally together."

I loved the way that sounded.

"In fact . . . I got something for you." He gestured toward the bed. "Go ahead, open it."

"For me?" I broke out in another grin.

He helped my pregnant ass to my feet. I walked over to the bed and took a seat, then reached for the beautifully wrapped package. "Let's see what's inside." I was giggling and feeling like a preschooler on Christmas morning. Once I opened the box, I pushed aside the tissue paper and gasped. "Oooh, baby! It's beautiful!" I squealed. It was the orange Christian Dior dress I had been admiring on a mannequin at Nordstrom. As well as the purple and orange Jimmy Choo's I had been whining about for weeks. "Thank you so much!" I rushed over to him and landed on his lap in a whoosh! "I love you. . . . I love you," I said between kisses.

He chuckled. "I'm glad you like it. Now put those pumps on for your man."

I was more than happy to model them. I rose and reached for the box and as soon as I pulled the shoes out, something dropped onto the floor. I looked down and my heart started pounding.

A small blue box from Tiffany's.

I looked from the box back up at Jrue, who was grinning. I was shaking so hard I couldn't even move.

"You know I love you, right?" Jrue rose and I watched as all that sexy chocolate came over to the bed. Goodness, he was gorgeous. He dropped down on one knee in front of me and held out the box.

"Aren't you going to open it?"

I felt like I was about to hyperventilate as I took the box from his hands and opened it.

"I wanted to show you how much you mean to me."

Obviously he didn't love me enough because inside were a pair of diamond studded earrings. There were at least two carats, but that was beside the point. I had been expecting an engagement ring.

"Thank you. They're beautiful." I tried to hide my disappointment. How much longer did I have to wait before he proved to me how much he wanted me and his baby?

"Not as beautiful as you, but definitely close enough." Jrue rose and then started unbuttoning my blouse. "I can't wait until I can buy you something even more precious that comes in a small box." He unsnapped my bra and moaned with appreciation when he saw my breasts spring free. They had been growing so much I had to buy new bras. Jrue caught a nipple between his teeth and I felt myself weakening. "I can't wait to put a ring on your finger and make you officially mine."

"What's stopping you?" I asked. Hell, as far as I was concerned, it was long past due. What in the world was he waiting on? I mean, sure, I couldn't wear the ring now, but at least knowing that he had every intention of leaving his skinny-ass wife and spending the rest of his life with me was enough for me. I loved him, but there was no way I was leaving the security of my marriage with Leon until I knew for sure my future was secure with Jrue. You know the saying, a bird in the hand is better than two in the bush. Neither he nor my unborn child was as secure as the future I already had. And I refused to settle for anything less. But I had no doubt that this baby was going to lure Jrue in. That and some of Ms. Netta's caramel goodness.

"Baby, you know why," he answered, and I could tell by the tone of his voice he was sick of talking about it all the time. Well, too bad. I was sick of waiting. "I can't leave her just yet. I need to make sure her cancer is still in remission before I ask her for a divorce. I promise you, baby, it's going to happen, but I'm just not that cold-blooded to simply dump my wife. I just need a little more time." His eyes were pleading with me to understand.

So sue me. I'm selfish and wanted him all to myself. Fuck his wife. Every time she brought her Olive Oyl–looking ass to the job, she looked healthy to me. In all honesty, I think Charlotte sensed she was about to lose Jrue and was using her health to hold on to him for as long as she could. Hell, the moment she found out she couldn't have babies and knew how badly he wanted kids of his own should have been a rude awakening.

"Don't keep me waiting too long. Otherwise, your daughter is going to be calling someone else daddy."

Jrue eased back and I saw that muscle just above his dimple tick with rage. "The hell she will."

Ticktock, mothafucka. I laughed to myself. I knew just what to say to piss his ass off. Good. Maybe he'll hurry his ass up because I was sick of waiting.

"We're going to be a family before you know it. I promise." That's my man. Always trying to reassure me.

Trinette Meyers-Jarmon. I just loved the way that sounded. And, of course, our daughter would be named Symphony. We were going to have a wonderful life.

He was kissing a trail down to my round stomach and my pussy was throbbing with anticipation when I heard his cell phone ring. It was Charlotte. Jrue groaned and rolled over toward his pants.

"Dammit, don't pick it up." How dare he stop after getting me all hot and bothered.

"Trinette, you know I have to take this call. Otherwise she'll blow up my phone until I do."

I lay there pouting while he retrieved his phone, went into the bathroom, and turned on the exhaust fan while he talked to her in private.

I was sick of being second. Me and the baby had to be first. It was time for Jrue to decide.

17

Nikki

I'd just finished giving a statement to the police when I spotted Tristan parking his Impala a few feet behind the police barricade. He stuck a long leg out of the car just as I rushed over to the driver's side.

"Tristan?"

He turned to face me, smiled, then sashayed his narrow ass in black skinny jeans, gold stilettos, and a sequin top that hung off one shoulder.

"Tristan . . . what are you doing here?" I asked, then glanced around nervously to see if anyone else had noticed. Then it dawned on me. Why would they? No one other than me, Donovan, and Tammy knew Lorenzo had been messing around with Tristan.

"Lorenzo was supposed to meet me at my apartment an hour ago. Since he wasn't answering his phone, I thought I'd stop through and see why. What the hell's going on?"

My heart started thundering heavily. I didn't know how I was going to tell him Lorenzo was dead. Tristan tried to walk around me so he could get a closer look through the window, but I grabbed his arm and urged him to stop.

"Tristan, wait! I gotta tell you something."

"What is it, Nikki?" he asked. Then his face changed as if he already knew what I was about to say was going to be really bad. Hell, I didn't even know where to begin.

"Tammy came by and . . . somehow she found out about you and Lorenzo."

"What?" His large eyes got round and his jaw dropped. "What did she say?"

"It's not what she said. It's what she did." I took a deep, shaky breath. *Ohmygod!* This was probably the most difficult thing I had ever had to do.

"She left here and went back to her car. She must have had a gun under the seat because she came back and shot up the place. They arrested her about fifteen minutes ago." *Otherwise, she'd be out looking for you.*

"Oh . . . my . . . God! No wonder the windows are all busted up. I bet Lorenzo is probably going clean the fuck off! I guess that explains why he hasn't answered his phone." His eyes scanned the area, obviously looking for him. At that exact moment two people from the coroner's office stepped out of the barbershop carrying a body bag.

"Oh no! What happened? Who got killed?" he cried.

"Tristan . . . I . . . ." I couldn't even find the words, but I guess he saw the answer on my face.

"No . . ." Tristan started shaking his head with disbelief. "Nikki, please tell me Lorenzo isn't in that bag . . . please tell!" he screamed.

I started crying real tears. "I'm sorry."

"No! No!" he shouted. Then before I could have stopped him, Tristan made a mad dash and flung himself on top of the body, screaming and clutching the bag to his chest. "He can't be gone!"

If it wasn't serious, it might have been funny; instead, it was like a bad dream. There was nothing humorous about watching my dear friend's heart breaking. I hurried over just as two police officers dragged Tristan away, kicking and screaming.

"This can't be happening!" he wailed. "Please tell me he's not dead!"

Donovan came rushing out of the barbershop and glared over at me. "What the hell's he doing here?" he demanded.

"Don, please . . . just leave it alone."

"Hell nah! Doesn't he know this shit's all his fault! You knew he was married!"

I grabbed his arm. "Baby, please, stay out of it."

"Nah! Nah! That was my boy. He was like a brother to me. Now he's gone, dammit, over some fag. Now he's gone!" And then he broke down and started bawling. I had never in my life heard my husband cry like that before. I hugged him close and tears started running down my eyes again. Tristan was sobbing as well while he stood off to the side with one of the officers, probably giving them more information than they were looking for. My heart went out to both of them. One had lost his best friend; the other had lost the best thing to happen to him in a long time.

That evening it was all over the news about Lorenzo having an affair with a gay man and his wife finding out her husband was on the down low and killing him. Some people said they would have done the same thing and that she had every right. All I could do was shake my head.

I put Aiden to bed, then went to check on Donovan. He'd been quiet most of the evening. Not that I blamed him. His best friend was dead and his wife now behind bars.

I stepped into the family room and found the television on, but he clearly wasn't watching it.

"Can I get you anything?" I asked and smiled, hoping that it would make him feel better. He just kept sitting there staring at the television like he had also died this afternoon. "Don, did you hear me?"

He looked to his right and glared at me. "How long had you known Lorenzo was gay?"

I shrugged. "Not that long. A couple of months."

"But you knew he was sleeping with Tristan?" He gave me this look like he was accusing me of pulling the trigger.

"I think it was more than just sex between them. Tristan was in love with him."

Donovan scowled. "Yeah, right," he said like I was lying.

I stepped farther into the room with a hand at my hip. "Why are you mad at me?"

There was that hateful look again. "I'm curious what secrets Tristan's keeping for you. I mean, you knew who he was fucking, so who's to say he doesn't know who you're fucking as well."

I rolled my eyes. "I know you're not trying to go there again."

"Yeah, I am, and I asked you a question. Who you been fucking around with?"

I refused to have this conversation, and part of me was afraid that if he looked at me long enough he would see the truth.

Yes, I had an affair three and a half years ago. It was during Donovan's deployment to Iraq, but only because I had thought our marriage had been over. After the death of our daughter, our marriage wasn't the same. We didn't talk, rarely made love. It was like we were two zombies coexisting. By the time his unit had been called up, we were both relieved for the distance. Six months into his deployment, Donovan wrote me a letter telling me he wanted a divorce.

Devastated, I ended up in the arms of a gorgeous widower, Kenyon Monroe, who I thought was everything I needed to help me get on with my life. Instead, he had turned out to be a psychopath. When Donovan and I decided to give our marriage another chance, Kenyon was livid and ended up trying to kill me.

But even after we got back together, I never told Donovan about the affair. At first I tried; then I thought it was irrelevant.

Kenyon had been sent to a state mental facility and was no longer in my life.

That was the one and only time I had ever had an affair, so his comment pissed me off. I turned and was heading out of the room when he sprung from his chair and raced across the room so fast I ran into the corner of the bookshelf.

"Oww!" I cried.

But instead of my husband coming to my aid to see if his wife was okay, he mean-mugged me. "What you rushing for? You got something to hide?"

"Seriously? I just banged my hip on the bookshelf and you're worried about what I'm hiding. I'm not hiding a got-damn thing!" I screamed. The pain in my side made me mad and gave me the strength to lie. At this late in the game, there was no way in hell I was telling him about the affair.

"Do you have any idea how many soldiers came home to find their wives gone . . . bank accounts drained . . . and kids that weren't even theirs? I was over there fighting for my country . . . providing for my family!"

Oh my goodness, this was starting to sound like a broken record. "Baby . . . I already know that, but what the hell does that have to do with anything?"

"It means I'm tired of sleeping with one eye open!" He was talking loud and I smelled the tequila on his breath. Donovan had been drinking again.

"I thought you promised to stop drinking."

He slammed his fist through the wall. "My best friend was murdered today and you're worried about me having a drink! Dammit, Nikki. Get off these nuts!" Donovan pushed past me and moved down the hall. I heard him climbing the steps. As soon as a door slammed upstairs, I fell to my knees onto the floor and cried. Other than prayer, I didn't have a clue how to save my husband or our marriage.

18

Trinette

"Hey! We need some more T-shirts over here," I shouted over my shoulder, then smiled down at the little girl in front of me and handed her the last small T-shirt.

"Here ya go," Zee said as she carried another stack over to the table.

I mopped my forehead. It had been a long, hot September afternoon, and wearing high heels had been a stupid move on my part. Although I would never admit it.

The Festival Art's carnival was the college's chance to shine and showcase everything we had to offer to the community with more than 100 educational sessions and hands-on activities. It was a free, fun, educational event with giveaways, arts and crafts vendors, and so much more. I had spent the entire afternoon handing out T-shirts and pamphlets about our department.

I'd been watching my baby's daddy all afternoon working at the other end of our booth. Jrue looked delectable in blue jeans, a John Tyler T-shirt, and that coochie-curling smile. I wanted to ask him to meet me in the ladies' room, but those nosy chicks at the table were bound to notice. Speak of the devil . . .

"Trinette . . . when was the last time you took a break?"
Jrue asked as he walked down to our end of the table.

I shrugged and tried to pretend like it had been a while.
"I'm okay."

He shook his head. "No, it's not okay. We're not going to
have you falling out on my shift."

"I know that's right," Zee said, and I saw the way her eyes
were traveling back between us like she knew something. I
thought we had already been over that?

"Have a seat," he said and pulled a chair over. My man was
thoughtful like that. Always thinking about me. That's why I
loved him so much.

Jrue moved over to the admissions' booth to see if they had
any more pamphlets left.

"He is so fine."

My head whipped around to look at Zee standing there
staring after him, watching his ass. I couldn't believe she was
admiring my man.

"You need to find something else to do," I said and tried to
keep the attitude from my voice.

"What? I'm just saying. Hell, if he's messing around on his
wife, why not mess around with me?"

See, it's always women like her wanting something they
could never have. Instead of fantasizing about my man, what
she needed to be worried about was that overweight boyfriend
of hers. "Trust me, as happy as that man looks, I'm sure somebody's responsible for that smile, which means *that* sistah's on
her job."

She laughed. "I know that's right."

We went back to handing out T-shirts and gift bags. Zee
was spending way too much time ogling my man. I couldn't
wait until we were finally able to go public with our relationship so I could check her ass.

I was waving good-bye to two small children when I spotted Jrue's wife sauntering her narrow hips in our direction.

"Who wears high heels to an art fair?" Zee hissed near my ear. I gave her a weird look, then glanced down at my feet. "Oops. My bad."

I rolled my eyes back in the direction of Charlotte and took a moment to check her out. The yellow pantsuit was clearly Liz Claiborne and the shoes were Louboutin to match the leather bag on her arm. Trust and believe I planned to drag Jrue to Norfolk next weekend so he could buy me the same, because there was no way I was being upstaged by that narrow wench. Although I could wear a paper sack and she still wouldn't look as delectable as me.

"Good afternoon, ladies." She greeted us with a warm smile and I looked at how neat her ponytail was. No weave, all natural, and not a hair out of place.

"Hello, Charlotte," I said, then paused to hand a pamphlet to a student and explain our program. The whole time I was talking, out the corner of my eye I caught that bitch staring at me.

"When's your baby due?"

I turned around, fighting a smirk. I wanted so badly to correct her. *You mean, when is Jrue's baby due?* I chuckled inward. In due time, Netta, in due time.

"In three months," I replied, and rubbed my stomach. There was no mistaking the envy in her eyes.

"Do you know what you're having?"

I paused for dramatic effect. "Not yet, but *he* wants a boy and I want a little girl," I said with a laugh. I was so enjoying this. "What about you? No babies in the forecast?"

Charlotte looked a little embarrassed. Good for her. "No, we've talked about it, but Jrue and I need to slow down our schedules first."

I arched my brow. "Really? Because the other day he told me he would love to have children. At least two."

Charlotte swallowed, clearly disturbed that I'd had such an intimate conversation with her husband. Oh my! She had no idea just how intimate we have been.

I shrugged and tried to act nonchalant. "My baby's father and I are so excited. I can't get him to stop talking about this child. He's been waiting a long time for this day."

"I can imagine he is excited." She looked past my shoulder, probably anxious to get away from me and my happy pregnancy.

"He's ecstatic." I leaned in, pretending like we were close friends and I was sharing an important secret. "Every man wants a child of his own. Believe me when I tell you, if a man can't get it from his wife, then there's always some other woman out there willing to have his baby. And I'd be damned before I let another woman steal my man."

Charlotte eased back and looked at me as if she wasn't sure if she should thank me or strangle me. That's good, because I just wanted to give her a little something to think about. Trust me, the day this baby is born is the day she better get ready for me to come knocking on her front door.

I spotted Jrue heading our way. His brow was bunched and he appeared nervous as hell. "Hey, baby."

I whipped my head around. "Hey, I—" I bit my tongue when I realized he wasn't talking to me. Instead, I watched him lean across the table and kiss that skinny wench dead in the mouth in front of me. No the hell he didn't.

Charlotte pulled back with this saucy grin on her face like she was telling me something. The bitch can't tell me shit. Hell, I was the one carrying her husband's child, not her. "I thought I would come down here and check on my husband and see if we were still on for dinner tonight." She was smiling up at him and I wanted to reach over and scratch her eyes out. Ticktock, bitch! Ticktock.

"We should be done in plenty of time." He was staring at her the way he looks at me and I wasn't feeling that shit at all.

That was my man. Not hers. I was supposed to be wearing that kilowatt diamond that was on her ring finger. What bothered me the most was that my man had forgotten that I was standing there. I guess it was up to me to remind him.

"Ouch!" I cried, then buckled over and gripped my stomach.

Jrue practically pushed Charlotte away and hurried to my side. "Trinette, you okay?"

"I just felt a sharp pain. Ouch! There it goes again!" God, I was good.

I leaned all my weight against him as he assisted me over to a folding chair. "I told you not to overdo it," he scolded, then dropped down on one knee beside me. I just stared into those beautiful eyes of his.

"Shouldn't we call an ambulance?" Charlotte asked with a frown on her face.

"No, I'll be okay. Just give me a minute." I flinched again for dramatic effect. "Sometimes this little lady likes to kick her mama in the ribs." I gazed up at Jrue again with a pitiful smile on my face and he took my hand in his.

Charlotte hurried around the table and moved beside her husband, looking suspicious. It took everything I had not to laugh at her barren ass.

"Take some deep breaths," Jrue suggested, and I did just as he said. This was just too good. "Charlotte, can you hand me a water from out of the cooler?"

She cut her eyes, then walked over to the cooler under the table and retrieved a bottle of water. Jrue quickly took it from her and pressed it up against my forehead.

"Mmm, thank you, Jrue," I purred.

Charlotte stood back and watched the two of us together. There was no way she could not see what was going on. It took everything I had not to laugh as I rested my forehead on Jrue's shoulder. "I guess I did overdo it today." And then my daughter must have known her daddy was near. "Oh!" I gasped.

"What's wrong?" My man looked so scared I almost felt bad for worrying him.

"Feel." I took his hand and pressed it against my stomach. "She's kicking me."

"Wow!" he laughed. "You got a little football player on your hands."

"Or a dancer." I winked.

You should have seen the look on his face while she kicked around. I stole a glance over at Charlotte, standing there like a lost puppy. "Charlotte, would you like to feel her kick?"

She quickly shook her head. Hater. I didn't want her bony fingers touching me no way. What Jrue and I were sharing she would never get to experience with him. And that's okay, because he wouldn't be her husband for long. That much I was certain of. This little girl I was carrying had already stolen her father's heart. And I planned to steal Charlotte's husband away. It was going to be easier than I had imagined.

19

Nikki

"Nikki, you're never going to believe this."

I was heading into the bookstore when I noticed I had missed a call from Trinette. I really wasn't in the mood to hear about her love triangle, but as crazy as my life was, it was nice to know someone else had problems other than me.

"What won't I believe?" I dared to ask.

"Donovan called me last night."

"What?" I almost ran through a stop sign and had to slam down hard on the brakes. "What the hell! When was this?"

"Last night. Girl, I tried calling you back, but you turned your phone off."

"That's because I caught Donovan going through my call history the other night. Not that I have anything to hide." When I confronted him about it, he admitted he was looking for proof that I was having an affair. I was so tired of him accusing me of doing something I was not.

"Well, he sounded crazy last night. Don't you know he asked me if while he was deployed if you had been messing around?"

No he didn't. "What did you tell him?"

"What?" Trinette gave a rude snort. "I can't believe you even asked me that! I told him hell no, because as far as I am concerned you hadn't. Technically, the two of you weren't even together at the time."

It was good to know my best friend was still quick as a whip. "Thanks, Netta. What else did he say?"

"That was it and he acted like he didn't even believe me. Said we were two peas in the pod, then told me to tell Leon to give him a call." Trinette started laughing like it was funny. She had no idea this situation was getting far from funny. "I couldn't believe he even went there."

Hell, I could. "You remember how he was when you were here? Well, he's starting to act like that again. One day he's normal, the next day he isn't. And now, ever since his best friend was murdered, he's back to acting like he has PTSD. It's like I'm starting all over again."

"He's probably just being paranoid. You know how those army dudes are. They come back from a long deployment and automatically assume someone's been sleeping in their bed. It's like Goldilocks and some shit. Who's been sleeping in my bed? Who's been sleeping in my bed?" Her crazy ass used different animated voices mimicking the three bears and had me laughing.

"You are stupid!"

She laughed. "Whatever, you know I'm telling the truth. To be honest, I don't know how you have the patience. I stopped dating soldiers when I was nineteen after I realized they're all broke and crazy."

I rolled my eyes even though I knew Trinette couldn't see me. "Well, we're not just talking about a soldier, we're talking about Donovan."

"I know, Nikki. And you know I love Donovan, but the best thing you can do for your husband is get him some professional help," she said as she tried her best to be more sensitive to my needs. I had to at least give her an A for effort.

"You're right. Prayer and couple's counseling just isn't enough," I admitted while I whipped around a slow car and made a right at the corner. "Enough about Donovan. How have you been feeling?" I asked, anxious to change the subject.

"Sick as a damn dog. I don't know why women do this to their bodies! All the throwing up . . . eating like a crazy person . . . It's just too much for someone to have to go through for nine months."

That girl is so dramatic that I had to laugh. "If women didn't do it, your ass wouldn't be here. I'm just glad you decided to keep the baby."

"Girl, me too. It's actually worked out better than I thought. The way those two men are behaving, I plan to milk it for everything that it's worth. Leon bought me that Pandora bracelet I'd been wanting. Jrue just paid off my Macy's credit card. I'm going to sit back and enjoy this shit!" She sounded so damn giddy.

We shared a laugh. I definitely needed that with all the crazy shit happening in my life right about now.

"When's Leon getting back from Germany?"

"Saturday." Trinette sighed. "Two weeks was not long enough. I have been enjoying spending time with Jrue without worrying about Leon sniffing my damn pussy."

"He doesn't do that!" I laughed. My girl was so dramatic.

"Yes, he does, right before he dives in for a snack. Now that I'm pregnant I can't keep that man off me. He likes sucking on my titties and slurping on my damn clit!"

I was laughing so hard I had to wipe my eye. "He's happy his wife is finally pregnant."

"Yeah, I know, and it's going to break his heart when I finally leave him." I was surprised that she actually sounded sad about it.

I still think Trinette would be making a big mistake leaving Leon for another man. She already knew what kind of life she'd have with Leon. Okay, so maybe he couldn't put it down in the bedroom like Jrue, but he loved her unconditionally and once that baby was born, there would be no limits to what that man would be willing to do. But I guess the heart wants what the heart wants, and at least for once it wasn't about money, so it made me wonder if maybe this thing with Jrue really was for real.

"You never know; before that baby is born you might even change your mind."

There was a hesitation before she finally said, "Maybe, but I seriously doubt it. I think Jrue's wife knows something is going on, so it's only a matter of time."

"Just be careful. You see what happened to Lorenzo."

She snorted rudely in the phone. "No offense to Tristan, but if I was Tammy and found out my husband had been fucking a dude, I would have shot his ass too."

So would I.

We chatted a few more minutes; then I got off the phone and thought about what she had said and decided that maybe it was time to go another route with this entire situation. Donovan would kill me if he found out, but I was running out of options.

I glanced down at the clock on the dashboard. It was barely eight. I had planned to arrive at the bookstore a little early this morning and work on inventory, but there was plenty of time for that later. Right now I had something a little more important to deal with. I headed down I-70, got off at Goodfellow Road, and drove until I reached a soldier standing on guard at the entrance. I flashed my military dependent ID, then pulled my car through the gate and up to the 138th Engineering Battalion.

Donovan had joined the National Guard during college. He had been attending on a track scholarship, but with me also trying to go to school, rent, and bills, we still were barely making it. Back then they had been giving $20,000 bonuses to join the Army National Guard, as well as money for education and books. Donovan had signed up without even telling me. That had been our first heated argument, mainly because I was scared and thought he was selfish for jeopardizing his life when he had a wife to think about. He was just getting ready to leave for basic training when I had discovered I was pregnant with Mimi.

I parked my car in the visitor's parking lot, then moved inside the building. I had been there enough times that I knew where I was going. I nodded as I passed several soldiers in their battle uniforms. It doesn't matter how often I see it, nothing is sexier to me than a man in uniform. I guess it's what the uniform stands for. The pride and the confidence all together seemed to give a man swag.

I moved quickly across the drill floor to the battalion headquarters and stepped through the door. There was a young light-skinned female private sitting behind the front desk.

"Can I help you?" she asked. I didn't miss the way she was looking me up and down. I guess wearing a uniform made it hard for a woman to feel feminine. I was rocking blue jeans, yellow pumps, and a white striped blouse. My locks I had pulled up in a cute ponytail. Yes, this sistah looked fierce.

"I'm Staff Sergeant Truth's wife. Is your first shirt here?"

I saw the way her light brown eyes lit up at the mention of my husband's name. I gazed down at the last name on her shirt. *Sanders*. I might have to bring her name up at dinner tonight and find out what her story was.

"Hold up." She rose and walked around the corner and a few seconds later returned and signaled for me to come back. "Clarke said to come on back."

I nodded and sashayed past her, leaving a whiff of my perfume for her to inhale. Just because she was wearing a uniform didn't mean she couldn't still smell good. I read the names on the doors until I spotted SERGEANT FIRST CLASS CLARKE.

"Mrs. Truth . . . please . . . come on in."

I nodded and greeted him with a warm smile. "Thank you. It's good to see you again."

"Yes, it is." His grin became a devilish smirk. I watched as his eyes gave me the once-over, stopping at my ass. I rolled my eyes inward. Like I said before, men ain't shit.

"Have a seat. What can I do for you this morning?"

I suddenly felt like I was betraying my husband by being there. The last thing I wanted was to put his business in the street, but at the same time he needed help and it was his unit's responsibility to make sure that he got that. I lowered into the stiff chair across from his desk and waited until Clarke had taken a seat before I spoke.

"I've been wanting to talk to you about Donovan. Did you receive any of the messages I left?"

He shook his head. "What messages?"

Something in his eyes said he was lying. He'd received my messages but felt he had better things to do than return the calls of one of his NCOs' wives.

"Never mind," I muttered while I tried to hold my tongue. "The reason for my calls and for dropping by your office this morning is that I really need to talk to you about my husband's behavior."

His brow rose and I could tell he was interested in what I was about to say. I hated feeling like I was betraying my husband, but Clarke was his supervisor, so he would know more about Donovan than anyone else. "Ever since he's gotten home from Afghanistan, he's been acting weird."

"Weird how?" he asked suspiciously.

I could barely steady my shaking hands. "Hardly sleeping, drinking too much, and really depressed."

He laughed. "Is that all? Everyone acts like that after a deployment."

No, he isn't making fun of me. I shook my head and tried to remain calm. "No, this is nothing like the way he had acted when he got back from Iraq. This time it's different. He's really distant and agitated."

Clarke leaned across the desk and licked his lips suggestively. "It sounds to me like it's nothing that his wife can't solve at home for him." He laughed again and then had the nerve to reach down for his cell phone and start texting. "All he needs is some loving. You can handle that, can't you?"

"Of course I can handle that!" I had to bite my tongue to keep from cussing his ass out. Satisfying my husband had never been a problem. What I couldn't handle was that nobody seemed to be taking this situation seriously. "But he's acting extremely paranoid and accusing me of messing around and trying to leave him."

Clarke tilted his head slightly and looked up from his phone. "Have you been messing around on him?" He had this look like he knew the truth. I quickly shifted on the seat.

"What kinda question is that?"

"Because you wouldn't be the first," he answered bluntly. "It takes a strong woman to stand by her man for twelve months. That's a long time to go without sex. Hell, I wouldn't have blamed my wife if she had."

I couldn't believe he was having this conversation with me. "Sergeant, I have never messed around on my husband . . . not that it's any of your business."

He smirked. "Sorry, but I gotta ask. I don't need one of my soldiers going off the deep end because he can't trust his wife."

Again, I regretted even coming to see this prick. What I wanted to do was reach across the desk and strangle his ass. Instead, I changed the subject. "Doesn't the National Guard have programs in place for your soldiers coming home?"

He nodded. "Yes, and each one of them is required to meet with the psychologist upon return. Donovan saw her and she signed off on his evaluation form that he was fit for duty. I guarantee you, if she had thought anything was wrong, she would have referred him for further counseling."

"That woman probably sees hundreds of soldiers a week. She doesn't have the time to spend with each one long enough to truly evaluate them."

"She's good at what she does," he insisted.

"Well, she made a mistake. My husband needs to be reevaluated. He had soldiers in his unit killed while in Afghanistan. Two weeks ago, he watched his best friend get gunned down at his shop. Donovan has experienced way too much trauma and it's affecting him and our marriage."

Clarke sat there staring across the desk at me for a long moment. "Weren't the two of you having marital problems a few years back?"

No he didn't. "What the hell does that have to do with anything?"

He shrugged. "I'm just saying . . ."

"Then next time check your facts. Our marriage has been stronger than ever! We were happy before he left on this last deployment. Now my husband's been back eight months and something still isn't quite right. It's like he lost his soul down there."

There was a brief pause. "How about I call him in and talk to him?" he said like he was doing me a favor.

"Talking to him is not going to help. You need to have him evaluated for PTSD!" I was screaming now. "Listen, you either do something or I'm going over your head and having a talk with the commander about you blowing me off. I'm sure the last thing he wants is for one of his soldiers to be on the evening news after he's snapped!"

Oh, that definitely got his attention, because the color drained from his face and he quickly sat up in the seat. "I'll contact the psychologist and schedule him for another evaluation. Then we'll see what she has to say after she meets with him."

"Yeah, you do that." I rose from the chair truly disgusted with the man. He's supposed to care about his soldiers and it seemed the only thing he wanted to do was brush the problems aside and pretend that everything was all right. "And don't be all day about it either. My husband needs help and he needs it like yesterday."

20

Trinette

"Jrue, sweetheart . . . park over there." I pointed to the empty parking space close to the door.

"I see it."

I couldn't begin to tell you how much I had been enjoying the last two weeks. Leo was in Germany, and Jrue and I had been taking advantage of every second of him having me all to himself. It gave us a chance to play house and experience what life was going to be like when we're finally together as husband and wife, raising our children. I was already considering having one more only because Jrue wanted two.

On Sunday, Jrue told his wife he needed to be in DC for a conference on Monday morning, and instead he came over and stayed the night with me. I knew it was wrong having another man sleeping in the same bed that I shared with Leon, but I paid for the bed, so technically it was mine. And when Jrue finally divorced his wife and I left Leon, I planned to take it with me.

"You ready to go inside?" he asked and shut off his Jaguar.

I nodded, leaned forward, and met his lips as he pressed them against mine. Like I said, I couldn't have been happier.

"Mmmm-mmm-hmm, you know you taste good."

Damn, this brotha was sexy as fuck! I gave him a sly look. "That's not the only thing that tastes good."

He chuckled. "How about I find out later?"

"I agree."

Jrue got out of the car and I waited for him to come around and help me out. Then together we walked up the sidewalk and through the doors for Dr. Sandra Brown, my obstetrician. I moved up to the desk.

"Hi, I'm Trinette Montgomery and I have a one o'clock." I ran a hand through my hair to make sure it was perfect. Even though I'm pregnant, I believe in keeping it cute.

The receptionist nodded. "Sure thing, Mrs. Montgomery. Has any of your information changed?"

I know it was a formality, but she asked me the same damn thing every visit. I shook my head. "No, nothing has changed." I handed her my insurance card and a check for my copay.

She reached for my folder. "Please have a seat. I'll give you your card back in a moment."

I noticed all the other pregnant women sitting in the waiting area eyeing my man like I wasn't there. I love for other women to stand back and admire what I got just as long as they remember that man belongs to me. Or at least he will when he finally divorces that needy wife of his.

As soon as we were seated on a comfortable love seat Jrue leaned close to my ear. "I think you're the prettiest pregnant woman in here."

My head whipped around. "You *think*?" He needed to try that again.

Jrue laughed. "Relax, baby. There is no doubt you are the finest thang in here."

"Much better," I cooed and met his lips halfway.

"Let me go use the restroom real quick before they call your name."

I watched him walk away, admiring his perfect ass in dress

slacks. I'd heard the expression clothes make the man, but in Jrue's case, the man made the clothes look good.

"Excuse me?"

My head whipped around to look at the blonde seated on a chair to my left. She was a skinny thing with stringy hair and a serious overbite. "Yes?"

"Is that your husband?"

I could see that look in her eyes as she stared off in the direction of the bathroom. I was tempted to reach inside my purse and give her a Kleenex to sop up the drool. "Of course it is," I lied. Hell, what choice did I have? If I told her the truth, the second I turned my back she'd be trying to slip Jrue her number.

She shook her head. "He's gorgeous. The two of you are going to have one beautiful baby."

"Thank you." At least she appreciated beauty when she saw it. I reached for one of those baby magazines and while I thumbed through the pages I thought about my unborn child. She was right. Jrue and I were two beautiful people whose children couldn't be anything but breathtaking. I could already see our daughter with her smooth chocolate skin and all of my fabulous qualities. I bet I could get her modeling in one of these magazines, which should be easy considering most of the babies were average looking.

Jrue returned and again I noticed the admiring looks. I just beamed with pride. Yeah, my man definitely looked good.

"Mr. and Mrs. Montgomery . . . follow me."

Smiling, I rose and moved toward the nurse waiting patiently. I was well aware that Jrue was frowning at the mistake. I could have corrected her, but what was the point. They thought he was my husband and soon enough he would be, so why confuse things if we didn't need to.

We were turning the corner when the receptionist called after me. "Mrs. Montgomery . . . you forgot your insurance card."

Jrue brought a hand to my waist. "Baby, I'll grab it."

He hurried over to the desk and I watched in slow motion as the chick reached across the desk, tipped over her coffee cup, and it spilled onto Jrue's slacks. He jerked back and cussed under his breath.

"Oh, I am so sorry," she said, and hurried out of her seat and around the desk with a roll of paper towels. I brought an impatient hand to my thick waist, then rolled my eyes. Goodness. She was so damn clumsy.

"Don't worry about it," Jrue said as if accidents like that happened every day. What he needed to be doing was demanding to see her boss.

She handed him a handful of paper towels. "Mr. Montgomery, I'm truly, truly sorry."

He held up a hand. "It's okay . . . really."

My man might not have had a problem with it, but I had every intention of complaining to the doctor about her incompetent staff. We were in a recession and there were way too many qualified people out there desperate for a job to be dealing with someone who should be flipping burgers at Wendy's instead.

The nurse escorted us into the examination room, took my vitals, then handed me a gown so that I could get undressed from the waist down. She finally left and shut the door behind her.

"Baby, what's up with that Mr. Montgomery crap?" Jrue scowled like his pride was hurt.

I batted my eyelashes at him. "Sweetheart, what difference does it make what they call you? You're still big daddy to me." I made a show of peeling the slacks down my legs and wiggled my hips. As I hoped, I shifted his focus back to me. The last thing I needed was for him to be tripping about being mistaken for Leon. "All that should matter is that this child growing inside me belongs to you." I slipped my panties down to my ankles, then kicked them away.

Lust brimmed in his eyes. "Damn, baby. You know my dick's hard, right?"

Of course it was. I backed over to the door and turned the lock. "Have a seat," I ordered.

"You're not serious?" he asked, although the hand unbuckling his slacks was already onboard with the idea.

It usually took my doctor fifteen minutes to make it to the room, which gave us plenty of time for a little quickie. "Absolutely, now unzip your pants."

I watched as he took a seat, then reached inside his fly and pulled out his beautiful penis. Nothing was more succulent than a dick that was two-toned—chocolate and caramel.

I straddled his waist and Jrue slid in with ease. Immediately, I started riding him. He planted his hands at my waist and guided me along his length. Oh, it felt good to be bad. Within minutes I was close to orgasm when I heard someone turn the knob. The second they found it locked, they started knocking. I pressed a finger to Jrue's lips and he started pumping hard.

"Mrs. Montgomery . . . are you in there?"

My eyes rolled in the back of my head as I came down hard onto his dick and Jrue brought his lips to mine just in time to stifle my cries. That man was so good at what he did. There was more knocking, but we ignored it. I think just the thought of getting caught had us both turned on. Seriously, what could they really say except that I was making love to my husband? He started driving harder, lifting my body up and down over his hard length, and before long he released a grunt and came.

I got up from his lap and grabbed a paper towel and wiped off. While he fixed his clothes, I took a seat on the table. He'd just fastened his belt when I heard keys jingling and the door sprung open.

The nurse walked in and glared at us. "What was wrong with the door?" she asked, then sniffed. I sure could smell sex in the air.

I shrugged and looked at Jrue. "You tell me. We tried to open it, but it wouldn't budge. You know . . . it's bad enough your clumsy receptionist spills coffee all over his pants, but then we get locked in a room and can't get out. I think I'm going to have a talk with the manager!"

That shut her up. She rolled her eyes, then turned and walked back out of the room. Damn, I was good.

"I guess you told her," Jrue said and winked.

"I guess I did." We then laughed.

"Wow! If I hadn't seen it for myself I never would have imagined."

Thirty minutes later, I linked my arm through Jrue's and beamed up at him as we exited the examination room. "I told you."

The experience had gone exactly the way I had hoped it would. Dr. Brown saw so many couples every day that it didn't even dawn on her that Jrue wasn't Leon. As soon as Jrue saw my baby on the screen, he was captivated. And when Dr. Brown asked if we wanted to know the sex, we took one look at each other and agreed. I'm having a girl! Jrue was so stunned it no longer mattered that he wasn't going to have a son. Now he wanted a little princess, who would have her daddy wrapped around her finger. Trust me, I couldn't have timed it better myself.

"I think this calls for a celebration," he suggested with that big silly grin still on his face.

"I agree."

We were walking through the lobby on the way out to his car when I heard someone calling Jrue's name. Turning around, I found a woman standing in front of the elevators. I looked up at him to see if he recognized her and the look on his face said he did. I never thought a dark man could turn white, but he looked as pale as a ghost.

"Jrue . . . who's that?" I asked.

He dropped my arm like I had leprosy and strolled over to the slender woman who was mean-mugging me. I was seconds away from asking her what the hell she was looking at.

"Hazel," he said with a grin, then hugged her.

"Jrue, aren't you going to introduce me to your friend?" she asked while looking in my direction. I was growing tired of her staring me down.

He whipped around and I had never seen him look as scared before in his life. Like he wished my ass would just disappear. Well, I'm sorry, but I wasn't going to be ignored.

"I'm Trinette," I said with attitude. "And you are?"

She brought a hand to her malnutrition waist. "Hazel. His *wife's* sister."

I looked her up and down and within seconds saw the resemblance. She was tall and skinny with a wide forehead and more moles on her face than makeup could hide. I was tempted to reach inside my purse and give her a business card to a good dermatologist.

"Uh . . . Hazel, Trinette and I . . . work together. She was having contractions and since her husband is out of the country on business, I rushed her in to see her doctor," he lied, and looked over at me pleading with his eyes for me to play along.

I was so sick of playing these games. If he'd just tell his wife the truth, we wouldn't be going through all these changes. But I sighed and decided that I would be the bigger woman, which, as skinny as Hazel was, wasn't hard to do.

"That's right. I've been having cramps all day." I brought a hand to my belly just so she'd see just how pregnant I was. She looked suspiciously down at my stomach, then looked from me to him. I gave a coy grin and stared up at him adoringly, then rubbed my stomach. I don't care what he said. I wanted her to know the baby I was carrying belonged to him.

"Yeah, I was just taking her to get something to eat. She's been feeling light-headed. I was holding on to her arm just to make sure she didn't fall before we made it back to my car."

"How far along are you?" she asked.

"Seven months," I said.

She nodded, then all the anger seeped from her face. "I know how you feel. I was the same way when I was pregnant with Ronnie."

Jrue's shoulders sagged with relief and I just rolled my eyes inward. This chick was dumb as a box of rocks. I see why so many women get played, because they only see what they want to see.

"Well, I better get Trinette something to eat and drop her off at her car. I'm making her take the rest of the day off."

"Gurrl, you better enjoy all the pampering while you can. Jrue, I'll see you Saturday for dinner," she reminded, then hopped into the elevator and waved.

Jrue was quiet all the way back to his car. I could see the wheels in his head turning.

"What's wrong?"

"What's wrong? I almost got caught! That's what's wrong."

"Okay, but you didn't." I waved, dismissing the issue. "You worry too much."

He raked a hand across his face. "This isn't a game, Trinette."

"Then do something about it. Hell, you've been telling me for over a year you're going to ask your wife for a divorce. Okay, then get it done."

Jrue shook his head. "It's not that easy."

"What's so hard about it? So what if the cancer comes back or that you'll have to give her half of everything you own. Big fucking deal. I'd rather be broke and happy than rich and miserable." I couldn't believe I was saying that, because once upon a time I put money over everything else. But since I met Jrue, all that had changed. It wasn't about the money anymore. For the first time I had met a man who had stolen my heart and I was willing to sacrifice everything to be with him. I just needed to make sure he felt the same way. As rich as he was, even if he gave Charlotte half there would still be plenty left for him to spend on me.

"I just need more time."

"Time is running out. Your daughter is going to be here in two months and she's going to need her daddy." I watched the way his eyes got all soft and misty at the mention of our unborn child. Oh yeah, having his daughter was going to be the best thing that could have ever happened to me.

Jrue reached across the seat and laced his fingers with mine. "You're right. I need to quit bullshitting and just tell her."

As he pulled off I was already plotting how I was going to help give him that little nudge to make sure that happened.

21

Nikki

"You are listening to Ms. Nikki Truth, the host of *Truth Hurts* on 97 WJPC. If you're just tuning in, things have been crazy around here. Tonight we're talking about relationships and the warning signs. When do you know when something just isn't right and it's time to question your relationship? The phone lines are open." Within seconds, the lines were lit up. Courtney, a radio intern, signaled through the glass for me to pick up line three.

"Caller, you're on the air."

"Hello, Ms. Nikki. This is Desiree."

"Hello, Desiree."

"I'm calling because I've been dating this guy I really like for about three weeks now."

"Oooh, a new relationship. Okay." I leaned in close, ready for the story to get juicy.

"He is gorgeous, romantic, and has even been by my house to cut my grass."

"He definitely sounds like a keeper."

"That's what I thought. Anyway, we have spoken every day since we've met. He even texts me hugs and kisses every morning."

"Sounds like you got the type of man my listeners would

love to take off your hands. So what's the problem?" I asked, trying to move this conversation along.

"The problem is he said he was going to visit his mother, who lives in southern Missouri. For five days I didn't get a text message or a single call. What hurt the most was I didn't even hear from him on my birthday."

"Ooh, I can understand why you're pissed."

"Exactly. He came back home on Monday like nothing happened and said the reason why I hadn't heard from him was because there was no cell phone reception. He and his family had spent the weekend celebrating his grandmother's hundredth birthday at their house on the beach and his phone doesn't work down there."

"And you don't know if you should believe him or not?" I interjected, trying again to keep the conversation moving along.

"Exactly. The second he kissed me I wanted so desperately to be-lieve him, but now I'm starting to second-guess everything he tells me."

"And you have every reason to. Relationships are hard enough out there and if trust is an issue for you, then it's easy to understand why you're having doubts."

"My ex-husband cheated on me. I always knew something wasn't right, but I put my trust in him and instead came out looking like a fool when he got this chick pregnant."

"I guess the biggest question is how much you like this man?"

She sighed. *"I like him a lot. Every time I see him my entire body heats up and when we make love, it's explosive. But I'm just not sure. I feel that he is hiding something."*

"Then follow your instincts. But keep in mind, sometimes we subconsciously find ways to ruin our relationship by think-ing there is more going on than there really is, but at the same time, we gotta follow our gut," I added, then slid my micro-phone closer. "My advice is to tell him how you feel and watch his behavior when he responds. He'll either try to do things to ease your mind or suddenly he'll really start slipping up."

"Okay. Thanks. I'm going to try that."

"Hold on. Let's see what kinda advice our listeners have. Caller, you're on the air."

"Ms. Nikki, this is Carmen. Desiree, girl, that dude is just playing with your mind! Been there, done that. Get away before he walks all over your heart."

"Thank you. Next caller."

"Desiree, he reminds me of my husband of thirty years. Girl, just let the relationship run its course. It might be just fear standing in the way."

"So you think she should stay with him?" I loved getting differences of opinion.

"Yes, I think she's letting fear stand in the way of true happiness."

"Thanks for calling. Next caller, you're on the air."

"That guy sounds just like Todd. We dated for almost a year with that same damn story about his phone reception. It was just a bunch of bull. Come to find out he was spending the weekend with his woman."

"How did you find out?"

"How you think? I found a gas receipt in his car from this little town on the other side of Kansas City, and the next time he said he was going to visit his mother, I followed his ass."

"Ooh! And what happened?"

"I saw him, his wife, and their two kids riding around in the family van. They went to the mall and I made sure I walked through so he could see me. He about choked when I stopped to admire his daughter and asked his wife where she bought her shoes. Bastard."

I laughed. "Thanks for calling. Well, Desiree, there you have it. You've gotta follow your heart on this one. Either you're gonna hang in there for true love or you're gonna bail out before you get your heart broke. This is Nikki Truth and love hurts. There is no doubt about that. The question is: Are you willing to take that risk? Good night and remember the truth will set you free."

I heard Rihanna playing just as I took off my headphones

and dropped them onto my desk. Another perfect show. If only I could say the same about my life.

Thirty minutes later, I stepped inside the Waffle House and spotted Tristan sitting at a table in the corner. I made eye contact, smiled, then headed his way.

"Hey, sweetie," I said, and leaned down and hugged him in a tight embrace. He hadn't been at the radio station in the three weeks since Lorenzo's death. I had to talk him out of coming to the funeral because I had been afraid of what Lorenzo's family and friends would have done if they saw Tristan. Instead, I saved him an obituary and gave him a recap of the service. It had been standing room only. I had no idea how many friends he'd had. A lot of them had been clients from the barbershop. I didn't get to talk to many people because I was too busy keeping my eye on my husband, who looked ready to jump into the coffin along with Lorenzo. I wasn't sure how much more pain Donovan could endure before he finally snapped.

Tristan removed his dark shades and I saw the heavy bags under his eyes. He didn't look good at all.

"How are you holding up?"

His bottom lip quivered and I watched while he tried to hold it together. "It still hurts. I never loved a man like I loved him. And I hate that I didn't get to pay my final respects and say good-bye."

"Don't worry. Whenever you're ready, I'll take you out to the cemetery so you can see where he's resting." I would have said anything to make him feel better.

He drew a deep breath and managed to get out a few more words. "It's just so hard for me. I really thought we had a future together."

The waitress arrived and we stopped talking long enough to order. I hadn't had a chance to eat before running to the station. Leaving the bookstore and picking up Aiden was really starting to take a toll on me and my already tight schedule.

"How's Donovan doing?"

I blew out a breath. "Not good at all. He's also taking Lorenzo's death hard. Gone into a depression. Last night, he paced the floors all night. I thought I was going to lose my mind. Then I spoke to Trinette and she said Donovan called her last night. He wanted to know if I'd had an affair while he was deployed."

"Oh my! You don't think he . . ." His perfectly arched brow rose.

"No, I don't," I remarked, although my stomach was all tied up in knots. "I think he was just fishing for information that Trinette would never give him."

There was a slight pause before he said, "You never told him about Kenyon, did you?"

Tristan watched my face to gauge my reaction while I finally shook my head. "No, and I'm glad I hadn't because he'd *really* be acting a damn fool right now."

He nodded. "You're probably right. I just hope he gets better. I really hate seeing you stressed out like this all the time."

It was so considerate of him to be thinking about me when he was hurting so much. "Thanks. I went to Donovan's unit today and told them they needed to do something to help him."

"Oh, good. I hope they can help him."

My eyes swelled up with tears. "So do I."

I made it home after midnight and the house was quiet except for Rudy jumping all over me. "How's mama's baby?" I cooed as I gave him some love, then put my keys on the counter and walked upstairs to check on Aiden. My little man was sleeping soundly on his back. I hated missing his bedtime, but I had to make a living, so on the weekends I tried to spend as much time with him as possible. I kissed his soft cheek, then went into my room and kicked off my shoes before going in search of my husband. As usual, Donovan was in the family room watching ESPN.

"Hey, baby," I said and was so happy when he winked back at me.

"Hey, sexy, come give your man some love."

I flopped down onto his lap and pressed my mouth to his. His kiss was so soft and delicious I wrapped my arms around his neck and he cradled me close to his body while the kiss deepened. "Mmm, what did I do to deserve all this?"

He pulled back and looked serious for a moment. "Baby . . . I know that I haven't been acting myself lately. I've been under a lot of stress and I want to apologize."

See, this was why I loved this man so much. How often does a man admit that he is wrong? "Thank you, baby. That means a lot to me."

"I promise to start acting better. I just need to get my head on right."

All I wanted was for him to hold and caress me and make me feel like things I used to feel between us. I wanted to feel loved. "I agree. You need to see a therapist to help you get past some of the things that have happened to you."

He barely hesitated before saying, "I agree."

I breathed a heavy sigh of relief. "I'm so glad you said that. I was feeling so guilty about talking to Sergeant Clarke. I thought if he insisted that you—"

Donovan cut me off right there. "Hold up. What the fuck you mean you spoke to my first shirt?"

I startled. That blank look was back. A muscle at his jaw was ticking. "I mean, I didn't know what else to do. I think you have PTSD and I was scared, so I asked Sergeant Clarke for help."

"Get off my lap," he said in this voice that was so calm it chilled. I quickly scrambled to my feet. If I hadn't, chances were I was going to end up on the floor.

I put my hands up in defense. "Baby, I'm sorry that I went to your first sergeant, but I didn't know what else to do."

"Not that!" He fumed and jumped up from the chair. "Do

you know how bad it makes me look that my wife went to my unit and told my command she thinks I have PTSD! Do you have any idea what you've done?"

"Would you quit yelling before you wake up Aiden?" Now he had me screaming.

"Fuck!" He dragged a hand down his face and walked around the room. This conversation was definitely far from over, but at least he lowered his voice. "How the hell could you do something like that to me?"

"I did it because I love you. Something is seriously wrong with you, baby, and I want you to get the help you need."

He shrugged his shoulders, indicating there was some truth in what I was saying. "Then ask me to go and see a private doctor. Not be evaluated by an army shrink. Hell, that shit stays in your permanent record. I'm up for promotion this year."

I hadn't thought about that. "I'm sorry. I've asked you to see a therapist before and you refused. Couple's counseling wasn't working, so I just didn't know what else I could do. Baby, I was only trying to help."

"Well, you helped a'ight." He glared over at me for a long uncomfortable moment. "Sometimes I think you're trying to get rid of me."

I rolled my eyes. "Oh brother, not that again."

"I'm serious! You're spreading rumors at my unit that I have PTSD. I mean, what had I ever done except serve my country and be a good provider for my family."

"I never said you weren't a good provider. Don, I just want things back the way they used to be. You have to admit things haven't been good between us since you've gotten home."

"Why is that? Come on, Nikki, be honest. You wish I never came back, don't you?" he taunted with this crazed look in his eyes.

"Of course not."

He shook his head. "It's a damn shame. Specialist Smitty's

wife was so devastated when her husband died, she miscarried and lost their baby and she's been grieving ever since."

He wasn't telling me anything I didn't already know. Jackie Smith had been an active member of the FRG when her husband was killed after stepping on an unsecure mine. Rae and I were the first wives by her side when she had received the devastating news. "What does Jackie have to do with us?"

"I'm saying . . . I've been by to see her on several occasions and she would do anything to hold her husband again. How come my wife doesn't feel the same way about me?"

Okay, he was being ridiculous. "What the hell are you talking about? When your unit returned from deployment, I was right there with Aiden. I remember holding you tight, saying I was never letting you go again. You can't compare the two of us because the difference between Jackie and me is that my husband came home, or at least part of him did, while hers didn't. But at least she still has her husband's spirit, because you lost yours while in Afghanistan and I need for you to go back and get it. I need the man that I fell in love with in junior high to come back to me!"

He was quiet. Probably thinking about how ridiculous he sounded. I just couldn't believe he had even gone there with the whole dead husband story.

"I'm going to bed. I'll see you upstairs." I was just too through with the entire conversation. I was heading toward the stairs when I heard him turn off the television and reach down for his keys. Quickly, I swung back around. "Where are you going?"

Donovan brushed past me and didn't bother to respond.

"Don . . . I asked you a question. Where are you going?" I followed him into the kitchen where he reached inside the refrigerator and grabbed another beer.

"I'm going for a spin."

"What? A drive? You've been drinking." Had this man truly lost his mind?

"I haven't had that much to drink."

He stepped out the side door and into the garage while I stood there with a hand on my hip in disbelief. I didn't think he was serious until I heard the engine start.

"What the . . ."

I raced out the door and stepped into the garage just as Don put the Escalade into Reverse and pressed his foot down hard on the gas. The vehicle slammed hard against the garage door and it went flying out into the yard.

"Don, what are you doing?" I screamed as he backed down the driveway. I raced out into the yard as his tires screeched to a halt; then he shifted the car into Drive and peeled down the street driving like a crazy person. Up ahead I spotted a VW bug turning onto our street and my heart leaped into my throat as I watched in horror as Don tried to whip around the car. He must have lost control of the wheel because he went plowing across the yard of the house at the end of the corner and crashed through the front of their house.

I screamed and went racing frantically down the middle of the street. The entire time I prayed no one was hurt.

22

Trinette

Leon and I were at the Cinebistro seeing the new *Batman*. I had been waiting for weeks to see the movie. As soon as they announced the start of the movie we followed the crowd inside. As usual we had perfect seats right at the center of the theater.

"What do you and my daughter want to eat?"

I looked up from the menu and met his proud grin. When he had returned from Germany, I had placed a small box on the bed. Inside was a cigar wrapped in cellophane paper that read, "It's a girl!" He'd had his chest stuck out proud ever since. Staring up at his kind face, I felt another moment of guilt. I hated what I was doing to him. But what choice did I have?

"I think I'll have the shrimp and grits and the chocolate cake."

While he gave the waiter our order I looked over toward the door and my stomach did a nosedive. Jrue and Charlotte were walking into the theater. I glared over at the two of them, waiting for Jrue to look up and notice us. As soon as he moved to the aisle in front of us I knew he was getting ready to occupy the only two seats available that were directly in front of where we were sitting. Jrue's eyes grew big and round. He was holding hands with Charlotte, and they were wearing matching turquoise and black outfits. I nodded and forced a smile at both of them.

Leon was the first to speak. "Hey, Jrue, man. Good to see you again." Smiling, he rose from the chair and bumped fists. The two had met at numerous campus functions.

"Good seeing you too." He nodded, then turned to his wife. "Leon, this is my wife, Charlotte. Charlotte, this is Trinette's husband."

"It's such a pleasure to finally meet you. Congratulations on the baby!"

Leon was beaming with pride. "Thank you. Thank you. Yep, my wife and I are excited. She just found out last week we're having a girl."

Jrue glared over at me and I just grinned. That's what he got for bringing that skinny bitch to my favorite movie theater. I told him before that Leon and I came here often. The least he could have done was call and verify I wasn't coming. Men can be so insensitive at times.

"That's wonderful," Charlotte remarked with this smug look on her face. "I'm glad my husband could be of service while you were out of town."

His brow ruffled. "What service?"

"Didn't your wife tell you?" she began innocently. "Trinette was having false labor pains and Jrue was kind enough to take her in to see her obstetrician. Isn't that right, dear?" She gazed up at him.

Jrue seemed to be gathering himself before he finally nodded. "Oh, yes. I almost forgot about that. Absolutely. I'm glad I was there to help. I would have wanted someone to do the same if I had been out of the country. How was Germany?" he asked, smoothly changing the subject.

"It was great. I spent most of the time in the office, so I didn't get to see too much." A waiter was coming down the aisle with our drinks. "We better get in our seats. It was nice to see you again."

As soon as I flopped down on the chair, I could see the wheels in Leon's head turning. Damn that skinny ho. By the time our waiter had left to check on our order, Leon swung around on his seat, not at all happy. "Why didn't you tell me you had contractions and Jrue had to take you in?"

I shrugged. "I didn't want to worry you. If I had told you, you would have been on the next plane back to the States. It was just false labor. Nothing to worry about."

I couldn't believe how disturbed he looked at not being there. "I don't care how big or small the pains are. From now on you need to call me. That's *my* child you're carrying and I don't want anything happening to either of you."

I nodded, although I wasn't paying any attention to what he was saying. I was too busy watching Jrue and his wife as they ordered their food.

All through the movie I couldn't stop looking at the two of them. Every time she leaned in close and whispered in his ear I wanted to scratch her eyes out. I had really been looking forward to *Batman* and had heard the action scenes were fantastic, yet I couldn't focus on anything but the couple in front of me.

I tried not to think about the two of them being together and instead focused on an upcoming event. The entire department was attending a Career Programs mini conference in Virginia Beach next month at the Embassy Suites. We all had rooms there, but I planned on being with Jrue alone for two nights. Leon and I owned a condo on the beach that we rented out. I had contacted the management company months ago and reserved those two days. That way we'd have somewhere private we could go and be alone without anyone finding out. Zakiya was already suspicious that Jrue was messing around on his wife. Until he was ready to leave her and finally be with me, I didn't need anything standing in the way of me being with my man.

Halfway through the movie, I excused myself and went to

the bathroom. One annoying thing about being pregnant was that I always had to pee. I was coming out of the bathroom stall when I spotted Charlotte standing in front of the sink.

"How are you enjoying the movie so far?" she asked as I moved to the sink beside her and lathered my hands.

"Plenty of action," I said, although I had been too busy watching her and Jrue to really notice.

She reached for the paper towels, handed me one, then grabbed another for herself. The whole time I watched her watching me.

"What?" I finally asked. I hated when women stare. Just say what's on your mind.

"I'm sorry if I keep looking at you. It's just I am so envious of pregnant women." She sighed and had this sad look. "Just between you and me . . . Jrue and I have been trying for years, but I can't seem to get pregnant." She sounded like she was glad to have finally gotten that off her chest.

"I'm sure it will happen in time." Like with someone other than my future husband.

"That's what I've been told, but I caught my husband standing in the baby section at Macy's the other day. And I know despite everything he's said about it being okay, deep down he really wants a child of his own."

My plan was working. I struggled to keep a grin from my face. "Really? How sad," I said. I truly am a good actress.

"Anyway, I finally decided it's time for me to go and see a fertility doctor. If in vitro fertilization is the only option, then so be it."

Hell no. The last thing I needed was for this heifer to finally get pregnant when I was so close to getting what I wanted. If Charlotte ever gave birth to a child, there was no way Jrue would ever leave her. And Ms. Netta was not having that. "That sounds like a wonderful idea. I hope it all works out for the two of you." Yeah right. My daughter didn't need any siblings who weren't born from my coochie. I planned on texting him as soon as I got home and give him an ultimatum. If he decided to fertilize a baby in a dish, then it was over and Leon and I were going to raise his daughter. I was sure that was all the push he needed to finally make his decision. I'd be damned if I went through months of throwing up and stretch marks for some other woman to step in and steal my shine.

23

Nikki

After Donovan and that whole drunk driving fiasco, he was so devastated by what he had done that he admitted himself into a mental hospital. The unit was now jumping through hoops trying to assist me, but at this point I didn't need their help. It took three days before a doctor finally diagnosed my husband with PTSD. I couldn't tell you how relieved I was. Not because I had been right all along about my husband having the disorder, but because he was finally getting the help that he so desperately needed and deserved.

For the first few days he wasn't allowed to have any visitors; then I was invited to attend his treatment sessions. A lot of his bitterness and rage surfaced during the session, but after two weeks I could tell that progress was finally being made.

I was at the bookstore setting up for a book signing. We had a new author Ashlie Kelly coming in to sign copies of her first novel, *Right Through Me.* It was an amazing story written by such a young woman. I had arranged chairs for a reading and question and answer session followed by the book signing. We'd been publicizing the event for weeks.

I was hooking up the mic when I heard the main phone ring. I looked at the line of customers at the counter. It was two-for-one, and those days were always busy at the store.

"Karen, stay at the register and I'll answer the phone in my office." I hurried to the back of the store and grabbed the phone on the third ring.

"Book Ends . . . May I help you?"

"Well, hello, Nikki."

I froze because there was no way in hell I was on the phone with that psycho, yet I knew that voice that sounded like nails on a chalkboard. "Kenyon?"

"Yes, baby, it's me."

I looked around to make sure no one was listening, then whispered, "What the hell are you doing calling me?"

"I earned a phone call and the only person I wanted to call was you."

"But I have a restraining order against your behind. Which means you're not supposed to be calling me."

"Baby, I just wanted a chance to let you know I've been thinking about you?"

"Why?" Lord, why now?

I hadn't heard from that fool since he'd been arrested for kidnapping and attempted murder. I remember all those weeks of trying to keep Donovan from finding out. Thank goodness he was just getting back from Iraq and was spending a great deal of time at the unit in processing. I had made sure my lawyer kept my identity a secret because I was afraid of my husband finding out the truth about my affair that had ended up being with a straight-up stalker. In the few months that we had been dating, Kenyon had become so obsessed with me that he refused to accept that my husband and I were trying to save our marriage. As far as he was concerned, the only woman in the world for him was me.

Eventually, he was arrested and found mentally incompetent to stand trial, and was sentenced to five years in a mental facility; in exchange, he was supposed to have absolutely no contact with me. By doing so now he was violating the terms of his sentence.

"Baby, I've tried to stop loving you, but I just can't."

"Well, I wish you would." I had enough problems without him calling me. Just the thought of me making love to this psycho made my skin crawl. I remembered thinking he was someone special and that maybe we had a chance. I guess that's what happens when you start dating when your heart had been broken by someone else. You think there is more going on because you so desperately want it to be.

"Kenyon . . . Do me a favor. If you really love me, you won't ever call me again."

"But I—"

"No buts, just don't ever call me again."

He was saying something when I hung up the phone. I hated to be rude, but you had to be with someone like Kenyon. He was like a freaking leech. If I showed even the slightest bit of weakness, he would suck me dry.

Thank goodness I had sense enough years ago to change my home and cell phone numbers. Nevertheless, I picked up the phone again and contacted my lawyer. I needed to make sure that nut never called the bookstore again.

24

Trinette

On Saturday I lay around napping most of the day. Jrue had gone to Baltimore with Charlotte's skinny ass for the weekend to visit her family, which left my fat, pregnant behind with nothing to do except watch movies and read a book.

I got up from the couch in my sitting room and padded across the plush carpeting into the bathroom. Lately, all the hell I do is pee, then pee again. This baby is getting so big she is always pushing on my bladder.

"Little girl, I wish you'd move over," I hissed and even tried to push her over off my left side, but her stubborn little ass wouldn't budge.

She is going to be just like her mother.

I had to smile at the thought of there being a mini me.

As I washed my hands I stared at myself in the mirror. Damn, I was huge.

I turned from side to side. I was wearing panties and a T-shirt that stretched across my big, inflated belly. Just the sight made me want to cry. I don't care what anybody says, there is nothing attractive about being pregnant.

"You're a pig," I mumbled, then little missy started kicking me in the ribs. I pressed a hand to my belly and stepped into the bedroom just as Leon was coming through the door.

"What's wrong?" His eyes got large with worry.

I groaned. "She's lying on my side. I don't know if she's kicking my ribs or what. All I know is it hurts."

"Here . . . let me help you." He rushed over and raised my swollen ankles onto the bed. "Do you need me to take you to the hospital?"

"No." I wished he'd just go back downstairs.

"I'm serious. If you're hurting, I want to make sure I'm there this time to take you in to see your physician."

Oh hell! Leon was starting to get on my nerves. Ever since Charlotte blurted out that Jrue had taken me to my OB appointment, he'd been going on and on about not being there when his pregnant wife needed him. For the last week he'd been calling me every hour, insisting that I do nothing, and while at home, smothering me. Now since I was feeling like shit, he was going to be asking every five seconds if I was okay. I wasn't sure how much more I could take.

"No, Leon. I just need to lay here a while."

I missed sleeping on my stomach. Since she had started growing I couldn't even find a comfortable spot. I lay on the opposite side the baby was pressed up against hoping that she would take the hint and roll her little ass over.

"Do you mind if I lay here for a few minutes and hold you?"

I was screaming inside, hell no! As big as I was getting, the last thing I wanted was to be touched, but I just closed my eyes. Leon reached inside the nightstand and rattled around in one of the drawers for a few seconds, then climbed onto the bed and rolled beside me.

I heard a humming sound. My eyelids flew open and I rolled onto my back. In Leon's hand was my vibrator.

"What the hell? Leon, the last thing on my mind is sex." Just like a man. If they find you in the bed, their dick gets hard and they are ready to get busy.

He shook his head and chuckled. "I'm not thinking about sex."

"Then why are you playing with my vibrator?" And how the hell had he known it was tucked away in a box of tissues inside my nightstand. I took a second to think what else was in there that I wouldn't want him to find.

"I had an idea. I think if we pressed this against your stomach, the vibration will make Little Bit move over."

Little Bit was the nickname he'd picked out for my daughter. "I'm so desperate I'm willing to try just about anything," I said with a tired laugh.

"Then roll back over."

I did as he said and he laid the device against my stomach and turned it up on high. And sure enough in a matter of minutes that little girl woke up and moved, relieving the pain in my side.

"Oh, my God. She moved!"

Leon laughed. "I had a feeling that might work."

"I'm just glad it did. I wasn't sure how much more of that I could take."

He turned off the vibrator and set it to the side and lay back on the bed. "Come here," he said, and I was glad to roll into the cradle of his arm. I closed my eyes and listened to his deep breathing.

"Have you been thinking about any baby names?"

How was I going to tell him that Jrue and I had already picked out a name for his daughter? "I haven't given it much thought," I lied.

"I was thinking that maybe we should name our daughter after my mother."

Leona. Hell no.

I tilted my head and turned up my nose. "Seriously? That's a name for an old lady. Girls nowadays need cute names like Serenity, Symphony, and Sage."

He frowned. "She needs a name that has class and represents strength. Think about when she finally hits the job market. We don't want her to be stereotyped."

One thing my daughter will never be is stereotyped. I guarantee she is going to be a diva just like her mother. "I think we need to find a name we both like." Like Symphony. I rolled away from him, found a comfortable spot, and shut my eyes, suddenly feeling sleepy. I was no longer getting the rest I needed and the bags under my eyes were proof of that. And Netta wasn't having that.

"Let me ask you a question . . . was Jrue in the examination room when you found out the sex of our child."

My eyelids snapped open. Shit. Where the hell did he hear that? "Hell no. What in the world made you think that?" I didn't dare look over at him.

"I was just asking. He was there with you at your appointment, but you never said if he was in the room with you or not."

"Good Lord, of course not. He waited in the lobby until my examination was over."

I felt his body sag with relief as he rolled over and wrapped an arm across my body. "I was just asking."

"Don't be ridiculous. Why don't we come up with a list of baby names and put them in a hat and pull from them?" I said, changing the subject.

"That sounds like a plan." He sounded pleased by my suggestion.

Maybe taking Jrue to see my physician had been a mistake.

25

Nikki

Donovan had been home for almost two weeks now and he was better than ever. He was on medication for depression and still needed to see a therapist every week, but at least he was now talking about what he had gone through emotionally during his deployment. And that was a plus. Now we were taking things one day at a time.

I hadn't been to the shop since Lorenzo's murder. Mainly because just driving down Page Street gave me the creeps, but since Donovan was back to scheduling clients at the shop, I figured I needed to quit being a punk and go have lunch with my husband.

I stepped into the shop, greeted the crew, and sashayed back to my husband's office with the mail in one hand and a pepperoni pizza in the other. I had decided to surprise him and hadn't bothered calling, which would explain why when I pushed open the door, some chick was leaning across his desk.

What the fuck?

Her face was only inches from my husband's and whatever they were discussing was intense. The second they heard someone coming through the door, she drew back and turned my way. I recognized her instantly. It was that chick from Donovan's unit. Sanders.

I wished I could say underneath that military uniform was a shapeless, manly body, but I would be lying. She was wearing black leggings, thigh-high red boots, and a long tunic sweater cinched by a wide belt that emphasized her tiny waist, and I couldn't even deny that she had ass and titties for days. I felt self-conscious in comparison and found myself wishing I had worn something other than my favorite purple sweat suit.

"Am I interrupting something?" I asked, staring both of them down. It was one thing to see her visiting him while he was in the hospital undergoing treatment. It's another to find her ass spread across his desk. "Excuse me . . . I asked a question."

Donovan slowly rose from his chair and shook his head. "This is Malinda Sanders. She's in my unit."

"I know who she is," I replied with attitude. "What I want to know is why she is in your office."

Her eyes traveled from mine to his while Donovan chuckled like I was the one being ridiculous. "Nikki, chill. Her son's out front getting his hair cut by my man."

That may be true, but that frown on Malinda's lips hinted at something personal just between the two of them and I didn't like that shit one bit.

"Mrs. Truth . . . good seeing you again."

I wish I could say the same.

"I better get back out there." She glanced uncomfortably at Donovan, then nodded her head and started walking toward the door. "Truth, I'll see you at drill this weekend." The whole time she avoided eye contact.

I waited until I heard her voice out on the floor before I pierced my husband with a hard stare. "What's up with that?"

His brow rose and he had the nerve to try and look confused. "What's up with what?"

"That chick . . . bent all over your desk. That's what." I snarled and tossed the mail on the desk.

He reached for the stack still avoiding eye contact. "Nothing."

"It sure the hell didn't look like nothing." My head was moving with straight attitude. "It looked to me like she was ready to slob you up."

He had the nerve to laugh like I was a joke or something. "Nah, babe. She was just stopping in, saying hello."

Yeah right. I had been around long enough to know when something was going on. And if there wasn't anything going on, Malinda definitely wished there was. "Look like y'all were saying a lot more than just hello. Matter of fact, she looked like she was upset about something. I wonder what the fuck that could be?" I had never considered myself a jealous woman until now. Probably got a lot to do with the fact that Donovan had been accusing me of messing around on him for months.

The disbelief on his face was priceless. Of course he was going to deny it. That's what men do. "Nikki, ain't shit going on. Why you tripping?" he asked, and finally looked me in the eyes. "She was just telling me about a problem she was having at the unit that I need to address this weekend."

I threw my hand up. "Then she should have saved that shit for the weekend instead of coming up in here disrespecting me."

Donovan shook his head as if he couldn't believe I was tripping. Okay, so maybe I was. After the whole Kenyon thing I was feeling paranoid that he was going to try calling me again. I had even contacted the phone company, the second time to a shift supervisor, just to confirm my home number was unlisted and that in no way could someone get access.

I guess seeing how beautiful Malinda was without the uniform had me on edge. Here it was I'd been trying for months to prove my loyalty and then to find someone who was obviously interested in my husband making a play on him. Okay, so maybe Donovan was too stupid to notice. All I knew is that despite all the bullshit of the last few months, I loved my husband too much to lose him.

"Baby, I don't know what you think you saw, but it ain't happening. I love you. It's always been about you."

I thought about pushing the issue, but considering how well Donovan had been acting since his discharge, I decided to just let it go for now. Last thing I wanted to do was be one of those wives who accused her husband of messing around without proof.

"I brought pizza," I said like he hadn't noticed the pizza box in my hand. I moved over to his desk and set it down on the edge, then reached inside.

He looked relieved that I had finally let it go. Trust me. All I had done was tuck the little incident in the corner of my mind. I'd revisit it later.

"Thanks, babe. How'd you know I was hungry?" Donovan grinned with the devilish twinkle in his eyes. I felt my nipples start to tingle and grow hard. It had always been hard to stay mad at him for long.

I nodded and tried to act nonchalant as I took a bite. "It's my job to take care of my husband's needs."

Donovan winked, then reached inside the box. "It most definitely is."

While we ate pizza we talked about what we wanted to do for Aiden's third birthday, which was two weeks after Thanksgiving. We were planning to spend the holiday at Mama's house next Thursday. While he thumbed through the mail, Donovan suggested taking Aiden to Chuck E. Cheese.

"What's this?" He looked puzzled as he ripped open a large white envelope. And his eyes grew even larger as they skimmed the pages inside. "Son of a bitch!"

"What?" I asked between chews.

"That sorry mothafucka!" he yelled.

"What? What?" Dammit, inquiring minds wanted to know.

He stabbed the page with his index finger. "According to

these papers, Lorenzo left his half of the barbershop to Tristan."

"What?" I was sounding like a damn parrot. "No shit! He left him the barbershop?" It was starting to become clear that Lorenzo really had cared about Tristan. "No way!"

With a heavy groan, Donovan pushed his chair back and stormed into the shop. I could hear him cussing as he went to talk to his crew. The second he was gone, I quickly grabbed my cell phone and dialed Tristan while I chewed. This news was too good to wait.

"Hello?" Tristan said after two rings and had the nerve to sound sleepy.

"Wake your ass up before Donovan comes back," I whispered loudly into the mouthpiece.

He gave a rude snort. "What? He's already acting a fool again?"

"Yep, but you'll never guess why?" I swung around on the desk and looked over at the door to make sure he wasn't coming back.

"Why? What's going on?" I heard the alarm in Tristan's voice.

I brought the phone close to my mouth while I eyed the door and said, "Donovan got a letter in the mail. Apparently Lorenzo left you his half of the barbershop." I expected to hear Tristan scream loudly in my ear; instead, my announcement was met by silence. "Tristan . . . you still there?"

There was a soft cry. "He believed in me. My boo believed in my dream!" He started bawling and I felt bad for telling him over the phone.

"Damn, Tristan. I'm sorry. I shoulda waited and talked to you later in person."

"Nope, I'm glad you told me. I was just laying here thinking about Lorenzo, wondering if he was alive if he would have really left Tammy. Now I know."

I had to grin. He was right. Lorenzo had truly cared about him.

As I listened to Tristan talk about Lorenzo and his generous gift, I didn't have the heart to tell him there was no way in hell Donovan was ever going to allow him to set foot inside the barbershop.

26

Trinette

"Finally!" With a sigh, I pushed open the door to my condo in Virginia Beach. Although it was mid-October, it was stuffy inside. I slipped out of my green pumps, then moved over to the sliding glass door and slid it open.

"This is a nice place," I heard Jrue say as he walked through the living room, admiring the space.

I smiled and took a quick sweep of the room. Every square inch had been decorated by me. "Leon bought it last year as a rental property. We have a management company that handles it for us. It pretty much stays rented."

"I can see why. It's a wonderful location close to shopping and the beach. I would love to find a property like this myself, especially with the real-estate market as low as it is."

My man definitely knew real estate. "Leon said the same thing. He wished he had bought two other units in this complex. This one pays for itself."

"I believe it."

Enough about real estate. That was not at all why I had come here. I signaled for Jrue to follow me to the master suite where I parked my rolling suitcase, then turned on the ceiling fan. His cell phone rang and I noticed him glance down at the screen.

"Hey, babe, it's Charlotte. I'm going to take this in the other room." He walked off before I could tell him what I thought of his skinny ass wife. I was tired of sneaking around and sharing him with her. The sooner he left her and proposed, the sooner I could finally let Leon go. Trust and believe, I wasn't making any moves until I was certain of what was waiting behind door number two.

By the time he had returned from making his call, I had slipped out of my dress and was standing there in my bedroom in panties and a bra with my swollen belly prominently on display. Every chance I got, I tried to remind him of his daughter growing inside me.

"When are you going to talk to your wife?"

"When are you planning to tell Leon?"

"What is this, some kinda game? One of us goes first and then the other follows? I already told you I plan to talk to him just as soon as I have this baby. The question is whether my daughter is going to have her real father's name on her birth certificate or Leon's?"

The muscle ticked at his jaw. I knew that would get to him. "I'll talk to her next weekend. I promise. I just have to be delicate with Charlotte."

Fuck Charlotte. I was tired of sharing my man with her. "Uh-huh," I said and made sure he knew I didn't believe a word that he said. Hell, how long had he been promising? "And when's that? After she finds out her cancer has come back or even worse, she finds out she's pregnant."

He shook his head. "Baby, we already talked about this. I'm not interested in putting my sperm in no damn dish. If she can't have a baby like normal people, then we just won't be having any."

"Mmmm-hmm." Like I said, I didn't believe a word he said.

"Trinette, I mean it. I'm going to handle it."

"You better," I said with enough attitude that he had to

know I was serious. Until he talked to Charlotte, there was no way I was telling Leon. Jrue didn't have anything to lose except that skinny-ass barren wife of his. I had a husband who was an excellent provider. I'd be damned if I left with nothing when I planned to have it all.

He snaked out an arm and pulled me close to him. "Listen, I might not say it enough, but I love you. I want to be with you and my daughter. Nothing or no one is going to stand in the way of us being together. I promise you that." He leaned down and kissed my lips. I tried to act like I was still mad, but eventually I softened and allowed his tongue to slip inside. All I dreamed about was our life together and I couldn't wait until I was officially Mrs. Jarmon.

Jrue backed me against the wall, then slid his arm around my waist. "I'm ready to taste that pregnant pussy."

"You are so nasty," I purred. I saw the desire burning in his eyes and my body quivered.

"Always when it comes to you." He blew out a low breath, then dragged me against him. "I gotta have you." He leaned down and kissed me and pushed his tongue inside, and I got lost in his tasty mouth.

I didn't know what it was about him, but he had this overwhelming power over me. It was hard to think with his warm body rubbing against me. Lust surged through me like new blood. With every stroke of his tongue my breasts tightened, and it wasn't long before I felt a familiar ache in my womb that traveled down to my kitty-cat and she purred.

"Jrue," I moaned in his mouth. His masculine scent invaded my senses and I felt dizzy . . . and anxious to have all of him inside me.

Before I could catch my breath, Jrue's hands were on my body, cupping my round breasts.

"Oh yeah," I whimpered, then arched my back, drawing closer, yet it still wasn't anywhere near close enough.

"Trinette," he groaned. "You like when I play with your titties, don't you?"

"Uh-huh," I murmured, unable to find the words to express how he made me feel. And as far as I was concerned, words weren't needed.

He pushed my bra strap over my shoulders while his lips traced a hot wet path over my cheek and down my neck. I gasped as his lips closed over an aroused nipple and sucked.

"You like that?"

"Dammit, quit playing! You know that I do." It felt so good my wobbly legs were about to give out. I wasn't sure how much longer I could stand. "Please," I whimpered.

"Please, what?" He got off on taunting me.

I ran my hands over the warm, hard expanse of his chest and along his rigid stomach. "Baby, I need you." I deepened the kiss, needing to feel everything my baby had. He moaned while his hands bit into my ass and he dragged me against him, lifting me and rubbing his dick against my kitty.

"Sweetheart, you've already got me."

He always knew the right thing to say. We frantically pulled off our clothes and tossed them aside. Then he reached down and parted my lips, and nudged at my opening.

"You're so wet," he panted. I rocked against his fingers, heightening the growing pressure that coiled between my thighs. One of the good things about being pregnant, we no longer needed to use protection. Jrue always felt good, but without a condom the real thing was incredible.

"Wrap your legs around me," Jrue ordered as he lifted me off the ground, then leaned my weight against the wall. Grabbing my buttocks with both hands, he entered me in one powerful thrust. I started rotating my hips.

"Trinette, dammit . . . don't move," he ordered.

I'd never been good at listening.

"Shit!" he cursed, then pulled out and surged into me

again with incredible force. My eyelids flew open in surprise as my kitty pulsated and contracted around his magnificent dick.

"Jrue!" I cried out, my nails digging into his forearms. He answered by pounding into me again and again, until I was spiraling toward orgasm so fast I thought I would lose my mind. Jrue continued to pump his length into me, long and fast, drawing out my orgasm. "Baby, yes . . . Oooh, yes!" I whimpered over and over, until with one final thrust he came. With his penis buried deep within me, I was still whimpering. I opened my eyes and what I saw over his shoulder made me scream.

"Leon!"

Jrue's head whipped around and the second he spotted my husband standing a few feet behind him, he dropped me to the floor and I fell on my ass. "What the fuck?"

Everything happened so fast I didn't even have a chance to catch my breath. Leon lunged at Jrue; then the two of them were punching and knocking over furniture.

"Stop it!" I screamed. Despite everything, I didn't want either of them to get hurt, but I was pregnant and helpless to break it up.

I was so shocked that I couldn't even move. I just sat there on the floor and watched the both of them punching and crashing into my furniture. There was no way this was happening. What in the hell was Leon doing here?

When Jrue turned his head to look at me, Leon threw a punch that sent his naked ass crashing into the 55-inch flat-screen television. Damn. I knew I should have had it mounted last winter.

"Leon, baby. Please!" I said. My lip was quivering so hard I thought I would throw up.

"Now you wanna act scared," he said in this voice that was so calm it was scary. "Get your ass up!"

I scrambled to my feet. "Leon, baby, what are you doing here?"

"Oh, so now I'm your baby. A few minutes ago you were calling Jrue baby."

Damn, he'd been listening that long?

Jrue rose from the floor. Blood was dripping from one cheek. "Look, dude, let's talk about this like men."

"I advise you not to say a damn thing to me." He narrowed his gaze on me. "I can't believe you've been fucking this nigga."

I looked over at Jrue, wishing he would just leave the room long enough for us to talk in private. But leave it to a man not to get the hint. "Leon, please . . . it's not like it seems. I can explain."

"Explain what? That this mothafucka just happened to trip and his dick fell inside you." Leon shook his head. "Nice try. You know, I thought something was wrong when I got a call from the receptionist at your OB office confirming your appointment next week. Before I got off the phone she wanted to say how much in love we looked and apologize again for spilling coffee on my slacks."

That stupid bitch. I knew I should have gotten her ass fired.

"But then I got an e-mail from the management company saying the condo had been reserved for personal use."

"Leon, I'm so sorry. It wasn't supposed to happen this way. I—"

He cut me off. "Save that shit for someone who cares. All I want to know is if the baby you're carrying is mine."

I looked from him to Jrue. All that hurt on Leon's face, I wanted so badly to tell him what he wanted to hear. But I couldn't because, in truth, it wouldn't have mattered. Leon would never forgive me. Not anymore. I could see it in his eyes. And I couldn't blame him. I had vowed to make our marriage work, and instead I had fallen in love with someone else.

"I can't do that. I'm sorry, Leon, but I'm carrying Jrue's baby."

I wanted to slap that smirk from Jrue's face. Leon looked like I had punched him in the chest and I felt bad. I had planned on ending our relationship, but not this way.

"The two of you have fifteen minutes to get the hell out of my condo. I also advise you to get all your shit out of my house before I return on Monday. I'll be staying at a hotel because I can't even stand to be in the same room with you."

When he turned and walked out of the room and out of my life, I knew this time it was for good.

27

Nikki

I have spoken personally to Mr. Monroe's case
manager, and they had assured me Kenyon
will not be contacting you again.

"Baby! What's taking you so long?" Donovan shouted
from the family room.

"Here I come!" I logged off my e-mail and hurried into
the kitchen to retrieve the bag of popcorn from the micro-
wave. At least that was one worry off my mind.

Ever since Kenyon had contacted me at the bookstore, he'd
been calling me every week just to say hello and let me know
how well his therapy was going, like I really cared. If I had my
way, that dude would never get out of the hospital. I thought
my husband had been acting crazy. Well, Kenyon was clearly a
lunatic.

My lawyer had been trying for the last three weeks to get
that problem under control. And since Kenyon hadn't contacted me in two days, my lawyer's e-mail was my stamp of re-
assurance that the problem had finally been eliminated.

Mama was keeping Aiden for the weekend so that Donovan and I could have some much needed quality time to-

gether. This would be the first weekend I had allowed my assistant manager Terrence to run the store. It definitely wouldn't be his last.

I dumped the bag of popcorn into a bowl, then hurried into the living room and flopped down on the couch beside my husband.

"Okay, what did I miss?"

"Damn, baby, there really were dragons in them eggs!" His eyes were wide with surprise as he laughed. "Hold up, let me rewind it."

Game of Thrones was one of the most popular books in the store. I decided to buy the first season DVD, and we spent the day curled up on the couch together. After the first episode, Donovan and I were hooked. He rewound what I missed, and we ate popcorn and enjoyed our time together. I was so tickled to have this side of Donovan again, yet I was afraid the slightest thing was going to send him back over the deep end and I couldn't have that. At the end of episode 5, he hit the Pause button.

"Why'd you do that?" I asked and sat up on the couch.

Donovan's face got all serious and for a moment I thought we were back to him tripping about Tristan owning half of his barbershop. The lawyer he'd retained confirmed the documents were completely legal, and his only option was to try and buy him out. Of course, Tristan refused.

"I want a moment to talk to you."

I took a deep breath and started getting all nervous. Six weeks of therapy and it still wasn't enough. "Sure . . . what about?"

"First . . . I wanted to take a moment and tell you how much I love you. Baby, I don't know what I would have done if you hadn't stood by me all these months and helped me get through some things. I know all the drinking and weird behavior was a bit much, and especially me accusing you of messing around while I was deployed. I know you were nothing but faithful to me all those months and want to just apologize." He brought my hand to his lips.

I felt a surge of relief that he was finally starting to believe that I was committed to our relationship. "Thank you, baby. That means a lot to me."

"Baby, I'm trying to take it one day at a time and hope that eventually I'll be back to the man you once loved."

I had tears in my eyes. How long have I been waiting to hear those words? "You are the man I love. There is no past tense about it. I just need you to talk to me and let me know when something is bothering you. We're in this together." I leaned forward and wrapped my arms tightly around my husband and kissed him with everything that I had. Just as things started to get heated, he eased back and grinned over at me.

"How about we go have dinner at The Cheesecake Factory?"

My eyes lit up. He knew how much I loved that place. "Ooh! That sounds like a wonderful idea!"

"Great. Then go on upstairs and start getting ready. You know how slow y'all women are," he teased. "I'll be up as soon as I catch the news."

I sprung from the couch and hurried to the bedroom. We hadn't gone out to dinner in ages. I was in my closet trying to find something to wear that was classy and super sexy at the same time. I wanted my husband to feel proud with me on his arm. The house phone rang. I went over and grabbed the cordless phone.

"Hello?" I was digging in my jewelry box looking for a pair of gold hoop earrings that it took a second before I realized someone was crying. "Hello?" I said again but louder.

"N-Nikki . . . Leon put me out!" Trinette wailed.

I startled. "Put you out? Why?" I didn't even know why I was surprised, but I was.

"Leon put me out of my house. Can you believe that?"

Nope, I couldn't, because when it came to Trinette, Leon was a damn doormat. "What happened?"

"What happened is that he changed the locks. Jrue said he would go with me to get my stuff, but after the two of them going to blows—"

"Okay, ho. Time out." I just hated when someone started at the middle of the story. "You need to start from the beginning."

"Okay, but you better not judge me," she managed between sniffles.

I groaned. "Of course I won't. Your ass might be fucked up in the head, but you're still my best friend. Now quit stalling and tell me what happened."

"Well, remember I told you my department was going to Virginia Beach for a conference."

"Uh-huh." I glanced at the clock and jumped up from the bed. Donovan was taking me to dinner and I needed to be getting ready. "Keep going. I'm listening," I said, and wiggled out of the sweatpants.

"Well, I decided that the only way Jrue and I would have any privacy was to go somewhere else."

I knew Trinette long enough to know she was stalling. "Uh-huh, and where was that?"

"Well . . ." There she goes, stalling again.

"Trinette. What the hell did you do?" I wasn't there, but I could see her sitting on the couch nervously twirling her wedding band around her finger.

"We went to the condo."

"What?" I screamed. Sometimes I think this girl is stuck on stupid. "Please don't tell me Leon walked in on you."

"I thought you weren't going to judge?"

"I'm . . ." I drew a calming breath as I walked into my closet and retrieved a burgundy wraparound dress. "What the hell have I told you about shitting where you sleep?" I paused and shook my head. "Netta, you don't bring another man to your husband's bed."

"Well, actually we didn't make it to the bed. Leon caught us in the living room." She had the nerve to say it like it was all right.

"It doesn't matter if it had been on the front porch. The condo? Goodness, Netta! That's that man's house. You had no right. No wonder Leon is pissed."

"I know . . . I know. I don't know what I was thinking except that I wanted to be alone with Jrue. Away from Zakiya sniffing around at him. I just never thought that Leon would find out that I was at the condo and come down. When he walked in, Jrue was in midstroke."

Goodness, sometimes she can be a little more graphic than I needed.

"You gotta be kidding?" This was better than any Lifetime movie. I put the phone down on the bed, grabbed the dress and slipped it on, then picked up the receiver again. "Okay, and then what happened?"

"Leon and Jrue started throwing punches and breaking shit."

"Oh, my God! Who won?" I'm sorry, but I just had to ask.

"You are silly." And she even had to laugh. We'd always been stupid like that, which is why I guess we managed to stay friends all these years. "Actually, Leon may be small, but don't let his size fool you."

"So Leon tapped that ass, huh?" I reached for a pair of chocolate stretch boots and took a seat on the end of the bed while I slipped my feet inside.

"Are you going to let me finish or not?"

"I'm listening." As soon as the shoes were on my feet I hurried into the bathroom. "I don't know why you didn't call me on my cell phone. I coulda used my Bluetooth." Getting ready with one hand was too much damn work.

"I did, but you didn't answer."

She was probably right. I had left my phone in my purse.

"Anyway, Leon told me I had until Sunday to move out of the house. Of course it was Thursday and there was no way I could get packed and find a moving company over the weekend." Trinette blew out a heavy sigh. "I went by an hour ago and the locks had already been changed."

I shook my head. "What about the baby?" I just hated all this was going on while she was pregnant.

There was a long pause. "Oh yeah . . . I forgot to mention something."

I had to close my eyes and count to three. "What now, Netta?"

"Leon asked me in front of Jrue if I was carrying his baby."

I felt a wave of uneasiness. "And?"

"And I told him the baby was Jrue's."

I gasped. What the hell? "No, you didn't."

"Yes, I did." She released a long, shaky breath. "I didn't have a choice. My marriage is over with Leon. He will never forgive me for messing around on him. But I love Jrue and he loves me, so at least I have a chance at a future with him."

I just didn't have a good feeling about any of this. "Maybe Leon will forgive you for the affair."

"Are you kidding? It's one thing for a man to suspect his wife's having an affair, it's another to have it thrown in his face. You said so yourself with Donovan. He only suspects you had an affair while he was gone. If he found out it was true, it would be a totally different ball game and you know it."

"You're right. I just hate all this is happening while you're carrying a baby." I heard the phone click. "Netta? Netta, you still there?"

"Yeah, ho. I'm still here."

My heart started to pound. I hoped she wouldn't answer. "Because I just heard the phone click like someone just hung up the phone."

"It wasn't me. I'm sitting on the bed in my hotel room talking to you on my cell. It must be someone at your house."

I hoped like hell she was wrong.

28

Trinette

I still couldn't believe Leon had put me out of the house. I mean, seriously. How did he know he wasn't the father of my child? Okay, so maybe I *did* tell him he wasn't and got caught sexing another man in our condo, but how'd he know I wasn't lying? As far as I knew, I had no idea who the father of my child was. I just hoped this little girl I was carrying really belonged to Jrue, because if she didn't, I was in for a world of trouble.

I pushed that ridiculous thought aside. Who else's baby could it be but Jrue's? I mean, come on. During our ten-year marriage, I'd forgotten to take my birth control pills on several occasions, and not once had my period been late. But the moment I started screwing around with Jrue, I'd had two false alarms and then *BAM!* I'm knocked up. That's why I was eighty-five percent certain this baby belonged to him.

Jrue was generous enough to have hired a moving company to remove all my stuff from the house; then he leased me a beautiful three-bedroom condo in Short Pump that was only a few miles from the 5,000-square-foot home he shared with Charlotte. Despite the outcome, things had actually worked out better than I could have ever planned. I now had my man coming to see me every single evening after work.

Soon our baby will be born, but I was tired of waiting for Jrue to talk to Charlotte. I figured I owed it to our daughter to give him just a little nudge.

I slipped into a pink and white running suit that I had spotted on display at a maternity store in the mall. It was the perfect little thing to wear to the grocery store or just to run about in the neighborhood.

I managed to get down on all fours and scramble around boxes of shoes until I found a pair of brand-new pink cross-trainer shoes. I think I may have worn them once. Not that I planned to do any running this evening. Instead, I was on a mission. As soon as the laces were tied, I took one look in the mirror and one word came to mind.

Perfect.

Grinning, I grabbed my keys and headed out to my car. It was shortly after six when I pulled into the parking lot at American Family Fitness. I've had a membership since I moved to Richmond and had barely used the location near my home. But tonight would be my first time at the Short Pump location.

And for good reason.

I rode around the entire parking lot until I spotted the red Porsche with CJ on the personalized plates. Grinning, I parked my car at the other end of the lot, then climbed out and wobbled my big ass inside.

"Welcome to AFF." The girl behind the counter was way too cheerful.

I handed her my key chain; she swiped and handed it back to me. Leon had signed us up for a three-year family contract so I was still good to go.

"When's your baby due?" she asked, staring down at my stomach. What was with all these women envying pregnancy? If anything, I wanted that perfectly flat belly that she had. I guarantee there wasn't a stretch mark in sight.

"In six weeks." And not a moment too soon as far as I was concerned.

I walked to the women's locker room, put my purse and keys away in the locker, then went in search of Charlotte Jarmon. I was making my third trip around the gym when I spotted her on the treadmill. The machines on either side of her were occupied, so I made sure she wasn't able to see me standing near the track, eyeballing her. She had her iPod on her arm and headphones in her ears. She was running and sweating like a malnutritioned hog on an August morning.

As soon as one of the machines was free, I hurried over to the treadmill and jumped in front of a short pudgy chick.

"Hey! I was waiting for that machine!" she protested.

I rolled my eyes. She clearly needed the equipment more than I did, but that was beside the point. "Are you really going to fight about a machine with a pregnant woman?" I said in a sickly sweet voice, then gave her a look like she was clearly being ridiculous. She glared down at my stomach and turned away.

I stepped onto the machine and pushed the Quick Start button.

"Hello, Trinette."

I looked to my left and acted surprised to see Charlotte. "Hey, girl! I didn't even see you over there. How's it going?" I smiled and started walking.

"I can't complain." She gave me a curious look. "I haven't seen you in here before."

"My doctor told me I needed to start getting a little exercise. This baby has me gaining way too much weight." I rubbed my stomach and watched her eyes travel down to my hands. There was that pang of envy again. What's with these women? "How're the fertility treatments going?"

Charlotte turned red and looked embarrassed. I gave her a look like she had nothing to be ashamed of. "They've been running tests but haven't started the fun stuff yet."

"Fun for whom? Your husband?" I asked all innocently, then gave a soft chuckle. "I don't know about Jrue, but if it were Leon . . . jacking off to a porn magazine in a private room would not be considered fun."

Oh, Charlotte looked ready to have a hissy fit. "Speaking of husbands . . . I bet yours can't wait to get his hands on that baby," she said, smoothly changing the subject.

I turned away long enough to conjure up a few fake tears, then drew her attention. "Leon left me," I replied, lip quivering.

"What?" She seemed clearly surprised and almost pleased to hear that my life wasn't as perfect as she originally thought. "What man leaves his pregnant wife?"

"One who discovers the baby she's carrying doesn't belong to him."

"What?" She was beginning to sound like a parrot.

I shrugged like it was no big deal. "I guess the truth would have come out eventually anyway. As soon as she's born anyone will be able to take one look and know who her father is." I gave her a coy smile, then increased the speed on my treadmill and stared at the TV monitor overhead. I could hear the wheels in Charlotte's head turning.

"Is it anyone I know?"

"Maybe. All I'm going to say is that he's married and until he leaves his wife, I can't reveal his identity. Trust me, once things are different, I plan to announce it to the entire world."

Charlotte stopped suddenly. Only the treadmill was still going and she almost fell on her pancake ass before she managed to catch herself. If she had fallen, that would have been some funny shit.

I chuckled to myself, then faked a sharp pain and brought a hand to the side of my stomach. "Oh my, maybe I need to take this workout thing one day at a time." I stopped the treadmill, then gave a two-finger wave. "See you around." Charlotte was standing there speechless like a freaking scarecrow. Damn,

I'm good. I whistled all the way back to the locker room. It was time to get back home and wait for Jrue to arrive.

It was almost eight when I heard the key turn in the lock. I flicked on the television and pretended I was engrossed in a movie when Jrue stepped into the room.

I smiled over at him. "Good evening, baby," I cooed and waited. I didn't have to wait long.

"Charlotte said she ran into you at the gym this evening." His comment sounded more like a question, as if he thought his skinny-ass wife might possibly have been lying.

I acted like I had to think about his comment a moment. "Yeah, sure. I saw her while I was out walking on the track."

He walked farther into the room. "Really? Since when do you go to the gym?" Okay, so now we were getting to the real issue.

I didn't dare look at him because he was sure to see my ass was lying. I decided to flick television channels. "I've gained five pounds since my last OB visit. I decided if I didn't get my big ass up off the couch, I was going to be fifty pounds heavier by the time this baby is born. Sorry . . . not having that."

Jrue was silent as he walked around the coffee table and took a seat on the couch beside me. I pretended to be watching the *King of Queens*. Don't get me wrong, I loved that sitcom, but my mind was more on what he had to say. I wish I had been a fly on the wall at his house, because I'm sure the second Charlotte had stormed home from the gym she had torn into his ass.

"Charlotte asked me if you were carrying my child."

It took everything I had not to grin. I had to count backward slowly, three . . . two . . . one . . . My eyes turned to him all wide and round. "What? Are you serious? W-What did you say?" Did I have talent or what?

"I told her the truth."

"What?" Okay, I wasn't acting now because what he had

just confessed was music to my ears. "You finally told her the truth?"

He nodded and looked at me. "Yes, I told her you were carrying my child." Jrue pressed his palm to my stomach. The look in his eyes was crystal clear. This little girl meant more to him than all the money he had in the bank. And that was all I could ask for. "I told her I was sorry for hurting her, but I loved you and wanted to be with my family."

Tears were streaming down my face. I couldn't believe that this day had finally come. Jrue had told Charlotte about us. He was all mine. "What did she say?" I know it was wrong, but I had to know every little detail. Like I said, I wish I had been a fly on the wall. I could just see her bottom lip dropping when Jrue confessed to her his love for me and our unborn child.

"First, she was hurt, and then she started throwing shit. I decided that it was time to go."

Yes, absolutely. The best thing to do was come home to your family. "Sweetheart, I'm sorry that things had to go down this way." It took everything I had to try and sound sympathetic.

Jrue shook his head. "No, as a man, I'm the one who owes you an apology. The day you told me you were pregnant, I should have made a decision to either be with you or divorce Charlotte instead of straddling the fence."

"If Charlotte hadn't confronted you, which would you have decided?" I already knew the answer, yet I still needed to hear it.

Jrue shifted sideways on the cushion and made sure he was looking directly in my eyes when he answered, "You. It's always been about your crazy ass." He gave a short laugh. "The day you walked into my office and interviewed for the job, I knew then I was in trouble."

I grinned. I would never forget that day. I had on a black Vera Wang dress and charcoal heels. It had been a panel of three, yet the only person I focused on was Jrue. I dominated that interview and his attention. Two hours later, he had called to give me a tentative offer pending the completion of a background check.

The rest is history.

Jrue took my hand in his. "What I'm trying to say is that I love you and it's time for me to step up to the plate and do right by you."

I can't even begin to tell you how long I had been waiting to hear those words coming from Jrue's mouth. Finally, after months of praying and hoping, I finally had my man all to myself. Yet why didn't it feel as triumphant as I had imagined?

29

Nikki

I was on my way to pick up Aiden from daycare when I decided to call Trinette and see how she was doing now that Leon had put her ass out.

"Girl, I'm not even thinking about Leon. I'm with my baby's father."

I didn't even know why she was trying to lie. "But you're not even sure he's the father of your baby."

"Well, I'm *almost* certain and Jrue thinks he is, so that's all that really matters."

Sometimes I wish I could record Trinette just so she could hear just how stupid she sounds. I don't care what she said, I know she still can't believe that Leon dumped her ass. Hell, I can't believe it either. I mean that man had been putting up with her shit for years and had taken her back despite all of the trifling things she has done. I told Trinette she was pushing her luck and that at some point Leon was going to have enough, but, of course, she thinks her coochie doesn't stink and look where it got her. Now she's shacking up in a condo paid for by her suspect baby daddy. I just don't get that girl. It wasn't like she even wanted the baby in the first place, and now she's playing house with a married man.

"I really think you need to just get your own place, at least until the baby is born and Jrue leaves his wife."

She smacked her lips. "Jrue left his wife last week."

"What?"

"Girl, yes! She confronted him about the baby and he admitted it was his."

"Okay, hold up. Confronted? What made her think you were carrying his child?" Like I said before, I hate when someone starts explaining at the middle of the damn story.

"Well," she paused and chuckled. "I might have been instrumental in making that happen, but all that matters is that Jrue is now all mine." I didn't even want to know what she had done this time.

"And how long do you think that is going to last?"

"Why are you being a hater?" she spat into the phone.

"I'm not hating. But one of us has to be realistic about the situation, and it sure in the hell ain't you. You need to start working on a backup plan because this shit isn't over. I guarantee you. It never is."

My response was met by a rude snort. "Nikki, you worry too much!"

"Maybe so, but I think in this situation you have more to worry about than just yourself."

I was still shaking my head long after I got off the phone. Trinette was more work than I had time for this evening.

I pulled up at Aiden's daycare center and climbed out of the car. I followed the cracked sidewalk around back where the kids played in the playground while waiting to be picked up. I scanned the area especially the jungle gym, which was Aiden's favorite, and didn't find him anywhere.

"Mrs. Truth?"

Coming toward my left was Jeannie, one of the childcare assistants. She was a tall, blond, child psychology major. I smiled. "Hi, Jeannie. Did my husband already pick Aiden up?"

I asked, although I swore Donovan told me he was working late tonight.

She frowned and shook her head. "No, Aiden wasn't here today."

"What?" I said, then I quickly pulled it together. "Oh, that's right. Donovan was taking him to the zoo today." I lied, then waved and turned away. Big Mama always said what happens between a man and his wife is their business. Last thing I wanted was for the daycare to know that I was having problems in my home.

As soon as I rounded the corner I grabbed the phone from my purse and dialed Donovan's cell. The longer the phone rang, the more frustrated I became. Stupid me. Something had told me to drop Aiden off myself this morning like I'd been doing ever since Donovan had been waiting for me in the parking lot of the radio station drunk; but instead, this morning I allowed my husband to roll me over onto my back for some good loving and then was running late. He was supposed to have dropped Aiden off on his way to the barbershop. When I got his voice mail again, I decided to call the barbershop.

"A Cut Above the Rest."

"Gabby . . . is Donovan there?"

"No, he was here about two hours ago; then he left." She had an annoying habit of popping gum in your ear between syllables.

"Did he have Aiden with him?"

"Nope, haven't seen him."

My brain started racing with possibilities. Where the hell were they?

"Hey, Nikki." There was a pause. "What's up with Don?"

Now it was my time to hesitate. "Why do you ask?"

"Because ever since Lorenzo died, he hasn't been himself. I know he's taking it hard, we all are, but . . . he's just been acting really weird."

"Can you blame him? His best friend was killed."

"I know." Gabby hesitated. "But even after going into the hospital something still seems off about him."

She had no idea how badly I wanted to agree. Only I was not about to discuss my marriage with Ms. Gossip Queen. "I'm sure he'll be fine. If you hear from him, tell him to give me a call."

"Sure," she said, and I ended the call.

I made a left at the next corner, then hit the highway racing down I-70. I dialed the house and got no answer, then kept dialing Donovan's cell. This time it didn't even ring; instead, it went directly to voice mail. I pulled onto our street and pressed the remote. The second the garage door rose and I saw Donovan's Escalade inside, I got mad.

"Ain't this a bitch," I muttered, then slammed the car door shut. He had scared the shit out of me again for nothing.

I stormed inside the kitchen and noticed that on the counter was a half-empty tequila bottle.

"Don!" I called as I moved up the stairs. I hurried into our bedroom and when I found it empty, I went across the hall into Aiden's and looked over at his bed. He wasn't there. "Don!" I screamed, then raced down the stairs and stepped into the living room.

"What took you so long to get home?"

Startled, I turned around so fast I bumped into the coffee table. Damn, I've been doing that a lot. Ignoring the stabbing pain at my shin, I stared at Don, sitting comfortably at the head of my dining room table with a drinking glass in his hand.

"Don, what are you doing sitting in here?" Especially since the only time we used the room was during the holidays. That $5,000 solid oak dining room set was strictly for show. Well, at least that's what I used to use it for because there at the center of the table was a long white envelope. But that wasn't what made my pulse race. Nope. It was the large butcher knife that had been jabbed straight through the paper all the way clear through my table.

I took a nervous step into the dining room. "Donovan, what the hell is going on?"

He took a sip before replying, "You tell me." His eyes darted to the envelope on the table; then he tilted his head. "Go ahead. Read it."

I was almost too afraid to walk farther into that room. There was a calm about him that was almost eerie. "Where's Aiden?" I asked.

Again, he brought the glass to his lips. "Why don't you read the letter first?" he replied in a voice that was as crazy as it was soft as he pointed to the envelope.

In my panicked state, I kept an eye on him as I moved cautiously over to the table, yanked the knife out of the table, and then reached down for the envelope. As soon as I saw the return address, my knees almost gave out.

Fulton State Hospital.

Kenyon had sent a letter to my house. I dropped it onto the table like my fingers were on fire.

"What's wrong? Your man sends you a letter and you can't even take the time to read it. I'm so disappointed." His voice was dripping with sarcasm.

I looked at Donovan and saw the anger in his eyes and face. "Baby, please, give me a chance to explain," I cried desperately.

"What the fuck is there to explain?" he asked, then tossed the glass back and finished it in one gulp. "While I was deployed you were messing around with that mothafucka, weren't you?"

Oh, my God. How in the world was I going to be able to explain something that I should have told him years ago? Back then we had been trying so hard to fix our marriage and make things work that I didn't know how to tell him.

"Yes, but that was because I thought our marriage was over, I swear to you. The second you called and we talked about working things out, I ended the relationship."

"You must think I'm fucking stupid!" he shouted, then jumped up from the chair so fast I flinched.

"Donovan, please! I swear to you. I ended it. After you returned I never talked to him again."

"Oh, really? Then why the fuck was he talking about how much he enjoyed your recent telephone conversations?" Donovan started walking around the table and I was so scared at what he might do that I snatched up the knife and gripped it for dear life.

"Because he's crazy! Didn't you notice the letter came from a mental institution?"

He stopped walking and quirked an eyebrow in my direction. "Why you got that knife in your hand?"

"Because I don't like the way you're looking at me." I backed into the living room while Donovan had the nerve to start laughing.

"You know I can take that knife from you, don't you?" I felt his anger from several feet away.

"Donovan, just listen to me! I have been committed to our marriage. I swear to you."

"That's what your mouth says, but your thighs tell a totally different story. Aiden is that man's son, isn't he?"

My eyes widened. No he didn't just say what I thought he said. "What? You sound like a fool! That's your son and you know it."

"How the hell I know that? I hadn't been home a month and next thing I know you're pregnant. For all I know, Aiden' could be that nigga's son."

I struck a pose and pointed the knife at him. "Now you're talking crazy! Aiden's our son. If you don't believe me, call Trinette and ask her about Kenyon's crazy ass."

"I ain't asking that bitch shit. She'd say anything for a damn dollar." His frown deepened. "Y'all just alike. I spoke to my man Leon last week and according to him Trinette tried to pull the wool over his eyes with the same dumb shit."

No, this wasn't happening. "Okay, so maybe Trinette did try to play Leon, but she and I are two different people. Now tell me where the hell Aiden is!" I demanded. I was tired of playing this game with him.

"Aiden's away from the bullshit," he replied; then he just stared. "You're just like all the rest. My boys were coming home finding out their wives had been fucking in their beds, but I was like, my wife wouldn't do that." He shook his head and took two steps toward me and I froze. "Come to find out not only were you fucking around, but you had a baby by another mothafucka." Donovan then snatched me up so fast I didn't even have a chance to blink. "Do you have any idea how much I loved you?"

Did he just use past tense? "And I love you, so please listen to me w-when I say I'm sorry. I-It only happened that one time and only . . . only because I thought our marriage was over. If I had thought we had a chance, I-I never would have dated him." I was pleading and hoping that I could get him to listen to me. "The second you came home, I ended the relationship. I swear to you."

Donovan reached down and I gave no resistance as he took the knife out of my hand. "Then why didn't you tell me?"

He had that crazy look in his eyes again. Quickly, I jerked free, putting a little space between us. "Because I didn't know how to tell you. We were trying to rebuild the trust, and I was afraid that if I told you about it I would have ruined any chance of getting my husband back. I'm sorry. I swear to you."

"So am I."

His expression was so cold that I decided maybe it was time to snatch up my keys and go get Aiden while he cooled off. Chances were my son was at Mama's. I was about to leave the room when Donovan reached underneath his shirt and pulled out a gun.

"What the hell . . . ?" My heart slammed against my chest. "Donovan, put that gun away. You don't have to do this."

He slammed his fist against the wall. "Yes, I'm afraid I do."

Trembling, I brought my palms together and pleaded with him. "Baby, you need help. Serious help. I promise to be there with you."

"Shut up. Just shut the fuck up!" he screamed, waving the gun in his hand. "You don't give a damn about me. All I am is a fucking joke to you!"

Then everything happened as if we were moving in slow motion. Donovan fired a shot that whipped past my ear and shattered the glass china cabinet. I dove behind the table and tried to miss the next two shots while I scrambled across the floor. And when he pointed the gun at me again, I jumped up from the floor and tried to wrestle it from his hands.

And then the gun went off.

30

Trinette

"I can't believe you did all this for me!" I cried when I stepped into Zakiya's house. It was Friday evening and everyone from my department was gathered around in her tiny living room for my baby shower.

"We wanted to surprise you." Zakiya beamed like the proud hostess and she should be. Everything looked fabulous. Food was on the table and gifts on the floor. "Come on in and have a seat over there on the couch while I get you something to eat. I invited the entire office, including Jrue. He said he'll drop by later if he can."

I had to hide a grin. We were so good those chicks still had no idea that they were having a shower for Jrue's baby.

The last two weeks had been amazing. Jrue and I were living together at the condo planning a future that included marriage. Nikki was just being a hater, which was why I had hurried and got off the phone with her. I can't understand why she just couldn't be happy for me. Instead, she wanted to pollute my happy world with negative energy. Fuck Leon, Nikki, and Charlotte. I was in love and nothing else mattered except me, Jrue, and our unborn child.

"All this for little old me?" I batted my eyelashes and acted innocent. I'd had a feeling when Zakiya had invited me to her house that she was planning something special. I just had no idea the evening would be all about me. Not that I was complaining. In fact, it really meant a lot that she had gone to so much trouble to plan me a shower because, besides Nikki, I truly never expected anyone to do something so nice for me.

I took a seat on the couch and played all the stupid baby games; then we ate finger foods that didn't do anything but make me crave a steak and potatoes. Trust and believe, I'll be sending Jrue out later for takeout.

The doorbell rang and Zakiya went to answer it while I opened another gift. Inside was a $200 gift card to a new baby boutique I had found in Ladue. Zakiya and I had discovered it during lunch one afternoon. "Thank you," I said, beaming with excitement. My baby was going to be rocking some slamming outfits.

I looked up at the doorway just in time to see Jrue standing there and I smiled over at him. "Welcome to all the fun."

He gave a nervous laugh as he glanced around at all the women's envious looks. Jrue had a reputation of being the hottest man on campus. Luckily, they were under the impression that he and Charlotte were still together; otherwise, all these heifers would be all over him. "Hello, ladies. I'm not staying. I just wanted to drop off my gift and talk to Trinette for a moment. That's if I can steal you away."

With a nod Zakiya took the box from his hand and added it to the others.

"Sure. Y'all excuse me a minute." With the help of one of the ladies, I rose from the chair. I made my way through all the gifts and followed Jrue out onto the porch. "Hey, baby, I'm surprised to see you here," I purred softly.

Jrue walked down to the bottom step before he swung around and I noticed his expression had turned serious. "We've gotta problem."

I didn't like the way he was looking at me. "Baby, what's wrong?"

He reached into his breast pocket and pulled out a folded sheet of paper and held it out to me.

"What is it?" I asked. I was suddenly afraid.

"Proof that the baby you're carrying isn't mine."

It took everything I had to keep a straight face. There was no way he said what I thought he said. Yet the moment I took the paper from his hands and stared down at it, I felt like my feet had slipped out from under me.

"Charlotte has been seeing a doctor for weeks about infertility." He paused for a moment while he paced the length of the porch. "A week ago, Charlotte agreed not to go after my inheritance in the divorce if I agreed to be tested. She knew. She knew all along there was no way you were carrying my child."

Sterile.

Somehow, I managed to stay calm. "The test isn't one hundred percent."

"Maybe not, but it's enough to make me question what is happening here."

I hoped I didn't look as panic-stricken as I felt. "What reason do I have to lie to you?"

"Every reason," he replied, then crossed his arms and gave me a cold stare. "Leon was under the impression you were carrying his child. I thought he was impotent."

"Well . . . I . . ." Damn, I was so busted.

Out of the corner of my eye, I noticed Zakiya looking between the vertical blinds. Nosy ass. The last thing I wanted was for any of them to know what was going on in my personal life, so I tried to explain in a low voice, "I didn't say we *never* had sex, I said he had a hard time performing even when he could get it up. Leon thought he had managed to get me pregnant, so I let him think that."

"Just like you let me think that baby you're carrying is mine."

"That's because it is!" I yelled at him, then remembered we

had an audience. "Why are you treating me like this? I love you."

"Listen, Charlotte and I are going to try and save our marriage, but the only way we can do that is if I end my relationship with you."

My heart lurched at the mention of his wife. "What? You can't be serious! I thought it was over between you and that skinny ho," I stammered.

Jrue had the nerve to sound exasperated. "I changed my mind. I'm sorry, but I need to save my marriage."

Tears clouded my vision as I realized how desperate I was. "What about me and the baby?"

He shook his head and gave me a cold look that sent chills down my body. I had never seen him this way before. "That's not my problem . . . or my baby. You need to be out of my condo by Monday."

I gave him a look to let him know he was being ridiculous. "Monday?" That's the same thing Leon had said. "How the hell you expect me to move my shit that fast?" I shot back at him.

He gave me a nasty smirk. "I guess you need to figure that out." He said it like all of a sudden he no longer cared about me, and that pissed me off.

The door opened and Zakiya stepped out onto the porch. "Is everything okay out here?"

"Yep, everything is fabulous." Jrue cut his eyes in my direction one last time, then turned and walked back to his Jaguar.

The entire time I watched him I felt like my heart had been sliced in two. Whoever had said it wasn't lying.

Karma is a bitch.

31

Nikki

I must have fallen asleep in the chair, because I opened my eyes and the second I saw Donovan lying in bed I knew it hadn't been a dream. He was still lying there in a coma. All I had tried to do was take the gun from him. We had wrestled to the ground; then it had accidently gone off and a bullet hit Donovan square in the chest.

I don't think I will ever forget that sight of my husband lying on the floor in a pool of blood. Not knowing if he was alive or dead, I was screaming and shaking so hard I couldn't even think straight. Thank goodness my nosy neighbor on the left sent her husband over to see what was going on. As soon as he spotted Donovan lying on the floor with the gun in his hand, he hurried back to his house and called the police. I was sitting on the floor shaking and pleading to God to let my husband live.

No matter how I looked at it, all this was my fault. Sure, my husband had pointed a gun at me and had even tried to shoot me, and if the circumstances were different I might have been ready to walk away from him and our marriage. Instead, that wasn't the case. Everything that had happened was a domino effect from my affair. I had brought the incident on myself. I never should have gotten involved in Kenyon. Donovan and I were still married. Sure, he had written me during his deployment and had asked for a divorce, but I should have waited until he returned from Iraq and told me it was over to my face. But instead, I had an affair. And you see where that shit got me. While staring over at his lifeless body, I released a shaky breath. I would do anything to go back four years and tell him the truth, but like I said, it's always easy to say what you shoulda, coulda, woulda done when it's too late to do anything about it.

I heard a knock at the door and looked up to see my mother stick her head inside the door.

"Come on in, Mama," I whispered, and cleared the frog from my throat.

Mama walked into the room. The second she looked over at Donovan lying helplessly in the bed, she gasped and brought her hands to her mouth. "Oh, my God!"

I rose and immediately walked over to her. Neither of us had been in a hospital since Big Mama had passed away, so I knew it would be hard for her to see him lying in a hospital bed like that. I wrapped my arms around her, glad she had finally made it. "Mama, thanks for coming."

"You know Don is like a son to me."

Yes, she always did love him like one of her own.

"I'm always here if you need me." She eased back slightly and met my watery eyes. "Have you found out where Aiden is yet?"

I was seconds away from crying again at the mention of my baby. I had been so worried about Donovan that for a while there I forgot that I had no idea where he was. "I have no idea."

After Donovan was rushed to the hospital and carted off into surgery, I called to see if Aiden was with her. And when she told me no, I started calling everybody I could think of, but no one had him or knew where he could be. I had no idea who else to call.

I didn't miss the pain-stricken look on her face. "I tried calling everyone I know as well, but no one seems to know where my grandbaby is."

Another sob rose to my throat. I couldn't remember when I had felt so scared in my life. My husband was fighting for his life and my baby was missing. It took everything I had to hold it together.

"Mama, I need to go down the hall and check my phone messages. Maybe somebody has been calling the house looking for me."

Mama squeezed my shoulder, then nodded. "You're right. You better go and check. Although I'm sure whoever has him can keep him until the morning. My little munchkin should be sound asleep by now."

It was almost ten o'clock when I hurried out of the room and down the hall to the lobby searching for a good phone signal. I was practically out in the middle of the parking lot checking my voice mail. As soon as I discovered I had two messages, I got all excited. My fingers were shaking as I was pressing the keypad so I could listen to the recordings. The first was from Trinette. I ended up deleting it before it had even gotten started. The last thing I wanted to hear about was her and her suspect baby's daddy when I had far worse problems of my own. Right now I needed to find my son. The second message was an unavailable number and there was nothing on the recording for three long minutes. I stood there the whole damn time waiting for someone to say something before the message finally ended. By then I was crying my ass off. The last time I'd seen Aiden was when I had left for the bookstore this morning. I had no idea what time Donovan dropped him off or where he could have taken him.

I walked across the lot to my car, climbed in, and drove to the police station to report my son missing.

32

Trinette

This couldn't be happening to me.

I went to work on Monday, ready to make Jrue's life miserable because nobody treated Ms. Netta that way.

After Jrue ruined my baby shower, I had returned to the condo in total disbelief that my man could treat me that way. Yet the rest of the weekend he didn't come by to apologize for being insensitive; instead, he ignored all of my numerous phone calls. Well, guess what? There was no way in hell he could ignore me at work. Today, whoever didn't already know we had been fucking—thanks to Zakiya's nosy ass—they were about to find out, because I planned to announce to the world I was carrying Jrue's baby.

I pulled my car into the parking lot and was pleased to find parking right in front of the building. Grinning, I figured with this kind of luck it was going to be a fabulous day. I made my way toward my building and noticed that my favorite security guard was standing right outside the double doors.

"Hey, Herschel," I said with a big grin. I was determined to show the world that even though my life was fucked up, I was going to be all right.

I watched the way he tried to suck in his gut before moving to meet me. "Excuse, Trinette. Can you follow me, please?"

I put the brakes on my four-inch purple pumps and rolled my eyes in his direction. "What? Follow you where?"

"To the security office. We were notified this morning about your termination and I have been asked to collect your badge and keys."

"Terminated?" I parroted with outrage. "Terminated for what?"

He looked like a middle-school kid with a big secret. "Stealing funds."

"What? Stealing? Trinette doesn't have to steal a damn thang. You know what . . . I'm going to get to the bottom of this." I tried to get past him so that I could go inside, find Jrue, and see what the hell was going on, but Herschel wouldn't let me through the double doors.

He held his hands up, palms forward. "I'm sorry, Trinette. I can't let you in."

I couldn't believe the balls he had. Hell, he needed to act like that with those students who insisted on parking in staff spaces, maybe then I wouldn't have to complain so much.

"Herschel, look . . . I need to speak to Mr. Jarmon. He'll tell you this is all one big misunderstanding."

He scratched his head and suddenly looked nervous as hell. "I'm afraid he's the one who told me you were no longer allowed on the campus."

"What the fu—?" I couldn't even get the last word out as I reached for my phone and called Jrue at his desk. After two tries there was still no answer. I even tried reaching Zakiya and Josie, but neither of them appeared to be at their desk either. I wondered if they were all in a staff meeting. So I started dialing numbers and got so angry that I left several nasty messages.

"Listen, you bitch . . . quit playing games and come and tell security it's been one big misunderstanding!" Okay, so maybe I shouldn't have called Jrue a bitch, but any man who runs and hides instead of facing the issue was a bitch as far as I was concerned.

"Please, Mrs. Montgomery, if you leave now, the campus won't press charges. Otherwise, I'll be forced to call the police and have you removed."

I looked up at Herschel. His eyes were shifting side to side, and I noticed two other security officers had arrived and were standing a few feet away waiting for instruction. There was no way this was happening.

"I have a box with all of your personal belongings from your office. If you come with me and turn in your badge and keys I can help you get the items in your car." Herschel was practically pleading with me to listen to him. Hell, what choice did I have but to follow him?

After I gathered all my things, I drove around for a while, then went to my nine o'clock OB appointment. I was disappointed that neither Leon nor Jrue showed up to hear my daughter's heartbeat. Afterward, I went back to my condo.

I was eight months pregnant and jobless. There was no way in hell this could be happening to me. Of course I didn't believe Jrue would throw the mother of his unborn child out in the street. But just as he promised, I pulled up and a moving truck was in the visitors' parking spaces. Even then I was still in denial until I noticed them coming out of my condo carrying my Italian leather couch.

I jumped out of the car as fast as my pregnant belly would allow, then waddled up the sidewalk. "What the hell are you doing?" I demanded.

The men looked like they had both been recently released from prison with tattoos all over their arms and necks.

"I asked you a question," I repeated.

They stopped and the tall one focused his attention on me. "Ma'am, we were asked by management to move all the furniture out of this place." He tilted his head toward my condo.

I couldn't believe it. Jrue had kicked me, his baby, and all my shit to the curb. I watched two more step out carrying a priceless painting and my Tiffany lamps. I was on the verge of crying, but there was no way I was letting them see me break down.

While they loaded the truck, I shuffled back to my car and went to work finding a storage facility. Thank goodness there was one only a couple of blocks away. I drove over, paid three months in advance, and collected the keys. While the movers transferred everything I owned in the world from one location to the next, I just sat back in my car in a daze. There was no way this was my life.

I had lost my husband, the love of my life, and my job all in less than a month. I was Trinette Meyers–Montgomery, dammit, a little girl from the project with big dreams to live a life that so many could only have dreamed up. I drove a Mercedes. Had every credit card one could name and was so beautiful Beyoncé had nothing on me. I had loved my life and had always been in total control, and that was the mistake I had made. I had lost control when I made the mistake of falling in love. The one emotion I vowed to never feel for a man. Why? Because without love, I felt safe, secure, and invincible. Love made me careless, nervous, and stupid. Now I was pregnant with a baby I didn't want, fat as a damn cow, and with nobody around to rub my swollen ankles.

I'm not going to lie. My heart ached for Jrue. I wanted him to talk to me and tell me to my face he no longer loved me, yet no matter how many calls I made, no matter how many messages I left on his phone, he had yet to get back with me.

It took forever before I realized my cell phone was ringing. Frantically, I dug around in my purse, grabbed it, hoping it was Jrue calling. My heart sank when I realized it was only my mother.

"Mama, I would love to talk to you, but now is really not a good time," I said as I watched the men remove the last of my stuff off the truck.

"I don't wanna hold you. I figured you're probably on the phone with Nikki. It's all over the news about Donovan."

She now had my full attention. "Donovan who?" I asked, even though I knew good and damn well whom she was talking about.

"Nikki's husband," she replied. "Didn't you hear? He tried to kill himself."

"What?" I screamed. You mean to tell me someone was having a far worse day than I? One of the movers was standing in front of my car, waving his hand, trying to get my attention, but I blew him off as I listened to Mama tell me what she had heard on the news.

"... and that's not all. Not only is he in a coma, but Nikki can't find Aiden."

33

Nikki

"Gabby . . . I need to know what Donovan was talking about when he was last here."

Sometimes I hate that chick. One minute she's telling me something is wrong with my husband and the next she is acting like she had fallen on her head.

"He didn't say much," she said while popping her gum.

I brought an impatient hand to my hip. "Okay . . . what is not much?"

She shrugged. "Just that he'd be out the rest of the day." Gabby went back to styling some chick's head like I was no longer standing there.

"Man, that's messed up what happened to him," said the chick in the chair. "Don was good people."

"What the hell you mean, was? Was? My husband isn't dead! He's in a fucking coma and my son is missing! Do any of you understand what that means?" I was standing at the center of the barbershop floor screaming at all four employees. I didn't give a damn that there were customers sitting in each of their chairs. I didn't care how far down the street my voice carried. "I don't know what planet y'all are from, but while Don is in the hospital, I'm the fucking boss! So when I ask a question, I expect a got-damn answer!"

Darrius, a short, stocky barber was the first to acknowledge me. "Yo, Nikki, chill. We know you're tryna find yo little man and we really want to help you, but really, we don't know nothing."

Lyndell, a gold-tooth, mack daddy wannabe waved a pair of trimmers in the air and agreed. "He's right, Nikki. My man Don had been bugging out for weeks. He rarely cut hair anymore."

Everyone got quiet and for a split second I almost felt guilty for taking my frustrations out on all of them. "Look . . . I just want my son back. If anyone has seen anything, even the smallest thing, please tell me." It had been three days since I'd last seen Aiden. Saturday after I had filed a missing person's report with the police, the Missouri Highway Patrol issued an Amber Alert. So far there had been no real leads and I was starting to lose my mind. Somebody had to know something.

I noticed the way Gabby looked at Darrius out of the corner of her eyes as if she was asking him something. "Gabby, if you got something to say, then just say it." I said it with attitude, but deep down I was pleading with that chick to tell me what the hell was going on.

She pursed her lips for a fraction of a second before Darrius stepped in. "The only time Don ever seemed like himself was when that chick dropped by."

I turned my head and looked up at him, brow bunched. "What chick?"

"That bright-skinned chick," Gabby blurted out. "She drops by the barbershop from time to time. She was in here last week."

"Sanders?" I asked, although I already knew she was the chick they were talking about.

Gabby shrugged, then started to look annoyed that I was still asking questions. "I don't know her name. She just comes in and they go back in his office to talk."

Soldier, my ass! I should have followed my female intuition

and asked fucking questions. I knew there had been more going on between the two of them than Donovan had hinted. I just didn't want to ask questions and rock the boat, especially since he had been doing so much better since his release. Had Donovan been having an affair? If he had, talk about being a hypocrite. The bastard. There I was feeling guilty about my affair with Kenyon that had happened years ago while my husband had been having an affair right under my nose.

I stormed out of the shop feeing like a damn fool. Here I was a woman who had been married to her husband since graduating high school, yet I had no idea what he had been doing the last few weeks of his life. Had he been having an affair? It was just too hard for me to believe. Our marriage had been good. Damn good until he had returned from that last deployment.

A year is a long time to go without some.

Sergeant Clarke's words had come back to haunt me. While being deployed, had Donovan and Sanders been having an affair? Part of me still refused to believe it.

"There's only one way to find out," I mumbled under my breath and stormed out to my car.

I drove like a crazy woman over to the battalion, then went inside and headed toward the headquarters office. I wasn't sure what I was going to say to Malinda Sanders except just get right to it and ask her point-blank if she was having an affair with my husband. I mean, I wasn't a complete idiot. I saw the way she looked at the mention of his name. I remembered the way they were leaning close that time I had stepped into his office. Even then I had known something was going on between them, and still I had chosen to ignore it. Well, now, more importantly, I needed to know if she had any idea where Aiden was.

When I stepped into the headquarters office Malinda wasn't at the desk. My eyes traveled over to the clock on the wall. 12:30 p.m. It was lunchtime. Damn. Maybe if I had called instead of storming down to the office like I was about to set it off up in here, I would have known. I stood there for a few seconds longer, then stepped back behind the desk and headed to see Sergeant Clarke. Ever since Donovan had rammed his Escalade through the neighbor's house, he had been calling me every other day checking to see how we were doing. I guess he wasn't as much of a prick as I had originally thought. Or maybe he'd just been kissing my ass because someone had told him to. Either way, I was glad he had finally gotten with the program.

I reached Clarke's door and paused when I saw it closed. It appeared that the entire office had shut down for lunch. I noticed the dry-erase board hanging on his door and decided to leave a note. When I reached for the marker and pushed against the door it opened slightly, just enough for me to hear voices inside. Being the nosy woman that I am, I pushed it all the way and found Sergeant Clarke sitting in his chair, eyes rolled at the back of his head with a female bouncing up and down on his lap. I don't know how long I stood there watching him. It was like my feet had a mind of their own.

"I'm coming . . . oh, Clarke . . . yes!" she cried.

By this time, he also came and looked over and spotted me standing there. I realized the woman straddling his lap was Malinda.

"What the—?" he said, startled.

Malinda's head whipped around and noticed me at the door. She jumped up from his lap and reached for her uniform pants that were on the floor in a heap beside the desk and quickly got dressed. Nasty ass. She didn't even bother to clean herself up first.

"Don't you know how to knock?" Clarke barked while he struggled to adjust his clothes.

"Don't you know how to lock your door?" I retorted. Today was not the day to be getting smart with me. "I came by to ask Malinda if she was having an affair with my husband, but I can see the husband she's fucking does not belong to me."

She had the nerve to look offended. "An affair? With Donovan? Puh-leeze. That man is too in love to mess around."

I tried to keep a blank face, although her words were exactly what I needed to hear.

"Look . . . I'm just trying to find my son." I had lost some of the attitude from my voice. After all, I needed them; they didn't need me.

Malinda looked confused. "Your son? What about your son?"

I stepped farther into the room. "He's missing." I quickly gave them the *Reader's Digest* version of what had happened the day before. "Don got shot before I had a chance to find out where he had taken Aiden. Now I don't know where else to turn."

She buttoned her pants and looked over at Clarke, who looked just as puzzled.

"Fuck! I had no idea. But as soon as everyone gets back from lunch I'll call a meeting and ask if anyone knows anything," Clarke offered as he fixed his pants.

"Thank you." I started to turn away, but then added, "Sorry for barging in."

"No problem," he called after me. "That's if . . . we can keep this just between us." He pointed to him and Malinda.

Like I said before, men ain't shit. "Sure, it will be our little secret." I gave him a sick smile, then turned and left the building.

I drove away thinking about my husband being deployed, watching members of his unit having affairs, and the ones who weren't able to come home at all. I just didn't get it. Was life that bad that my husband had been willing to end his life and mine? And if so, whom would he have left Aiden with? He didn't have any family. His father had recently died of kidney failure, although the two had been estranged for years. He distanced himself from the rest of the clan of misfits that he stopped claiming as family years ago.

I drove around for a while, not sure where the hell I went. All I knew was that I had used a fourth of a tank of gas trying to sort out my thoughts and come up with answers. I wasn't sure what else to do. The police were out there looking for Aiden, yet there was no way I could just sit back on my ass and wait.

So what now?

Tired and hungry I pulled up to my house and raised the garage and the second I looked at Donovan's wrecked SUV, I just lost it. I put my car in Park and started bawling for my family.

I cried until I didn't have anything left in me; then I got out of the car and was getting ready to lower the garage door when I noticed a white Mercedes pull into my driveway.

Trinette.

By the time she had managed to wiggle out from behind the wheel, I was already hurrying down the driveway to meet her.

"What are you doing here?" I asked, and wrapped my arms around her the best way I could. I was so glad to see her.

"Dang, girl, I can't breathe," she said with a laugh, then hugged me back. "Mama told me what happened, so I gassed up my baby and drove home."

It's amazing how she can be a bitch one day and then be so caring the next.

"Have they found Aiden yet?" she asked, clearly worried.

I shook my head and didn't even bother trying to wipe away the tears that rolled down my cheek. Hell, this was my girl, I didn't need to.

She shook her head and gave me that determined look of hers. "They're going to find him. Watch and see."

God, I hoped she was right. "You know . . . even though

he is missing. I feel it in my heart that wherever Aiden is he's okay."

Trinette nodded. "So do I." I helped her carry her bags inside and she flopped down in a chair in the kitchen.

"You are big as a house," I said with a sad smile. I remembered when I was carrying Aiden. Just thinking about my baby made me feel sad all over again.

"I can't wait for this baby to be born." She rubbed her stomach, then must have seen the look on my face. "How's Don doing?"

I shook my head. "He's still in a coma. But he's stable."

"That's a good sign."

I released a long, shaky breath. "I just wish he'd wake up long enough to tell me where my baby is."

"What all happened? Why did he try to kill himself?"

I took a deep breath and said, "Actually . . . he was trying to shoot me."

"What?" she exclaimed.

I poured us both a glass of lemonade, then took a seat across from her at the table as I told her about his behavior since Lorenzo's death, the drunk driving incident, and my fears that my husband suffered from PTSD. By the time I was telling her about him pointing the gun at me, I was reaching for a napkin to dry my tears.

Trinette squeezed my hand. "He's going to pull through and you're going to find Aiden."

"I-I hope so. I just want my family b–back and everything to be the way it should be. Is that asking too much?" I stammered between tears.

"For you . . . absolutely not. Me, on the other hand, it's asking a whole helluva lot. Wait until I tell you what happened to me. . . ."

34

Nikki

I left the bookstore a little early so I could go by the hospital to see Donovan. I hated going to St. John's Hospital before five because there were never any parking spaces, so once again I was forced to park at the top of the parking garage. I climbed out and made it up to the ICU with plenty of time left to speak with his doctor during their evening rotation. All I wanted was for Donovan to come out of that coma and tell me where Aiden was.

I moved down the corridor and found his door opened. When I stepped around the curtain I found a woman sitting beside Donovan's bed with his hand pressed against her cheek.

"What the . . ." I started, and then I realized who the woman was. "Jackie?"

Smiling, she slowly dropped his hand and rose. "Oh, Nikki, I was hoping I would get a chance to see you while I was here. Rae called an FRG meeting and told us Donovan was in here. I came down to offer words of comfort to both of you."

"Thank you. I appreciate that." I stared her up and down. Jackie was fair skinned with freckles and short, reddish brown hair. She looked cute in dark jeans and a yellow peasant blouse.

I was looking over at my husband's lifeless body when I

heard her mumble, "I hope you don't mind me being alone with him."

My head whipped around. "Why would I mind that?" I needed her to explain.

Jackie shrugged. "I don't know," she began; then I noticed the tears clouding her eyes. "You have no idea how much your husband has meant to me these last few months."

Okay, she was saying fighting words. "No, but I bet you're about to tell me," I said with enough attitude that her head jerked back.

"What? Oh, you got it all wrong." She started shaking her head. "It's nothing like that. Your husband saved my life. After Smitty died and I lost the baby, I didn't know how to go on with my life, but your husband helped me get through it."

I saw a tear run down her cheek and I felt bad for accusing her of . . . well, I'm not sure what, but a few minutes ago there definitely had been something running through my mind. Only it shouldn't have been that. Jackie and I used to be close. When she had first found out she was pregnant, I was one of the few people she had contacted. I also remembered when she had called me wondering if I had heard from Donovan because she hadn't spoken to her husband in two days. As soon as the notification came that Smitty had been killed by an IED, I had hurried over to comfort Jackie. However, after that it was just too hard to be around a grieving widow because the same thing could have happened to my own husband at any moment. I'm embarrassed to admit that I started acting like death was contagious if I got too close. By staying away from Jackie it was my way of shielding myself from the same possibility. It had been my way of preventing something like that from happening to my own husband.

"I'm sorry I haven't been by to see you since . . . since Donovan came home. I've been so busy with the bookstore, Donovan, and Aiden. You know how it is," I explained.

"No, I'm afraid I don't know how it is," she said, and there was no mistaking the sarcasm in her voice before she forced another smile.

Damn, I guess she wouldn't know. Both her husband and child were gone. I felt like such an ass.

"Did you know your husband's been by to see me almost every week since his return from Afghanistan?" She didn't even wait for an answer. "Well, it's meant a lot. It's hard being without Smitty. Talking about him helps keep his memory alive." Women like her needed a man in order to survive.

I had no idea my husband had been visiting her. For a brief moment, I wondered what else he had been hiding.

"Jackie . . . Aiden is missing, and since Donovan is in a coma he can't tell me where he is. You spent so much time with my husband . . ." It took everything I could to keep the jealousy from my voice. ". . . would you have any idea where Donovan might have taken him?"

She gasped. "Missing? Oh my! You mean to tell me you have no idea where Aiden is?" Jackie looked just as upset as I felt. "No, I have no idea. He's brought him by the house before, but it's been a while." She shook her head. "You must be losing your mind!"

"I am. The only person who knows where he is is Donovan." I sighed with despair. Four days and still no sign of my baby.

"I pray that Donovan wakes up and your son comes home to you." Jackie looked so sad and pathetic. That woman was just too fragile.

"Thank you," I said, and I meant it.

Her bottom lip quivered; then she briefly turned away. "I can't help but think that if I hadn't given him Smitty's gun, none of this would have happened."

"Hold up! You gave him Smitty's gun?" I had wondered how he had gotten another gun so quickly. After the shooting incident at the barbershop, I had taken Donovan's gun and hid it in a box in the garage.

"I'm afraid so." She nodded. "Last week, he had come out to the house to see me and asked about Smitty's gun. Donovan knew exactly where he'd kept it in the attic. I don't like guns in the house so I let him have it. But I n-never expected him to use it on himself."

Neither had I, and now my husband was lying in a hospital bed and my son was missing. "Well, he did." I wished she'd just leave. It wasn't like I could sit there and talk to her about my problems. The woman was too much of a basket case. All she would do is get all emotional and make me feel even worse than I already did. "Thanks for coming by, but I would really like to be with my husband . . . alone."

She flinched as if I had struck her. I guess the word *husband* hit a cord. "Yes, I guess you would. I would give anything to see my Smitty again. But I guess that won't happen again." There was a bitter edge to her voice.

Okay, so here we go with that again. It wasn't like I wasn't a sympathetic woman, but her husband had been dead more than a year. I know some people grieve longer, but I had my own problems to deal with. Finding my son was my top priority. My husband waking up from his coma was second.

"Anyway, if you need anything . . . I mean *anything,* please let me know." Her smile was sincere and for a moment I felt guilty for rushing her off. "Before Smitty died we bought this old house in Belleville, so I've been slowly trying to renovate it the way I know he would have wanted. I'll be out there if you need anything."

"Thank you." I hugged her and waved her good-bye.

After Jackie left, I moved over to the seat she had vacated and stared at my husband lying in the bed with all those damn tubes attached to him.

"Donovan, please . . . if you can hear me, please give me

some kinda sign. I need to know where Aiden is. Please . . . I need to find our baby."

And then he squeezed my hand. My heart started pounding heavy and I looked up at his face and saw a single tear coming from the corner of his eye. "You can hear me, can't you?" I jumped from my seat and screamed for the nurse.

35

Trinette

Nikki was sitting in the large recliner with Rudy in her lap. "I know what I saw. Don was trying to give me a sign!"

I felt so sorry for Nikki. She had been so sure her husband was coming out of the coma when he squeezed her hand. But according to the doctor, it was just a reaction from the medication they were giving him. "He probably was trying to find a way to tell you something. I've seen movies where people have said they were in a coma and could hear everything that was being said around them. One woman was stupid enough to think since her husband was in a coma she could whisper in his ear that she was riding his best friend's dick in his bed until his return."

"What?" Nikki screamed and then started laughing. I was trying to cheer her up, so that was exactly the response I had hoped for.

I reached for another slice of pizza. "Yeah, girl. He woke up from that coma two days later and repeated everything she had said to him word for word."

"Hmmm. I wonder if he'll remember me telling him about my relationship with Kenyon." Nikki rubbed her hand along Rudy's coat. That dog was so spoiled.

"Maybe." I paused, then asked, "What do you think was

running through Donovan's mind after he read Kenyon's letter?"

Nikki shook her head with despair. "Betrayal, hurt, even revenge."

Yep. The same way Leon had felt after he found me screwing Jrue at the condo. "Nikki, I wouldn't be surprised if Donovan went to confront Kenyon."

Her head whipped around, eyes wide with surprise. "Drive to Fulton? Do you really think so?"

I shrugged. "I don't know. You'd have to check the date on the envelope, but there's no telling how long Donovan had that letter. He could have been thinking about you messing around, waiting for the right opportunity. Hell, if he was anything like me, I would have wanted to get all my facts straight first. Then I would have paid Kenyon a visit."

She just sat there staring off in space, probably thinking about what I had just said. "Anything is possible. Netta, I'll never be able to forgive myself for not telling him sooner."

Her eyes were all red from all the crying she had been doing since she'd gotten back from the hospital. "Back then you didn't think he needed to know about the affair. Hell, there were a lot of things I never told Leon."

She gave a rude snort. "And you see where that shit got you. So what's your plan now?"

I chewed my pizza and shrugged, because I really had no idea what the hell I was going to do now. I had no job, no place to live, and was a tank of gas away from being broke. I wasn't sure what I was going to do at this point. "I don't know. I guess I'll stay with Mama until after the baby is born."

"Really?" Her brow rose with surprise. "Are you feeling well?"

"It's not like I have much of a choice. I can only stay here so long. Eventually your husband and son will both be home."

Nikki released a long sigh. "I sure hope so."

"I figured I could stay with Mama. Until this baby is born

I can't even look for a job." My little savings will be long gone before then. I guess that's what I get for never bothering to prepare for a rainy day. All my life I have lived from one man's payday to the next and spending mine in between. It is so sad. I am a woman in her thirties with absolutely nothing to show for it. All my life I have climbed on the shoulders of some and stepped on the toes of others. As a result, I am homeless and Nikki is the only friend I have left.

"You wanna go and see a movie or something?" I suggested.

Nikki gave me a gloomy look, then shook her head. "No, my mind is on too much. I wouldn't at all be good company."

I met her sad smile. "Okay. I understand. Just trying to find a way to cheer you up."

"I just appreciate you being here. Although I'm starting to think the only reason why your pregnant ass drove nine hundred miles was because you didn't have anywhere else to go."

I laughed. "I guess that's partly the truth. My black ass sat there watching my furniture get loaded on a truck and realized I had finally hit rock bottom." I shook my head. Just talking about it made me realize just how pathetic my life was. "But you're my girl and I woulda been here regardless—even if I had a man at home laid up in the bed waiting on me."

"Wow! That means a lot coming from you." Nikki gave a sad laugh and then hugged Rudy close to her body. "I just wished Donovan would wake up just long enough to tell me who has my son. That's all I ask."

"I guarantee my godson is just fine. Don loved that boy and he would never have done anything to hurt him. Speaking of hurting . . . once again my bladder is full. Dammit. I can't get a break for nothing." I pulled myself up from the couch and was walking around the table when I felt something wet running down my leg. "What the hell? Now I'm peeing on myself."

"What?" Nikki jumped up from the chair and moved to

take a closer look. Just then I felt a huge gush and I completely wet the floor.

"Oh, my God!" I gasped.

For the first time since I arrived, Nikki gave me that goofy laugh of hers. "Netta, honey. Looks like you're in labor."

After that everything started happening so fast. I contacted my OB office back in Richmond and the receptionist assured me she'd have Dr. Brown contact labor and delivery with my medical history. By the time we finally arrived at Barnes Jewish Hospital and I was admitted to a private room, I started freaking out while Nikki just got a kick out of the entire scenario. People were sticking me in my arm and strapping devices to my belly. It was way too much. And let's not forget the pain.

"Nikki, what the hell is happening to me?"

"Netta, you're having a baby."

I wanted to slap that silly smirk off her face. What the hell was there to be happy about? Here I was about to become a single parent with some demon child trying to rip out my insides. There was no way this shit was happening to me.

"Hurry and get it out of me!" I growled.

Nikki came over and started stroking my cheek. "It's not time yet. You've only dilated six centimeters."

I closed my eyes and took several deep breaths. The pain was gone for now. I didn't know what in the hell possessed a woman to ever want to give birth a second time, because this was the worst pain I had ever felt in my life. My legs were jackknifed along my stomach, I was sweating like crazy, and there was no doubt I looked a hot mess. What woman in her right mind would want to endure these kinds of cramps?

My nurse walked into the room. "How's she doing?"

"How the hell you think I'm doing? My insides are being ripped out and no one cares!"

The nurse gave me a sympathetic smile. Like I wanted her

pity. If anything, I should feel sorry for her and that jacked-up weave on her head. I guess God don't like ugly because another contraction hit me and this one was worse than the last. I screamed and Nikki took my hand and I squeezed it.

"I want something for pain!"

The nurse shook her head. "I wish we could, but you're too far along. The baby should be here pretty soon."

This was not happening to me. Here I was lying in a hospital bed having a baby with no father by my side to tell me how beautiful I looked and that everything was going to be all right. It just wasn't fair.

There was a knock and I glanced up long enough to see Mama coming through the door with a small flower arrangement. What the hell did I need with flowers? What she should have been doing was sneaking in some drugs.

"How's my angel doing?"

Nikki gave a rude snort. "Acting like the devil."

She chuckled gleefully. "I can't wait to hold my little granddaughter."

The doctor came in and introduced himself as Dr. Kevin Mason. The second I was hit by another contraction, he poked around inside my coochie and I screamed. "Dammit, get this baby out!"

He removed his hand and grinned. "I think we're ready to have this baby."

"About time," I murmured. I was already getting tired. Having a baby was just too much damn work.

I laid there while they disassembled the birthing bed and my feet were finally in the stirrups.

"Just relax. You're almost there," Nikki said, trying to make me feel better. She had been a good friend and I don't know what I would have done without her. It's funny, but at the end of the day all you really got is family and friends, 'cause a man ain't dependable for shit.

"Trinette," the doctor said. "With this next contraction I want you to push."

I just started nodding my head when that pain shot through my pelvis. "Awwww!" I screamed and squeezed Nikki's fingers.

"Push, Netta!" my mother said. She was standing behind the doctor staring at my stretched-out kitty-cat.

"Dammit, I am pushing!" Oh, the shit hurt so bad I started crying.

"You're doing just fine," Nikki said.

I fell back against the bed and exhaled and barely had time to take a few short breaths before the pain hit me again.

"Trinette, I need you to keep pushing," the doctor said like he had somewhere else he needed to be. Who the hell did he think he was, rushing me?

"Netta, I can see her head!" Mama was clapping her hands and getting all excited. "She's got a full head of hair."

Who cares? I leaned forward and pushed as hard as I could, but I was tired, dammit.

"That's it," Dr. Mason kept saying. "Keep pushing."

"I'm too tired!"

"Netta, dear . . . listen to your Mama. You have to push, baby."

"I can't do it!" I cried. "It hurts too bad!" I wailed and wished they would all just get out of my room and let me rest.

"Netta, the faster you get that baby out, the better you'll feel. Now push, dammit!" Nikki said, trying to be the boss of me. As soon as the pain hit me again I leaned forward and pushed with everything I had. I don't know how long I lay there panting and pushing before I finally heard a baby cry.

"It's a girl! A little girl!" Mama cried. "And she's beautiful."

Of course. I didn't expect any less.

"You did good, girl," Nikki said with that silly grin and then kissed my cheek.

I lay back against the bed breathing heavy and was so glad it was over.

"Oh, she is beautiful!" I heard Nikki shriek.

I closed my eyes while the doctor stitched me up. I could hear the baby crying and my breasts tingled. I guess that's that weird maternal bond shit I had read about in magazines. A woman's body knows the child who lived in there for nine months.

Nikki and Mama were oohing and aahing, and next thing I knew I felt something on my chest.

"Congratulations, Mama, you have a beautiful little girl."

The moment I opened my eyes and stared down at my daughter, I don't know what happened to me. It was like my world started swaying beneath me and I felt this tug that was ten times stronger than when I met a gorgeous man. All I kept thinking was I had brought this little life in the world. She was lying there looking so helpless and beautiful. I don't think I'd ever seen a baby that breathtaking before, and I'm not just saying that because she belonged to me. She truly outshined any baby I'd ever seen before.

Mama's eyes got all misty. "Netta, she is so beautiful."

I struggled to find the words to speak. "Yes, she is."

I couldn't stop staring at her. All I could think about was protecting this precious little creature from all the evils in the world. And the second she opened her eyes, I gasped and knew who her father was.

Leon.

I started to weep because I had taken this little girl's daddy away from her. And she would grow up like I had, never knowing what it felt like to be truly loved by her father.

"She's got Leon's eyes."

I glanced over at Nikki and nodded. "And his forehead." I started laughing and crying at the same time.

This was my daughter. I was now a mother. Now ain't that some shit?

★ ★ ★

I must have dozed off because I woke up hours later to find the lights dimmed and my mother asleep on the couch in the room. I turned to my side and groaned the second I felt those stitches down low.

Mama stretched, then opened her eyes. "You're finally up, sleepyhead?"

I smiled. I remembered she used to call me that when I was a little girl. It's funny that for the first time I actually remembered the bedtime stories and the few and far between moments we had shared together when she wasn't chasing after the next high.

"Where's Nikki?"

Her eyes got all misty. "She still has a missing child to find."

In all the excitement, I had forgotten all about Aiden. I felt so bad for her. Here I was having a baby and hers was still out there somewhere.

"Why don't you go home and get some rest?" I suggested. Mama's hair was matted on her head and her clothes were wrinkled from sleeping on the couch.

"Your brother Travis's gonna pick me up at nine when visiting hours are over. I need to first find out how my daughter is feeling."

"Not bad, considering I just had my coochie stretched wide enough to birth a watermelon." Mama laughed and I joined in.

"While you were sleeping I had a chance to hold my grandbaby."

I felt my lips tilting upward.

"The whole time I was rocking her in the chair I was thinking to myself this little girl is my chance to get it right. I made a lot of mistakes raising you, but I want to be there for my grandbaby."

"That's good to hear because I'm going to need your help. I can't do it all by myself." Hell, I didn't know the first thing about taking care of no baby.

"Look who's finally awake!" My nurse came through the door holding a little bundle in her arms. She leaned over and I held out my arms and cradled her close. She was all cleaned up and smelled like baby lotion. I loved that smell.

"Are you planning to breast-feed?"

I flinched and scrunched up my face. Goodness, the last thing I wanted was for my breasts to sag, but as I listened to the nurse explain the health benefits to breast-feeding, I eventually decided to give it a chance.

"Okay, so make sure she latches on."

The nurse took my breast in her hand and manhandled my nipple. I was growing impatient and was ready to cuss her ass out, but instead I decided to just let it go for the sake of my child. It took a few moments as she showed me how to get the baby to latch on. I started to get frustrated because she was heavy handed and my breasts already felt sore. Then finally my daughter grabbed on and started sucking.

"Mama, look, she's doing it!" I exclaimed and then started crying again. Having a baby definitely throws your hormones all out of whack.

"Let her suck for a few more minutes, then try the other side," the nurse instructed.

I nodded and turned my attention to my daughter while my nurse went to check on another patient.

Her little hand squeezed my finger. "She is so precious," I whispered in awe. I still couldn't believe she was mine.

"You're gonna be a good mother. I'm certain of that. Better than I ever was." A tear rolled down Mama's cheek and I dropped my eyes briefly, allowing her a moment to pull herself together. Feeling sorry for my mother was a new emotion for me. But it sure felt better than hating her.

"Thanks, Mama."

She shook her head. "I made a lot of mistakes while you and your brothers were growing up, and they say the scars of the mother become wounds of the children. I messed all your heads up with the drugs and the men and never being around when y'all needed me. And the rape . . ." She got choked up. "I'll never forgive myself for allowing that to happen to you. But what I plan to do is to try and protect that little girl as much as I can because I don't want her to have to live the life I lived or to go through the things you did."

I nodded and felt my eyes getting all misty-eyed. "Mama, that's all in the past. Today marks a new beginning. We got three generations of Meyers women in this room."

She grinned at my statement. "Yes, I guess we do. Have you thought about what you want to call her?"

"Well, when I thought she was Jrue's, I wanted to call her Symphony, but now that I know for sure she's Leon's, I think I would like to name her Leona."

Mama appeared pleased by my answer. "Leona is a pretty name. Leona Montgomery."

"Leona Darlene Montgomery."

By now the tears were flowing down my mother's face. "That's the nicest thing anyone has ever done for me."

I finished feeding her on both sides, then handed her over to my mother, who burped her. "I guess I better get downstairs. Your brothers will be up with me in the morning to see the baby." She kissed my cheek and I lay there in the bed staring down at my beautiful little girl as she slept. How could I already be in love with someone I had just met?

What I felt for my daughter I couldn't even begin to explain, because it surpassed anything I had ever felt for any of the men in my life. I thought I had loved Jrue, but it didn't even come close to what I was feeling as I gazed down at my little precious angel. I heard a light knock and I looked up and had to blink twice just to make sure I wasn't seeing things.

"How are you feeling?" Leon walked slowly into the room like he was almost afraid to be near me.

"I've been better." I looked up into his face. He was growing a goatee and it looked amazing on him. I never had been able to get him to grow one and now he was. I couldn't help but feel a stab of jealousy that he was doing it for someone else. "How did you—"

He cut me off. "Nikki called me this morning and told me you were in labor."

My stomach did a flip-flop. "And you came all this way to see me?"

"No . . . I came to see my daughter."

"She's . . . she's right here." I pointed to the side of my bed. Leon came around and I watched his face as his eyes landed on his daughter for the first time. A huge smile tipped his lips.

"Can I hold her?"

Smiling, I nodded. "Of course you can."

I watched as he lifted her into his arms as if she were priceless china.

"She looks just like you."

For the first time he looked down at me and gave me a real smile. "Yep, she does." He chuckled softly, then brought her to his lips and kissed her. "Hey, Little Bit. I'm your daddy."

I knew I had no right, but at the moment I thought about the three of us being a family. If I had never messed with Jrue or had even ended the relationship when I had first realized I was pregnant, Leon and I would still be together.

"Does she have a name?" Leon asked.

I looked at him and nodded. "I named her Leona Darlene, after your mother and mine."

He nodded. "Wait until she hears that." He laughed and brought her cheek to his lips and kissed her again. "Mom and Dad wanted to come down, but I told them to just wait until we're back in Richmond."

We're. My heart started pounding.

"Leon, I—"

Again he cut in before I could even explain. "Trinette, there is nothing you can say that will change what you did to me and our marriage. But this is my daughter and I'm willing to do whatever it takes to make sure she has a good life. The kind of life she was supposed to have had with two parents."

Leona must have known we were talking about her. She started fussing, and I held out my arms. "She's probably hungry." I unsnapped my gown and whipped out my breast. I noticed that Leon tried to look away. My DDs were one of the things he had loved most about me, so I knew there was no way he was going to be able to look away for long. While my daughter sucked hungrily, he just stood there and watched with fascination.

"I can't believe you're breast-feeding."

You ain't the only one. "The nurse said it's important and I want this little girl to have what she needs."

I knew he was surprised to hear something like that from a woman as selfish as I was, but nothing was going to mean more to me than this little girl, and if he'd just give me another chance I would prove it.

"Leon, just seeing my daughter . . . our daughter . . . made me realize just how stupid I had been. I want her to have two parents."

He nodded. "I agree."

What did he just say? I didn't want to get ahead of myself, but was he saying what I thought he said?

Leon moved over to the chair beside my bed and took a seat. "I want you to come back to Richmond."

"Okay." Yep, he did, and I was seconds away from leaping out of that bed and over onto his lap if I wasn't nursing my daughter. I moved her so she could nurse from my other breast and got ready to speak, but Leon spoke first.

"Wait a second. Before you say anything, let me finish." He shifted on the seat. "You hurt me, Trinette. Not once, but twice, and I'll never be able to forgive you for that. I've already filed for a legal separation and my lawyer should be getting in touch with you."

"Excuse me?" There was no way. I just gave birth to his

daughter. "Didn't you just ask me to come back to Richmond?"

"So we can share joint custody."

No he didn't. "I'll have to think about it."

Leon leaned closer and I noticed the fire burning in his eyes. "Well, I advise you to think long and hard, because if you refuse to return to Virginia I plan on fighting you for custody."

"What? Custody?" I gave a nervous laugh. "No judge in the world would tear a child away from her mother."

"They will when they see the video of you and Jrue. Oh yeah, I forgot. You had no idea, but I installed a video camera in the condo out on the deck. I wanted to make sure our tenants were respecting the property. I just never expected to see a video of my wife fucking another man."

Busted.

"I also spoke with Jrue and told him I'd let him know if he was the father. In exchange, he has agreed to appear in court as a witness if there is a custody battle."

Leona finished eating and I put her over my shoulder and burped her as I thought about Leon's threat. It seemed like I hadn't much of a choice.

"I don't have a job. I can't afford to move back to Richmond."

"I plan on letting you keep the house, which I will pay for. As well as a more than generous monthly child support payment." He rattled off an amount that made my bottom jaw drop.

"In exchange, I want joint custody of Leona."

I pretended like I was thinking about his offer when really it was the only option I had other than living with my mother in her one-bedroom apartment. And that definitely was no way to raise a child.

"Can my mother live with me?" Just being in the big house all by myself with a baby already scared me.

Leon looked surprised, then nodded. "As long as she's off the drugs, she's more than welcome."

I nodded and didn't know what else to say.

Reaching over, he stroked our daughter's face. "Well, now that that's settled, I'll be back next week to take the two of you home." He leaned over and kissed Leona, then rose, walked away, and didn't once look back.

36

Nikki

I parked my Lexus near the back of the parking lot near the gate, then took a long, deep breath. The moment of truth would soon be at hand. A state mental hospital was the last place in the world I wanted to be. But it had been ten days and the police still hadn't found Aiden, and Donovan was still in a coma. So what options did I have?

I climbed out of the car and looked at my reflection. I made sure my hair hung loose just the way Kenyon liked it, although just the thought of trying to please that man caused the acid to rumble in my stomach.

I had ten minutes to get inside. I straightened my dress and hurried in pink pumps into the building toward the front desk.

After I showed my ID and signed in on the log, I moved into the visitors' room and waited. While I sat on the hard bench I felt agitated and nervous as hell. It had been almost four years since I last saw Kenyon, and that was across the courtroom before he pleaded not guilty due to mental insanity. The last thing I wanted to do was to sit across the table from the nutcase, but I had run out of options. If going to see Kenyon meant getting my son back, then it would definitely be worth it.

The door knob turned and I felt like my heart had jumped

through my throat. And then I turned my head and there he was.

Kenyon.

I guess I had expected him to be wearing a straitjacket with his hair wild all over his head and deep, dark bags under his eyes for years of being medicated. Only that wasn't the case at all. In fact, it was the exact opposite. All that dark chocolate still looked good in a white T-shirt that clung to his broad chest and loose-fitting jeans.

"What's up, Kenyon?" I greeted him playfully the moment he walked into the room.

He looked pleased by the warm welcome, especially when I rose and allowed him to hug me. As he held me against his strong body, I quickly had to remind myself that this was the same psycho who had kidnapped and threatened to kill me.

"You're still as beautiful as ever." He slowly released me and gave me a knowing look.

"Thank you."

While he took the seat across from me, I admired his good looks again. It was such a waste. How could someone who looked that good be so crazy?

"When my doctor told me you wanted to see me, you have no idea how shocked I was."

Probably nowhere near as shocked as I was that my lawyer had gotten me permission to see him, especially since I was the reason Kenyon was locked up in this facility for eighteen more months.

"Well . . . you talked about finding closure and moving on, so I figured it was only fair that I come and give you a chance to do just that." I gave a nervous laugh.

"Baby, I'm so glad to hear you say that." He leaned across the table and grazed my fingers with his hand. I was ready to cringe when someone tapped on the glass. Touching and any other physical contact was allowed only when the patient initially entered the room. Kenyon pulled back. "I missed you."

I frowned because I didn't even want to go there with him. Yes, we'd had some good times together in the months that we were a couple, but I never stopped loving my husband, and that's what kept us from ever really being together.

"How have you been?" I asked, because it was important for me to let him think I cared about him. It wasn't a total lie. I didn't hate him. I don't think I ever could because he really wasn't a bad guy. He was just crazy as hell.

"Baby, I've been taking it one day at a time. You'll be happy to know I finally let go of my mother."

About time. The woman had been dead for over eight years.

He had this far-off look in his eyes. "Yeah, I was happy to hear she was in heaven with your grandmother."

Like I said, he was crazy. Kenyon knew how much my grandmother had meant to me. "That's good to hear." I was anxious to get this interview under way.

"Yes, but she still talks to me at night. Just don't tell my therapist that," he added with a wink. "Otherwise, he'll think I'm crazy."

Hell, I thought he was crazy.

"Seriously, Nikki, I wanted to let you know that I am sorry for everything I had done to you. When you didn't accept any more of my calls, I put my feelings all into a letter to you."

"You did?" I said and decided to play dumb.

He frowned. "Baby, didn't Donovan tell you he read my letter?"

My heart started pounding. "How do you know that?"

He kept his eyes locked on mine like he was searching for the reason why I was really there. "Because he came down here to see me."

"What?" Trinette had been right. Coming to see him had been the right decision.

He nodded. "Yes, baby. He was here last week."

Okay, he was starting the *baby* crap again. It was one thing he used to do that drove me crazy. However, right now he could call me whatever the hell he wanted to call me.

"What did he come to see you about?" I asked like I didn't already know.

He shifted on the bench. "First, let me ask you a question . . . Is Aiden mine?"

I didn't hesitate. "Hell no. He's not! Aiden is Donovan's son."

Did that freak of nature really think I had a baby by him? Goodness, we'd practiced safe sex. Okay, so maybe we were careless once or twice, but I had gotten my period. That I was pretty certain of.

"That's too bad. Although . . . I've done the math and if my calculations are right, there's a slim chance that Aiden is my son. I'm not ready to let go of that possibility."

"Well, dream on. Aiden's Donovan's, not yours!" I sneered. There was no way in hell I was even going to allow him to plant that seed in my head. I know who's my baby's daddy.

There was no mistaking the disappointment on his face. "Whatever you say," he mumbled, even though he didn't seem convinced.

I was sick of his pathetic ass already. "Listen . . ." I tried to keep the panic from my voice. "What did you tell Donovan?"

Kenyon gazed up at the ceiling like he was collecting his thoughts. "Baby, I told him the truth."

"Which is . . . ?" Damn, this was too much like pulling teeth.

He grinned. "That we were in love."

I was seconds away from jumping across the table.

Kenyon sensed my anger. "Baby . . . baby, I couldn't lie. Part of my therapy is telling the truth, and I thought by being honest with your husband I could move past the betrayal."

This was way too much. How I wished I had just been honest and told Donovan about the affair when he had first returned from Iraq. If I had, none of this would have happened.

Instead, I had to deal with the lies, deceit that led to my own husband trying to kill me.

"Kenyon, I—"

"Baby?" he cut me off.

My brows rose. "Yeah?"

"Can you call me your baby? Just once."

Had he lost his mind? I had a hard enough time believing I used to have sex with him. I wasn't about to call this nutcase baby. That was before he sulked on the seat and suddenly looked bored with the entire conversation.

"Kenyon . . ." When he frowned, I quickly started again. "Baby . . ." Oh, that nut was grinning brighter than a ninety-degree day. "Baby, please, I need to know what Donovan talked to you about."

"Well, he wanted to know if Aiden was mine and when I neither admitted nor confirmed that he was, he got angry."

"Angry how?" I asked, nibbling nervously at my bottom lip.

"He said something about serving his country and this being the thanks he got. That he had friends who lost their lives and their wives left to raise their child on their own and one woman had lost both her husband and her baby."

I was so sick of Donovan singing Smitty's wife's praises all the time like she was the only one who had gone through anything. At least her husband had died in combat. Mine had come back broken. I wasn't sure which was worse.

"What else did he say?" I asked, growing impatient.

"He asked if I had any family and when I told him yes, I have five sisters who live in Hannibal, he got up and left."

Family, what the hell was he planning to do, drop Aiden off with one of them?

"Baby, is something on your mind?"

Kenyon always could read me. But there was no way in hell I was letting him know any more than he needed to know about my personal life. If Donovan didn't pull through,

Kenyon might think we had another chance to be together again. I definitely couldn't have that.

"Kenyon, I hope you get better so you can finally get out of here and get on with your life."

He stared across the table at me with those beautiful chocolate eyes of his and I felt myself remembering again some of the good times. "Baby, can I call you when I get out?"

I shut my eyes. "No, you can't call me and I'm not your baby. I am the woman responsible for putting you in here! I came here so you can get your closure, so shut the door, dammit, and don't ever open it again."

"I'd really like to come by your bookstore sometime."

"No!" I screamed. "If you want a book, then go to Walmart. Just stay away from my family and me. Listen . . . I love my husband and my son."

"But your husband said he wasn't going to be raising another man's son."

"But Aiden isn't another man's son." I felt like I had stepped through the twilight zone because this conversation was one big circle. "Wait a minute. When did he say that?"

Kenyon looked puzzled by my question. "He said it just before he rose and stormed out of the room."

37

Nikki

"You're listening to *Truth Hurts* and if you're just tuning in, tonight we've been talking about deadbeat dads. Yeah, I said it. Deadbeats. A sperm donor. Women have no choice but to be strong because we've assumed the roles of our children's fathers." At *children,* my voice cracked. I cleared my throat, then continued, "Ladies, the phone lines are open. Call and share your stories." The phone lines were lit up and Tristan signaled for me to pick up the first line. "Caller, you're on the air."

"Good evening, Ms. Nikki, my name is Jae."

I loved it when my listeners remembered to address me as Ms. "What's going on, Jae? Let me guess . . . you got a deadbeat daddy?" I asked, getting really close to the microphone.

There was a long pause and for a moment I thought maybe she had hung up. "Hellllo . . . Jae, you still there?"

"Yes, I'm here."

"Please, tell us about your baby's daddy."

"He's locked up."

"Oooh! Another one of those." I laughed. "What did he do?"

"Murder."

I startled and my eyes snapped to Tristan. "Excuse me?"

There were sniffles and an eerie chill came over me. *"He killed my daughter Miasha."*

I wanted to hang up the phone and end the call. The whole reason why I had picked deadbeat dads tonight was because I needed something amusing to lift my spirits so I could stop thinking about Aiden. There was no way with the thousands listening that I didn't allow her to continue her story. "Jae . . . I'm so sorry for your loss."

"It's been three years, but it still hurts." She got quiet again and I waited, giving her a chance to get herself together. I had an idea of the pain she was feeling. I felt a fraction of it every time I thought about my daughter . . . and Aiden.

"Can you tell us what happened?" I urged.

"He didn't want to pay child support. Can you believe that shit? He was behind two years in payments. So when he got a good job with the state, they started garnishing his check."

"Was he present in Miasha'a life?" I had to know if he had at least been a father to this child, even though that revelation would have only made understanding that much harder.

"Oh yeah. He and his girlfriend came around every other weekend and spent Saturdays with her. Our relationship ended long before she was even born, so I didn't have a problem with it, but then one weekend he picked Miasha up and didn't bring her back." Her breathing grew heavy. *"I called him, went by his house and nothing. I couldn't find him anywhere. I was going crazy looking for my daughter, and yet no one knew where she was."*

I sat frozen in the seat, hands shaking. "And then what happened?"

"I went to the police and filed a report, but they couldn't find him or my daughter. Then three days later, his girlfriend called and told me she thought something bad had happened to Miasha, and to look behind this old abandoned gas station off of Hanley Road. I was so scared I called the police and had them meet me out there." She was crying softly into the phone and a chill ran through my veins.

I wasn't sure if she could go on and I didn't blame her if she couldn't.

"It took them less than fifteen minutes to find her wrapped in a sheet in a storage closet!" she wailed into the phone.

"I'm s–so s–sorry." I was shaking and tears were running down my face. "No mother should have to go through that."

"He strangled her. He said he did it because he was sick of paying child support. Can you believe that shit! He didn't want to pay child support." The phone line went dead and I was so stunned I couldn't say or do anything except stare across the glass at Tristan. Within seconds I heard Adele coming on the air. I dropped my microphone and slid back away from the desk.

Ohmygod . . . ohmygod . . . ohmygod . . . what if Aiden is dead?

I saw Tristan rise from his chair and dash over to my room. "Nikki . . . gurrl, you okay?" He immediately wrapped his arms around me and held me close while I cried hard against his chest. "Oh my goodness, you're shaking!"

I tried to speak, but my lip was quivering so hard I just couldn't put what I wanted to say to words. I didn't need to. Tristan already knew what I was thinking.

"Listen to me . . . Aiden is not dead. He is out there some-where waiting for his mama to come and get him."

I knew he was trying to make me feel better, but I was sick of waiting for someone to find my son. It had been almost two weeks. The longest twelve days of my life. I wanted Aiden back safely at home where he belonged.

"I don't know what to believe anymore. Something is . . . is terribly wrong with this whole situation. If he was out there, then w–why hasn't anyone brought him to me? W–Why haven't the police been able to find him!" My teeth were chattering.

Tristan drew a deep, shaky breath. "I don't know why, but he's out there. I feel it in my gut."

He was right. I felt it as well. My baby wasn't dead. A

mother knows when something was wrong with her child, and I didn't feel like he had been harmed. So then where was he?

Tristan released me, then gazed down at my face, his forehead creased with concern. "How about I put on a CD for the rest of the show?"

I sniffed, then shook my head. I had a brilliant idea. "No, don't do that. I want to go back on the air."

Tristan gave me a weird look. "Oh, Nikki, I don't know. You sure about that?"

"Yes, I'm sure. The police can't help me, but I am confident that one of my listeners out there can."

He hesitated, almost too afraid to leave me because there was no telling what might happen if he did. I swung my chair back over to my desk and signaled for him to go back to his office as I put the headphones over my head.

At the close of the song, Tristan put his fingers in the air and signaled four . . . three . . . two . . . one . . . "You are tuning in to *Truth Hurts* and I am your hostess with the mostest, Nikki Truth. Tonight we had a startling story about a deadbeat father that I'm sure ripped at the hearts of many of us. I know it did for me. My prayers go out to Jae and her family. No one can begin to describe how much it hurts to lose a child. As most of my listeners know, several years ago I also lost a daughter when she ran out into the street and was hit by a car." I paused a moment to catch my breath. "Right now, I'm going to change it up a bit and we're going to talk about a good man." I reached for a Kleenex and mopped my eyes as I spoke. "I am married to a good man. He's such a good man he dedicated his life to serving this country. As most of you already know, my husband has been down range twice, once in Iraq and the other in Afghanistan. He's been home almost a year, yet it took months before I realized he suffers with PTSD. Mood swings, heavy drinking, insomnia, and the tragic nightmares. His case was so severe that almost two weeks ago he tried to shoot me, but instead he accidently shot himself." My voice had trailed off to a whisper, so I cleared my throat. "Now he's lying in the hospital in a coma fighting for his life. The big problem is before he was shot, he took our three-year-old son somewhere. Where? I don't know, and I haven't seen my baby since. I have no idea where he is and my husband isn't conscious to tell me. And even if he wakes up tomorrow, there's a chance he might not even remember. Now I'm grieving for not only my husband, but for my son . . . Aiden. I have no idea where he is or . . ." my voice broke. ". . . or where else to look, but I'm hoping someone out there knows something and can help me find him. So please . . . if you know something . . . anything . . . please call me. All I want is m-my b-baby back." I ripped the headphones from my ear and leaned back onto the seat and tried to pull myself together. I'd dealt with difficult issues on the show before, but this one was truly my biggest yet.

The phone lines lit up and I couldn't bear to pick up the receiver. I guess because I was afraid I would hear something I didn't want to know. Thank goodness Tristan and two of his assistants manned the phones while I called the hospital to check on Donovan to see if there were any changes. There was none. Then I called the police officer handling my son's case and had to leave a message.

By the time Tristan came over into my office I saw the long face and already knew there had been no luck at finding Aiden.

"Sweetie, everyone's calling with their love and support, wanting to let you know they are out there doing everything they can to help you find your son."

My throat was so dry all I could do was nod. I don't know why I thought after being on the air Aiden would magically appear. I guess I was just desperate.

"At least I tried," I said, and a single tear rolled down my cheek that Tristan reached over and wiped away.

"You did more than *try*. I had Courtney post Aiden's picture on our Web site. Someone is bound to remember something."

I nodded and thanked him, then reached for my purse out of the drawer. "I think I'm going to stay at the hospital tonight with Donovan."

"You want me to drive you?" he offered.

I shook my head. "No, I'll be fine," I lied. I was far from fine. I was more like a walking zombie.

At the close of the show Tristan walked out of the building with me. It was December and I was bundled up tight in a bomber jacket with a hood. Christmas was barely two weeks away, yet the holiday season wouldn't feel the same until my family was back at home. As we moved toward my car I spotted a woman standing there waiting in a long white winter coat and hat. It wasn't until she swung around that I recognized her.

"Who is that?" he asked.

I frowned. "Malinda Sanders. She's in Donovan's unit."

As soon as she spotted me coming her way, she walked around the car. "Hello."

I looked at her wondering why the hell she was here so late.

"You want me to stick around?" Tristan asked.

I stopped as soon as I reached my car and shook my head. "No, I'll be all right."

"Too bad. I think I'll stick around a few minutes." He stared Malinda up and down before he snapped his fingers twice and then pivoted on his heels. I watched as he walked over to his car across from mine, then leaned against the trunk with his ankles crossed and waited. He was such a good friend.

I finally swung around and faced Malinda. "Why do I get the feeling that you're here to tell me something I don't want to hear?"

"Because I am."

I took a deep breath, then leaned back against the hood, trying to mentally prepare myself. "Well?"

"I think my sister has your son."

I stood up straight. "What? Your sister? Why would she have him?"

"She was married to Smitty."

"Jackie? Jackie is your sister?" She nodded. "Why in the world would she have my son?"

"Because Sergeant Truth felt he owed her."

I was clearly confused. "Okay, hold up. You're gonna have to start over because I have no idea what the hell you're talking about."

Malinda took a deep breath and stared down briefly at her feet. "Our team was sent out on a reconnaissance mission to locate an area for a possible staging base for returning troops. We found a location that Truth believed to be the perfect area for the base. But when Smitty moved over to occupy that position, he tripped an IED . . ." I guess I looked confused because she paused to clarify. "It's an explosive device. Something your husband should have easily been able to identify."

"So what are you saying?"

Malinda shifted uncomfortably as she spoke. "Because of Truth's lack of judgment, three lives were lost." I flinched at the comment and her expression softened. "Look . . . Truth thought he should have been one of the ones to have died in the explosions. And he's been feeling guilty ever since."

I was gasping and trying to catch my breath. Why hadn't Donovan said anything to me about what had happened out there? All the hours I spent asking him questions, even during the counseling sessions, never once did he mention his involvement in Smitty's death or any overwhelming feelings of guilt.

"When my sister lost the baby, Donovan blamed himself. No matter how much I tried to tell him the miscarriage wasn't his fault, he felt personally responsible. Instead, he allowed guilt to eat at him for the rest of the deployment."

"Anybody could have made that mistake," I replied defensively.

"Anybody?" She looked offended by my comment. "He was the assistant convoy commander! Because of his lack of judgment three families' lives have been destroyed. That's not just a *mistake.*"

Tears burned at the backs of my eyes.

"Donovan promised Jackie that while in Afghanistan he would keep Smitty safe and bring him back home to her and the baby. The only reason why he had allowed Smitty to be on the team was because he thought it was an easy recon mission." Malinda pulled her collar up around her neck and shrugged. "After Sergeant Truth got home, he visited Jackie practically every week, trying to apologize for failing to keep his promise."

I had a hard time stomaching my husband being so personal with another woman. I was jealous and angry all at once.

"That day you saw me in his office, I had dropped by to talk to him about my sister's behavior. She was starting to get too attached."

"What do you mean?"

"I mean . . . she *expected* him to come by and when he didn't she'd fall apart."

I was so stunned by her confession that I didn't know what else to say except for the obvious. "What does this have to do with my son?" I didn't mean to sound like I didn't care, but I needed to first deal with finding my son; then I would focus on the source of my husband's pain.

"I think they both were grieving and trying to find a way to cope. Most times he took Aiden over there with him."

"So you think he left my son with Jackie?" I wanted so desperately to think that Donovan left Aiden with her while he went out to the mental hospital to ask Kenyon about the letter. But if that was the case, why the hell hadn't she brought him home to me yet?

"I've been trying to reach Jackie for days and tonight she finally returned my call. We were discussing my father who had recently been in the hospital, when I heard a child in the background crying. When I questioned her about it, she hung up on me."

My heart skipped a beat. "Do you think it was Aiden?"

She shrugged one shoulder. "I really don't know." There was a long moment of silence before she spoke again. "You have to understand, my sister kinda snapped after losing not only her husband, but their baby as well."

"I don't have to understand shit! That bitch has no right keeping my son."

Malinda jerked back. "Listen, you don't have to call Jackie a bitch. I'm just here tryna help."

"And I appreciate it." I should have known something was up the way she had been holding my husband's hand. Last week Jackie's ass was all up at the hospital smiling in my face while she was hiding my son. "Take me to her. Take me to my son."

She shook her head. "I don't know where she's at. I drove by her house on the way over to the station, but she wasn't there."

I suddenly remembered something. "Wait a minute . . . she had said something to me about renovating some old house, that it was therapeutic."

Malinda was quiet and I could tell she was thinking about what I had just told her before a frown marred her forehead. "They had bought a fixer-upper in Belleville before Smitty was deployed. But I thought she decided to sell that house."

Obviously she didn't know her sister as well as she thought. "Do you know where it is?"

She nodded. "I'm sure I could find it."

"Good, then I'll follow you." I hurried over to Tristan. He

was sitting inside his car, with the music playing, waiting. I was shaking so bad I could barely speak.

"What she say?" he asked the second I climbed in on the passenger's side.

"S-She thinks h-her sister has Aiden."

"Oh my goodness!" he cried and waved his hand. "Hallelujah!"

I pointed in the direction of the white Kia Sorrento. "Just follow her."

My heart was pounding so hard I had to take several deep breaths just to slow it down. The drive to Belleville would take thirty minutes and I wasn't sure I could sit still that long. I was both nervous and upset as I replayed the conversation with Tristan. The whole time I couldn't help but wonder, what if Malinda was wrong and Jackie didn't have Aiden?

"Hey, you okay over there?" Tristan took his eyes away from the expressway long enough to look my way.

"It depends on how you define okay. I wish this car had wings so we could be there in seconds, but at the same time I'm afraid to get there and find Aiden isn't."

Tristan reached over and squeezed my hand. "Uh-uh! We're having none of that, girlfriend! You just need to think positive. He's there. I can feel it in my bones."

I released a long, shaky breath. "I sure hope so."

There was a long moment of silence before he spoke again. "I went by the shop today," he said, and I appreciated him changing the subject.

"Really? How did that go?" I couldn't imagine the crew giving him a warm reception.

"I strutted in making sure everyone saw the diva that I am." He grinned. "I said, 'Your new boss is in the house!' and, girl, you could have heard a pin drop as quiet as that place became. All eyes were on me . . . just the way I like it."

"Hell nah! No, you didn't!" It felt so good to laugh.

He nodded his head. "You know I did. Uh-huh. Girl, I'm

thinking about bringing in a few stylists and maybe even putting a small boutique in the front. You know women love shopping."

I had to chuckle. "You know my husband ain't going for that shit, right?"

"That man is stubborn." He pursed his lips. "Like I told Donovan when he offered to buy me out, we are partners, so he needs to look at the bigger picture. Together we can make the shop a success . . . if he'd just take the time to see my vision. We can add some color to the walls, install new lighting, and knock out a wall or two. . . . We could have the hottest spot in all of St. Louis!" He did a three-finger snap and I laughed. Although it sounded fantastic, there was no way in hell Donovan was agreeing to something wild and flamboyant. He had offered to buy Tristan's half of the business, but my bestie told him there was no way he was letting go of his final gift from Lorenzo. I had to agree. Obviously Lorenzo wanted him to have it.

I laughed a little longer, then watched as we crossed over the Martin Luther King Bridge and into Illinois. "Do you think I should call the police?"

There was a long pause before Tristan finally shook his head and said, "No, not yet. We don't even know for sure that woman has Aiden."

He was right. I wasn't sure, yet I was hoping and praying that my gut was right.

Sanders pulled off at the Green Mount exit and as soon as Tristan moved up the ramp, my heart started racing again.

"Please let him be there," I mumbled under my breath. "And after I have my son safely in my arms, I'm going to be at that ho's ass."

"I know that's right!" Tristan shouted, and I realized that I had said it out loud.

I gave a shaky laugh and focused on the Kia. It seemed like it had taken forever before Malinda finally turned onto a wide street with homes just like you'd see in the movies with long driveways, large porches, and plenty of curb appeal. It was well after midnight and the street lighting wasn't the best, so when she pulled up in front of a large house, I had to really focus to see the two-story structure hidden behind large oak trees with a balcony coming off the master bedroom overhead.

"Damn, that's a nice house," Tristan muttered under his breath.

"Wait here. If you hear someone scream, call the police." Quickly I leaped out of the car and followed Malinda up the walkway to the door. She glanced over her shoulder and frowned when she spotted me.

"Why don't you let me talk to her first?" she suggested.

That wasn't happening. "How about we go and talk to her together." I didn't even wait for her response and walked up to the door and rung the bell. It seemed like forever before I heard footsteps and the lock turned and swung open.

The second Jackie spotted her sister and me standing at the door, the smile left her lips. "Nikki . . . Malinda . . . what are you doing here at this time of the night?" I didn't see what difference it made. It wasn't like she had been asleep. In fact, she was dressed comfortably in sweatpants, a hoodie, and running shoes, like she was about to go somewhere. I also noticed how she kept glancing nervously over her shoulder.

"Because you hung up on me. Why are you all the way out here?" Malinda asked.

Before Jackie could even speak, I blurted out, "Do you have my son?" I mean, really, why waste time with idle talk.

She gave me a confused look. "Your son? Why would I have your son?"

I placed a hand on my hip and stared straight at her. "Because Donovan left him with you." I didn't know that for sure, but it sounded convincing enough. Malinda turned to look at me, brow bunched. Goodness! Why couldn't she just play along?

"I have no idea what you're talking about. The last time Donovan came to my house was when he asked for Smitty's gun."

I still couldn't understand why that chick gave another man her husband's gun. Did she not realize his state of mind? "I think you're lying."

"What I need to lie about?" she retorted.

I was ready to drag that chick out of her house. I took a step forward and she took a step back and immediately Malinda moved in between.

"Hold up . . . we didn't come here for this." She rolled her eyes at me and I rolled mine back at her. I didn't care what she said, Jackie was lying.

"Look, sis . . . when I called you yesterday I heard a child in the background."

She gave her a blank stare. "Child? Girl, that was the television!" she said and then had the nerve to laugh.

"Jackie . . . I didn't drive out here in the middle of the night to play games. Aiden is missing, so if you have any idea where he is, please tell me!" She might have been my last hope.

She looked at me for a long moment, eyes getting all misty, and for a second I thought she was going to cry before the stupid smirk returned to her lips. "Nobody cared about me when I lost my child."

"You miscarried . . . my child is missing. Big fucking difference!"

She disagreed. "What's the difference? Losing a child is losing a child."

I was seconds away from wrapping my fingers around that crazy chick's neck. "Look, either you know where Aiden is or you don't?" I asked and brought a hand to my hip again.

Malinda stood there also waiting for Jackie to answer. I was sure she was hoping she had been wrong about her sister.

"Sorry, but as much as I wish I could tell you where your son is, I can't help you."

I don't know why her words hit me hard, but they did. I clearly thought she had Aiden or knew who did. "Well . . . thanks."

I turned and was heading down the steps to climb back into the car with Tristan when from inside I heard a heart-wrenching scream.

"Mommy!"

I swung around and noticed Jackie's eyes had grown large and wild.

Aiden!

38

Nikki

I raced back up the steps, anxious to get inside, but Jackie managed to step back into the house and slam the door in my face. "Open the door!" I screamed and looked at Malinda. "Did you hear that? Jackie has my son!"

Her eyes got large like she wouldn't have believed it if she hadn't heard it herself. "We don't know that for sure."

"Okay, then, who was that crying, 'Mommy'? It sure in the hell wasn't Casper the Fucking Friendly Ghost!" I barked. That chick was working my last nerve. "I know my son's voice." I rolled my eyes and screamed across the yard. "Tristan! Tristan . . . Call the police!"

There was no way in the world I was leaving there without my son. Even if I had to peel back every piece of aluminum siding, my baby was going home with me. I started banging on the door and ringing the doorbell like a lunatic.

"Jackie, dammit! Open this door!" I screamed.

Malinda removed her cell phone from her purse and started dialing. "Let me try calling her," she suggested. After a brief moment I heard her say. "Jackie, sweetie, you need to open the door and give Nikki her son. Jackie . . . listen . . . Jackie . . . that's not true. I'm not trying to hurt you."

All that baby talk was getting on my damn nerves. I snatched the phone from her hand and barked. "Listen, you crazy bitch. I want my son!"

"He's my son!" she screamed. "He's mine. Donovan took my baby away and brought me another one."

I didn't know what sick game was running through her mind, but that's my son. "I'm not playing with you!" It wasn't a threat; it was a promise. "The police are on their way."

"Well, then . . . if I can't have him, then no one can," she said, then hung up the phone.

"What the hell did she mean by that?" I muttered, then tossed Malinda her phone. "Your sister is a freaking nutcase." I ran up to the door and kicked it with my heel. "Ow!" That shit hurt. "Get your sister to open that damn door!" I turned on the heel of my sore foot, limped out to the curb, and climbed back into the car long enough to warm my hands.

"Did you call the police?" My teeth were chattering.

"Yes. What happened?"

I slammed the car door shut harder than I had intended. "That bitch won't let me inside so I can get my son."

Tristan clapped his hands. "So he is in there?"

I nodded and forced a smile despite how pissed off I was. "Yes, Aiden's in there. He cried, 'Mommy,' and I know my son's voice anywhere." My eyes flooded with tears, but at least they were happy tears. The police would be there soon and I would be able to get my baby and finally go home.

"Oh, lawd! Thank goodness. I was so afraid we might have been wrong."

I shook my head. "No, you were right. I just don't understand why Don left Aiden with that lunatic." I glanced over at the house and watched as Malinda knocked on the door. She obviously had no influence over her sister's behavior. I leaned back onto the seat and told Tristan about what transpired on the porch with that crazy woman.

Tristan was shaking his head. "I still can't believe she gave him her husband's gun."

"She probably wanted him to kill himself." There was clearly no way to know what had been going through her sick mind. I've heard of women snapping, but that shit was crazy as hell.

I reached down inside my purse and retrieved my cell phone, getting ready to call the police and see where the hell they were, when I noticed I had a missed called. One look down at the phone number caused my heart to bounce against my chest. "Tristan, the hospital called." I could barely get the words out as I redialed the number.

He swung around on the seat. "They must have news about Donovan."

I just prayed it was good news. The hospital wouldn't have called unless there had been some change with my husband's condition. The phone rang forever before I had someone at the front desk transfer me up to the ICU. I was practically hyperventilating by the time his nurse came onto the phone.

"Mrs. Truth, I've been trying to reach you for the last half hour," she scolded like she was my mother.

"I . . . was unavailable." I don't know why I even felt like I had to explain. Where I was or what I had been doing was none of her business. "Is something wrong with Donovan?" In other words, get to the point.

"Your husband is awake."

"What?" I gasped and met the worried look on Tristan's face. "He's really awake?"

"Yes, he's up and been mumbling something. We were hoping you could come to the hospital and tell us who he's talking about."

"What's he saying?" The least she could do was give me some kinda idea. For all I knew Donovan was still tripping about Kenyon.

"He's talking about someone named Aiden."

"Aiden's our son!" I blurted in a rush of words.

"Okay, then that helps. He also mumbled something about going to Jackie's house."

I was laughing and crying at the same time. My husband was trying to tell me where to find Aiden even though I had already found him on my own. But his confirmation made me feel so much better. Of all the things he could have said when he had come out of the coma, he wanted me to know where to find Aiden.

We talked a few more minutes and I promised to be at the hospital as soon as possible; then I ended the call.

"I'm so glad Donovan's okay." Tristan was grinning and rubbing my arm, showing me comfort. What would I have done without his friendship?

"Yes, he's awake and talking. At least that's a start, hopefully to a full recovery," I managed between sniffles.

Malinda was shouting and pounding hard on the door. I looked out the window, between the trees toward the front of the house, and what I saw made my heart stall. Jackie was standing out on the balcony with Aiden in her arms. "What in the world is that woman doing?" I said aloud; then it hit me.

If I can't have him, then no one can.

I sprung out of the car and hurried up the sidewalk where Malinda was still banging on the door. "She's out on the balcony with Aiden! Jackie! Jackie, what the hell are you doing?" I screamed as I hurried up the driveway.

Malinda swung around with tears streaming down her face. "I don't know what's gotten into my sister. I'm so sorry."

"What the hell you mean *you're* sorry? Help me! We gotta get inside!" I scrambled around the yard until I spotted a large brick. Quickly, I raced over, picked it up, and flung it through the front window.

"What's going on?" Tristan said; then he drew closer and gasped. "Why is she holding Aiden over her head?"

Sure enough, Jackie was standing near the rail, holding Aiden high above her head.

"Stay back! If you try to come in here, I swear I'll throw him!"

My heart was pounding so hard I was seconds away from passing out. "Please . . . Jackie, please, just give me my baby back!" I pleaded, hoping she would show some compassion.

"He's mine! Stay back!"

"I'm calling the police!" Malinda yelled. She was standing on the bottom step crying while dialing numbers.

"Please, just don't hurt him," I begged.

Tristan rushed over and stood beside me. "Nikki, what are we going to do?" he asked with this worried look on his face.

"I don't know." It was cold and a shiver skipped down my spine while I stared up at the balcony that beamed with floodlights. Jackie was no longer holding Aiden over her head and I was at least grateful for that.

"Jackie, it's cold outside. Will you please take Aiden inside where it's warm?" I asked. He was in pajamas and his feet were bare.

"What kind of fool do you take me for? The second I walk back into the house you're going to try and take my baby from me!" That fool then leaned forward holding Aiden over the railing.

I held up my hands in surrender. "O-o-okay. I'll s-stay back, just, please, don't drop my baby."

The moment Aiden spotted me standing in the front yard he started crying and holding out his arms toward me.

"Mommy! I want my mommy!"

I wanted so desperately to rescue my son and hold him in my arms again. Twelve days was a long time.

Jackie finally clutched him to her chest. "There, there . . . nobody's gonna hurt you," she cooed while Aiden struggled to be released.

Malinda started pacing around the yard. "Would you go sit down somewhere?" I hissed, because the last thing I needed was for Jackie to become agitated again.

"Jackie, please, just give me my son back."

She wildly shook her head. "He's mine now. Donovan asked me to keep him. When he came over to the house that day, he was upset about some letter he'd received and wanted to know if I would watch Aiden until he got back. I told him sure, no problem, and then he shot himself and didn't come back to get him. It was a sign that Aiden was supposed to be with me."

I was right. Donovan had stopped by her house on his way to see Kenyon. "Jackie . . . please! Aiden has a mother. My son is supposed to be with me."

She gazed down at me with this sick smile on her lips. "See, that's where you are wrong. When Donovan told me he thought you had messed around on him while he was in Iraq, I gave him the gun hoping he would use it."

"What?"

I heard Tristan gasp, then mumble, "No she didn't," under his breath.

"Why would you do that?" I asked, hoping that if I kept her talking long enough the police would show up.

"Why? *Why?* Because it's Donovan's fault my husband and son are gone!" she boomed. What right do you have to have a perfect life when all the people I have loved the most are gone. I wanted the two of you to feel my pain." She then climbed up onto one of the chairs on the balcony, holding Aiden over her shoulder as he struggled to be freed.

"No! Lemme go!" he cried.

"Jackie, please," I began with a sob in my throat. "My heart goes out to you, but your child is gone and nothing is going to bring him back. But my son is alive and he's scared and wants his mommy. You gotta let him go."

"Get over losing my baby?" she shrilled and held Aiden over the edge again, his little legs dangling wildly in the air while he cried. "*That* baby was the only thing I had left of my husband. And they're both gone. All because of your husband

and his stupid, stupid mistake. How could he miss that IED? It was his job to secure the area; instead, he was careless. Then the army had the nerve to rule it as an oversight. *Oversight?* You should be the one grieving over a dead husband . . . not me!"

She was getting agitated again and I allowed my eyes to shift to the far right of the balcony just as Malinda stepped through the French doors.

"How the hell she get up there?" Tristan shrieked.

"I have no idea." My eyes shifted down to the window I had thrown the rock through. A patio chair had been dragged directly underneath. While I was focused on the balcony, Malinda had gone inside.

A police car pulled to a stop in front of the house and a fire truck could be heard not far away. Nosy neighbors had come out of their homes and were gathering in the street, watching and whispering.

Malinda took a step out onto the balcony and Jackie swung around so fast, Aiden slipped from her grasp. I screamed and then breathed a sigh of relief when she quickly snatched him close to her chest again.

"Ohmygoodness!" Tristan cried.

"Stay back, Malinda!" Jackie bellowed. "You take one more step and I'm tossing him. I swear to you!"

"Malinda, dammit . . . Stay back!" I shouted.

Malinda held up her hands in surrender. "Jackie . . . sis. I just came up here to talk to you," she assured her.

Out of the corners of my eyes, I spotted two officers moving across the lawn toward the house.

"Stay back!" Jackie screamed. "If one person comes near this house, I swear I'm going to jump."

One of the officers tried to ask me questions, but I shooed him like a bug. There was no way I was taking my eyes off what was going on on that balcony.

While Tristan explained everything to the police, a fire truck pulled up at the house. Within seconds there were bright lights pointed at the balcony and they were removing their equipment.

All I could do was stare up at my baby boy, who was still crying for his mommy. Jackie and Malinda were going back and forth at it. I could barely catch a word they were saying, but I noticed that with every comment Malinda crept closer to where Jackie was standing. Everything was happening at once. Firemen, cops, and EMTs were everywhere while I listened as a negotiator tried to talk Jackie down from the balcony.

"Stay back!" she yelled. "I said for everyone to stay the fuck back!"

Next thing I knew, Malinda raced over to where her sister was standing and tried to wrestle Aiden away. I screamed and heard Malinda shout, "No!" Then Jackie was throwing herself over the balcony with my baby in her arms.

39

Trinette

Five months later

"Thank you *sooo* much, Ms. Brennan, and I'll see you in three weeks." I hung up the phone and shouted at the top of my lungs as I went rushing down the steps. "Whoo-hoo! Mama . . . Mama, guess what?"

She was downstairs in the living room, changing Leona's diaper. "Chile . . . why are you shouting?"

"Because, Mama . . . St. Mary's Hospital just called . . . I got the job!" I was so excited I had to force myself to breathe. "Can you . . ." My voice trailed off when I spotted Leon standing in the living room. I knew he was coming to pick up Leona for the weekend, but I had no idea he had already arrived. If I had, I would have taken a few minutes to fix myself up.

It was unbelievable the way children change you. Ever since Leona was born, I had slowly been giving up the designer outfits and stilettos, and settled for anything easy to slip on and throw in the washing machine. Can you believe it? Ms. Netta wearing polyester? Yep, it's true. That little girl had changed me so much I can't remember life before her.

"Hey, Leon, I didn't know you were here." I brushed a

hand across my hair. I could no longer afford my $300 weaves and with a baby, who had time for all that maintenance? Instead, I was wearing my hair natural. And I loved it. Mama washed and braided my hair, and after a few days I'd take it down for a nice curly look. Low maintenance. And not to mention the style looked fabulous on me. Who would have ever guessed?

He smiled while I noticed how handsome he looked in navy slacks and a white polo shirt. "I thought I would beat the traffic and pick up Little Bit on my way home."

"Well, she's almost ready. Let me go upstairs and put her in a clean dress." Mama smiled and lifted her granddaughter into her arms. I dropped a kiss to my daughter's cheek; then she brushed past me and went upstairs. I don't know how I would have done it all these months without my mother. She has been true to her words and has done everything she could to make life perfect for Leona. Our relationship was stronger than ever before.

"So did I just hear you say you got a job?"

I nodded and in no way could contain my excitement. "Yes, finally! Lord knows I've been trying for months. I was offered a position as a social worker at St. Mary's Hospital."

"That's wonderful. I'm happy for you." He gave me that grin that had gotten more adorable. Like I said before, the goatee looked amazing on him. It gave him that distinguished look. It was all salt and pepper like the hair on his head was getting.

"I'm so excited to be finally getting back to work. Lord knows I was starting to wonder if I'd ever get another job." I know I was ranting, but I felt nervous standing there talking to the man whose heart I once had under lock and key. Now he pulled all the strings. He was responsible for the house I lived in, the new Mercedes I drove, and all the money that made it possible for me to live comfortably.

Leon looked at me for a long, lingering moment. He'd

been doing that a lot lately. I don't know if it's the hair or the extra pounds that I've been too exhausted to try and shed. He had that look again like he was trying to figure something out. I wanted so desperately to think that maybe he had noticed how much I had changed and even missed having me sharing his bed, but I refused to let myself think like that anymore. It only made our impending divorce that much more difficult. Our lawyers had finally ironed out all the terms and in a few weeks it would be official.

"I know you've been really trying to find another job, so I'm proud of you."

After Jrue blackballed me, I had to hire an attorney who'd threatened to sue the college if he said one more unflattering thing about my character.

"Thank you." Hearing that he was proud of me truly meant a lot. "How's work?" I asked, because men love when you ask them about their day.

"That's something I wanted to talk to you about." He moved around the room and was starting to make me nervous. I went over to the couch and took a seat.

"Leon . . . what is it?" Lord, don't tell me this man was about to lose his job. I don't know how Leona and I would survive if he did. At least until I started working long enough to earn a living.

"I've got an emergency in Germany and I need to leave on Monday. I should be gone about ten days."

I nodded. "No problem. You can just bring Leona back early on Sunday."

He finally lowered onto the couch. Thank goodness, because he was making me dizzy.

"Since Little Bit came into my life you know the last thing in the world I want to do is leave town." He laughed. "I don't know if I can be gone that long without seeing my little girl."

I had a feeling where this conversation was going, but I was hoping that wasn't what he was about to say.

"You think it would be okay for her to fly thirteen hours?"

I knew it. What he needed to be asking was if I was going to allow my daughter to be away from me for that long. "I'm not sure." I shifted on the couch. "Leon . . . listen . . . I know we have joint custody, but you're not the only one who needs to be with Leona. Even though I'm no longer breast-feeding, she still needs her mother. Besides, who's going to watch her while you work?"

"You are."

"But I—" I stopped in midsentence. Did he just say what I thought he said?

He smiled. "I'd like for the two of you to come with me. That's if you aren't starting your job right away."

My heart slammed against my chest. He wanted to spend ten days in Germany with Leona and me. "No, I don't start until after Memorial Day."

Leon looked relieved. "Good, then how about it? Will you and Leona come with me?"

Did he know how long I'd been waiting for him to dangle me just one branch that said I had a chance of winning my husband back? I knew I was getting ahead of myself, but just an opportunity to spend some time with Leon was all I needed.

"That sounds nice," I said, trying to sound nonchalant. "I always wanted to go to Germany."

"Then it's settled." He smiled and then had that look again that you give your mother when one day you look at her and realize she is starting to look old.

"What's wrong?"

He hesitated, then finally shook his head. "It's nothing."

Oh, it was something that he wanted to say. But I guess I wouldn't find out what it was today.

Mama came down the stairs and Leon rose.

"The little angel is knocked out." She lowered her into Leon's arms, then slid the diaper bag over his shoulder.

"All right, I better get going. You think you can have suitcases packed by Sunday evening?"

I nodded. "I'll be ready."

Mama waited until he was out the door and loading Leona
in her car seat before she asked, "You going somewhere?"

"Yep, I'm going to get my husband back."

The divorce wasn't official yet, so there was plenty of time
to prove to Leon that I had changed. This time when I get my
husband back, I'm never letting him go again.

40

Nikki

There was a knock at the door. "Nikki, how long you gonna keep a brotha waiting?"

I turned the knob and stepped out of the bathroom and grinned up at Donovan's nervous face. "It's positive. Baby, I'm pregnant." I held up the home pregnancy test for him to see.

"Whoo-hoo!" he shouted, then lifted me into his arms and spun me around the room a couple of times. "We're having another baby."

"Yes, we are." I started laughing and noticed that Aiden was dancing around happily like he knew what we were talking about. "Aiden, you're gonna have a little sister."

"A lil' sister?" he repeated.

"Or a brother," Donovan mentioned as he lowered me onto the floor and pressed his lips against mine.

I'm not going to lie. The last few months have been rough. Donovan came out of the coma with very little memory of what had happened, and to be honest, I was relieved. The less he remembered about that terrible evening he'd tried to terminate my life, the better. Since then he's been undergoing a great deal of therapy trying to get his head on right. The episodes had become less and less that life was almost the way it used to be. On occasion I still saw him staring off in space probably remembering Smitty and the other soldiers on his team who had lost their lives, but he's learning how to cope and I was glad. Because I just couldn't imagine a life without him.

"We better hurry up and get ready. The grand opening is in less than an hour," Donovan said, then hurried into the bathroom to take a shower.

I stood there with a hand at my hip and shook my head. A Cut Above the Rest was reopening with a new vision. Tristan's vision. While Donovan was recovering, he had allowed Tristan to implement several of his ideas, and finally realized he was impressed. Tristan was just what that shop needed to finally expand the business. The two had since forged a business partnership and would be reopening with three hairstylists, as well as a boutique with purses, sunglasses, and other things women love to buy.

Of course, a couple of the barbers refused to work with Tristan and made a big scene before they quit, but it all worked out in the end. The newly renovated spot was chic and truly *a cut above the rest*. I think the shop was finally about to start showing some serious profits. I also believe Tristan has finally found his niche.

I handed Aiden his sippy cup, then kissed his little cheek.

"Thank you, Mommy," he said with a handsome grin.

"You're welcome, sweetheart. Why don't you watch cartoons while Daddy and I get ready?" I suggested.

"Okay!" He jumped up onto my bed and took a seat while I reached for the remote and found the cartoon channel. While he watched SpongeBob, I stared over at Aiden and said another prayer of thanks.

Shortly after Jackie Smith was released from the hospital with a fractured arm, she had been taken into custody. Thank goodness the fire department had their net in place when she had jumped from the balcony. Jackie was still behind bars, awaiting trial for kidnapping and attempted murder.

I hurried over to my closet and retrieved a brand-new black pantsuit I had purchased at the mall over the weekend. Pregnant? I was giggling with excitement. I couldn't believe it. We weren't even trying to have another child, but I guess the stress of the last few months had finally taken a toll. It was truly a blessing, and maybe my unborn child was what we needed to bring us even closer together.

I had just slipped on a pair of slacks when I heard my cell phone ringing. I reached over and retrieved it from my purse, then glanced down at the number. It was my attorney.

"Hey, Katherine. Do we finally have a court date?" I was ready for the Jackie episode to be over.

"No, not yet, but that's not why I'm calling."

Something in her voice made me suddenly stop. "What . . . what's going on?" I was almost afraid to ask.

There was a long pause before she finally said the words I wasn't prepared to hear. "I just received notice from the parole board. Kenyon Monroe was released last week."

I collapsed onto the bed. No way. There was no way she was correct. There had to be some kind of mistake. "But he's supposed to be in there at *least* another year."

"It appears he was released for good behavior."

I didn't hear anything else she had to say at that point and when I finally ended the call and put my phone back inside my purse, I was shaking. What did this mean for me and my future? What if Kenyon turned up and started demanding a paternity test?

That will never happen.

By the time Donovan had stepped out of the shower, I had pulled myself somewhat together. I shifted on the bed and took a deep breath, then turned and faced him. "Baby . . . there's something I need to tell you . . ."

CONSEQUENCES

Sasha Campbell

ABOUT THIS GUIDE

The questions that follow are included to enhance your group's reading of this book.

1. Should Nikki have been honest in the first place with her husband about the affair she'd had with Kenyon?

2. Was Trinette truly in love with Jrue Jarmon?

3. If you were Nikki, would you have stuck it out with Donovan after he came home from the war a different man? Would you have waited so long to ask for help from his unit?

4. Trinette had no idea which man was the father of her child. Who did you think was the father of her unborn child? Should Trinette have gone through with the abortion?

5. Do you think Trinette deserved everything that happened to her?

6. If you were Nikki, would you have forgiven your husband for trying to kill you?

7. Do you think Leon is going to forgive Trinette and take her back again?

8. How do you think Donovan will react to Kenyon being released?

9. Now that he's released, do you believe Kenyon will start stalking Nikki again?

10. Now that Kenyon has planted the seed, is there a chance that Aiden really *is* his son and maybe Nikki just isn't ready to admit it?

11. With all decisions there are consequences. Who made the bigger mistake: Nikki or Trinette?

Meet Nikki and Trinette for the first time in

Confessions

In stores now!

1

Nikki

"It's ten o'clock and you're listening to Nikki Truth, the host of the most talked about radio show in the Midwest, *Truth Hurts*. As my listeners know, I don't believe in holding your hand. If you want my advice, then you better have the balls to accept the truth . . . even if it hurts. Caller, you're on the air."

"Hi, Ms. Nikki. My name is Kimberly."

Obviously, Kimberly had been listening to my show, because everyone knows if I'm not referred to as *Ms. Nikki*, I have straight attitude. "Hello, Kimberly. What can I do for you?"

"I've got a little bit of a problem."

I leaned forward on my seat, ready to hear what crazy drama was about to unfold. "I'm all ears."

"Well, Ms. Nikki, I've been married to my husband for thirteen years, but for the last year our relationship has grown distant. I tried talking to him about it, even suggested maybe we get counseling, but he refused, saying nothing was wrong with our marriage. But I knew something wasn't right, because we haven't had sex in four months."

"Yep, that would do it. So what did you do?" I asked while adjusting my microphone.

"Well, something told me my husband was messing around."

"Something like what?"

"Like locking his cell phone, coming home at all hours of the night."

"Hmmm, those are definitely some signs."

"Well, yesterday I waited for him to get off work and followed him to this house. When I knocked on the door, guess who answered?"

"I hope for your sake it was a woman and not a man," I said with slight laughter, trying to make light of the situation.

"Oh, it was definitely a female. He came up behind her in his underwear. I confronted him. He screamed at me and acted like we've been separated for years instead of still living in the same house!"

"Okay, wait a minute. The brotha tried to pretend the two of you weren't even together?"

"Oh, yeah, and I went off!"

"Good for you, Kimberly."

"I finally asked him to choose, and he told me on her front porch in holey draws and a dingy wifebeater, he was in love with the other woman."

"Ouch! Girlfriend, say it ain't so."

Kimberly breathed heavily into the phone. *"Yep, I'm afraid it's true. I was devastated. I got back in my car and drove home."*

"Daaayum, girl! I wouldn't wish that kind of drama on anyone. So tell me, what did you do when he got home?"

There was a noticeable pause. *"Nothing."*

"Nothing?" This female was stuck on stupid.

"Ms. Nikki, that's the problem. I love my husband and I'm willing to do whatever I can to save our marriage. That's why I called. Because I need someone out there to tell me what I need to do to bring him back to me."

I shook my head and glanced through the glass at my producer, Tristan, who was shaking his head as well. There are some women out there who allow a man to get away with just about anything.

"Kimberly, honey, obviously you don't know anything about respecting yourself, 'cause if you did, instead of calling me, you would be packing his shit and burning it in the nearest Dumpster. Why in the world would you want a man who obviously doesn't want you?"

"He's the father of my kids." Don't you know she had the nerve to sound defensive?

"And that's supposed to make it right? Men can only get away with what women allow them to. He disrespected and played you in front of another woman. That's more than enough reason to dump his sorry ass." Tristan was going to have to do a whole lot of bleeping tonight.

"Hold up, Nikki. I love him, and I don't appreciate you talking negatively about my husband!"

"Excuse me, but it's *Ms.* Nikki to you, and if you love him that much, then why you even call my show? Next caller." I ended the call. Damn! I hate to say it, but women like her deserve what they get.

"Hi, Ms. Nikki. My name is Tasha, and my family thinks I need to leave my man."

Oh, Lord, not another. "Why is that?"

"Well . . . uh . . . a couple of weeks ago we were at my cousin Boo-Man's birthday party, and one thing led to another and my man hit me. I know he didn't mean it, and he swears he won't do it again."

It must be something in the air, because that night everybody was acting cuckoo for Cocoa Puffs. "Let me tell you something, Tasha. Any woman who takes a man back after he hits her, all she's doing is telling him it's okay to do it again."

"But he's going to counseling!"

"Good, he needs to. And what you need to do is find a man who respects you."

"He can't help it. His father used to abuse him."

"And that makes it right? Girlfriend, you have to respect yourself first before you can expect a man to show you respect."

"I know, but I've prayed on it and God wants me to take him back. I'm certain of it."

"Nooo, the Lord helps those who help themselves. If you

go back to a man that hits you, that means you don't feel wor-
thy of a man who won't."

"I believe everyone deserves a chance to change!"

What was up with these defensive women? "True, but are
you willing to risk your life on it? What if he really hurts you
next time?"

*"That ain't gonna happen, I'm certain of this. He's been trying
real hard to work on our relationship. In fact, last week he asked me to
marry him and I accepted. So there's no way I'm letting my family or
anyone else stand in the way. I just wanted to go on the air and say
that, 'cause I know my cousins Alizé and Lingerie listen to yo show."*

"If you're adamant about staying with him, then all I can
do is wish you the best of luck. In the meantime, do me a
favor . . . take some boxing classes." I ended the call, and the
phone lines lit up with callers anxious to put in their two
cents. "This is Nikki and you're on the air."

*"Tasha, you are pathetic. I would have taken a frying pan to his
head!"*

I had to laugh at that one. "I know that's right, girl."

*"Trust and believe, I used to date a man who hit me. I used to
think it was my fault. That maybe if I did things the way he asked me
to instead of the way I wanted, maybe he would love me more and stop
hitting me. But you can't change people like that. The more I tried to
make him happy, the angrier he got and the beatings got worse until
one day he hit me in front of my son."*

"What!" I cried, adding dramatic effect. "Girlfriend, what
did you do?"

*"Ms. Nikki, something in me snapped. I picked up my son's base-
ball bat and I swung and knocked that fool hard in the arm, then I
kept on swinging. I had him running out the door in his draws screaming murder!"*

"Good for you." I laughed, trying to lighten the mood. "I
like to hear about a woman standing up for herself."

"Humph! I might be a big girl, but I know I deserve better."

"Yes, you do. Next caller."

"Ms. Nikki, this is Petra, and I'm calling in response to the call you got from Kimberly. Yep, that was me she was talking about. I'm the other woman, and as far as her husband is concerned, I'm the only woman in his life. Kimberly, get it in your head, daddy ain't coming home!" Click.

"Oops, there you have it! Kimberly, dear, if that don't give you a reality check, then I don't know what will." I noticed Tristan waving his arms in the air. As soon as he had my attention, he signaled for me to take line two. "Caller, you're on the air."

"Hello, Ms. Nikki."

I groaned inwardly the second I recognized the voice. If it had belonged to anyone else, I would have considered the sound sexy and soothing. Instead, I was on the line with Mr. Loser.

I looked through the glass at Tristan, who was cracking up laughing, and stuck up my middle finger high enough for him to see it. "Caller, please introduce yourself," I said as if I didn't already know.

"Ms. Nikki, you hurt my feelings. I just knew you would never forget my voice."

I rolled my eyes. "Sorry, Charlie, but I hear hundreds of voices every week. I can't remember just one."

He chuckled. *"It's me . . . Junior."*

"Hellooo, Junior!" I said, trying to sound excited to hear from him. This man was like nails on a chalkboard—annoying as hell. "Long time no hear. What's it been, a month, maybe two?"

"It's been one month, two weeks, and three days, to be exact."

"Oh, boy! I take it your newest relationship didn't work out either."

He sighed. *"No, and I don't understand it because she was per-fect. I really thought she was the one."*

"If my memory serves me right, as far as you're concerned, they're all 'the one.' " Junior had gone through so many relationships it was pathetic. Nothing ever worked and it was always the woman's fault. He was what the show *The Biggest Loser* should really be about. He would have no problem winning, because he was definitely a big, fat loser.

"No, this woman was crazy."

Listen to him tell it, they all were. "Come on, Junior. Tell me what happened, even if the truth hurts."

"What's there to say? I loved her, still do, and part of me wished she'd come back to me. I just don't understand why she ended it. I was there for her, giving her everything she needed and then some, but she had the nerve to say she needed some space."

I stuck my finger down my throat. Men like Junior were sickening. "Maybe you were smothering her."

"Nope. As soon as she said she needed room, I gave it to her. I guess I just loved her too much."

"Ugh! You're turning me off. Come on, Junior. A woman likes excitement and a little mystery."

"I gave her excitement! I bought her roses, surprised her with a massage. I cut her grass, washed her clothes."

I cut him off. "Like I said, all that catering is a turnoff. That seems to be a pattern of yours."

"What do you mean?"

"I mean you can't keep a woman! I know the truth hurts, but if anyone's gonna be honest with you, it's Ms. Nikki."

He laughed. It was a soft, eerie sound. *"That's what I love most about you."*

Just like everyone else. "Junior, you call every month to tell me how you've gotten dumped. At some point you have to realize they can't all be crazy. Maybe it's time you started looking at yourself."

"I'm a nice man."

"Didn't you get the memo? Nice guys finish last. As sad as it may sound, women don't want a man who wears his heart on his sleeve."

"I don't understand that. Women are always talking about how

they want a good man, yet when they get a man who isn't trying to take their money or drive their car, they don't want him."

I sighed dramatically. "You're right, and it's a damn shame. However, we do know what we don't want, and that's a clingy man."

"I'm not smothering."

"Gotta be. You've been dumped five times in the last six months."

There was a noticeable pause. *"Wow! You've been keeping track. You obviously care more than I imagined."*

"Nah, don't get the shit twisted. I just got a good memory and you, my friend, are unforgettable."

"I'll take that as a compliment."

"Why? I wouldn't. True, there are some women out there who appreciate a good man who's also needy. Unfortunately, me and the hundred females I know don't. However, I'm gonna let the listeners be the judge. Let's see if there is one female listening tonight who'd go out with you. In fact, I'm gonna open up the phone lines and see if we can possibly make a love connection. This is Nikki Truth with *Truth Hurts,* and for any listeners who are just tuning in, I'm on the phone with Junior. Junior, say hello to the listeners."

"Hello."

I almost laughed at the way he tried to sound like Barry White somebody. "Junior is one of my faithful listeners. He is also a *good* man, who is unlucky with love. If there are any single women out there looking for a *special* kind of man, give me a call, because I'm about to hook you up." I couldn't help emphasizing *special,* because Junior was definitely a head case.

"I-I prefer picking my own women," he sputtered. I guess he was uncomfortable with me trying to help him out.

"Maybe that's the problem. You might be picking the wrong type, but I'm gonna hook you up."

"Damn, Ms. Nikki," he began with a chuckle. It was obvious I was making him nervous. *"I respect your advice, but why you*

always have to be so hard? In fact, why you gotta put a brotha on the spot?"

"Hey, I'm just telling it like I see it. In the meantime, keep your head up and take my advice for a change." I depressed the button, then took a few more calls and read several e-mails, but no one phoned in interested in going out with Mr. Loser. Not that I was the least bit surprised. By midnight my head was hurting and I was anxious to wrap up the show. "This is Nikki Truth at Hot 97 WJPC, ending another evening. When things get tough, remember the truth will set you free. Until next time." I leaned back in my chair as I took off the headset. By the time I placed it on the table, the sound of Jennifer Hudson was bellowing over the air. Tristan always knew what song to play at the end of each show. Sitting back in my chair, I had to smile. Tonight had been another fulfilling night. My producer came running over to my desk.

"You did it, girl! Another fabulous night." Tristan snapped his fingers. He's sweeter than a Krispy Kreme doughnut, but he is one hell of a producer and has been one of my closest friends for years.

"Thank you, sweetie."

He blew me a kiss, then pursed his cherry lip-gloss lips as he draped a hand at his narrow waist. "After Georgia comes on to take over the quiet storm, you wanna go grab an apple martini? I bought these shoes and I'm dying to be seen. Girlfriend is looking fierce!" He struck a pose, and I couldn't do anything but laugh. One thing Tristan knew was clothes. And even better, he knew how to get them cheap. Whenever I was in the mood for shopping, I took Tristan because he knew where to find every bargain from St. Louis to Chicago.

"Nah, I got an early day tomorrow at the bookstore. I was planning to go home and take a hot bubble bath and curl up under the covers."

He pursed his lips with disapproval, then sat his narrow ass on the end of my desk in front of me. "Miss Thang, I ain't even gonna try to beat around the bush about it. You need some dick in your life." I got ready to speak but he held up a heavily jeweled hand. "Hold on. Let me finish. Nikki, girlfriend, it's been six months, girl. Enough is enough. It's time for you to move on."

Tears burned at the backs of my eyes, and I let one roll down my cheek. Tristan was one of the few people I allowed to see me this vulnerable. He was right. I needed to start facing reality, but deep down, I wasn't ready yet to admit my marriage was over. "I know. You're right."

"Of course I'm right," he said with a toss of his fabulous weave. "Let's go get our drink on. I promise just one and we're out."

Tristan and I had been friends for almost five years, and that was long enough to know he wasn't going to give up until I agreed. I slipped into my winter coat, said good-bye to the rest of the night owls, then strolled out of the studio to my silver Lexus. Every time I saw my car it made me smile and gave me what I desperately needed—something to smile about. As I climbed behind the wheel and pulled out of the parking lot, I couldn't help but think about what Tristan had said. I needed to give up hoping and finally move on. Deep down, part of me knew my marriage was over, but a part of me still hoped and prayed we still had a chance. But I needed to do something because wondering what the future held was starting to drive me crazy. Luckily, I had my bookstore, Book Ends, and the best job in the world at WJPC radio. I still don't understand how I had been so lucky professionally.

I was already working for the station as an intern when the general manager agreed to let me liven up the first half of the quiet storm. I had this crazy idea to serve the needs of the hundreds of lonely listeners who tuned in at night by giving them the opportunity to call in and express their feelings. Hell, all the show required was common sense and my own style of bold, in-your-face advice. The crazy idea earned me thousands

of loyal listeners. Even though it's part-time, I love the hell out
of my job. Giving advice is something I'm good at. Instead of
getting a degree in radio broadcasting, I should have majored
in social work like my girl, Trinette. Nevertheless, giving advice is what I do best. I don't hold punches. But no matter
what I say or, better yet, *how* I say it, the listeners love me, and
the calls and letters keep pouring in. That's why I was pulling
out of the parking lot in a pretty-ass silver IS 350 convertible
with butter soft leather interior. The proof is in the pudding.
It's a damn shame. I could give other people advice about their
lives while my own was a damn mess.

My husband and I are separated, or at least we have been
since Donovan's unit, 138th Engineering Battalion, was acti-
vated and sent to Iraq. Lord, please forgive me. But his being
sent to war was actually a blessing. We'd been having problems
for some time, and the night before Donovan left, the two of
us decided that maybe time and distance would give us a
chance to decide if we wanted to either stay together or file for
divorce. I guess he decided on the latter, because despite all my
letters and care packages, I haven't received a single call or letter, nothing but a sorry postcard the first week he was there. I
know his ass is all right, because my girl Tabitha's husband is in
the same unit and she makes it her business to come to the
bookstore just so she can rub it in my face how often she talks
to her fat-ass husband.

After six months of nothing, I need to start facing the fact
that my marriage is over and has been for quite some time. Yet
a part of me still was not ready to let go. I don't know if I am
just being stubborn or plain stupid like half the women who
call in to my show.

Tristan made a right at the next corner, and I rolled my
eyes when I realized where he was headed. I thought we were
going to a bar close by and having one drink. Yeah, right. I
should have known he was going to take me to his favorite
hangout. Straight Shooters. A gay bar. Not that I mind. Hell, I

sometimes have more fun with gay men than I do with straight mothafuckas, who are too busy trying to run game.

I climbed out just as Tristan came over switching his skinny ass toward me in knee-high, red leather boots. I'm hating, because he's got a walk that's out of this world, like he's related to Ms. J from *America's Next Top Model*. He's wearing black jeans, a white blouse and a red leather jacket with a wide belt cinched tight around his small waist. Tristan's five foot ten with mile-long legs. I'm barely five six, so he definitely makes a statement walking beside me.

I frowned with annoyance. "I thought you said one drink."

"We are!" Tristan batted his eyelashes, trying to look innocent. I know there is no way he's leaving early. Thank goodness I drove my own car. "I hope you ain't using me as an excuse to hook up with Brandon tonight."

Tristan pointed his long nail in the air. "Gurlfriend, puhleeze! He's yesterday's news."

"Since when?"

He snapped his fingers. "Since I found out he was messing around. Don't you know that sneaky bastard left a message for another bitch on my damn answering machine?"

"What!" I tried not to laugh but couldn't help myself.

I could tell he didn't see anything the least bit funny. "I guess he thought he was calling that bitch's house."

I shrugged. "At least you found out early."

"You right, because I was ready to rock his mothafuckin' world." He winked and signaled for me to follow him inside.

The club was real tasteful and clean with small intimate tables and chairs and low lighting. There was a big stage in the middle. Tristan moved to a long table in the back that was occupied by friends of his. Two of them I had met before. Coco and Mercedes. Both men were prettier than me.

Mercedes glanced down at the watch on his wrist. " 'Bout time you bitches got here."

"I know that's right." Coco gave Tristan a high five as he slid in the seat next to him.

"Sorry I'm late, but if y'all weren't listening, let me tell you, the show tonight was off the hook! Matter fact, let me introduce the rest of y'all to the hostess with the mostess, Ms. Nikki Truth."

I waved and took the chair at the far end.

The other he/she I didn't know started squirming in his seat. "Oooh! Girlfriend, your show is the bomb! I never miss it."

Mercedes gave a rude snort. "She ain't lying. You've even answered her calls a few times."

I gave the one with the blond weave a long look. "Oh, yeah? When did you call?"

She looked uncomfortable. "Last month."

Mercedes filled in the details. "Girlfriend, here was Oasis. She called telling you her man insisted on the cat sleeping in the bed with them."

Laughing, I nodded my head. "Oh, yeah, I remember. I told you to tell him to get rid of the cat or you were leaving his ass."

"Yeah, and the next day he packed his shit and left," Oasis announced with disgust.

"Damn. I'm sorry."

"Wasn't your fault," she said, and made an exaggerated show of fanning herself. "I think that cat was licking a lot more than just his paws under those covers."

The table roared with laughter. Tristan signaled for a waiter and we both ordered a martini. The deejay was rocking some old school. I had gotten my drink and was having fun with the others when I felt someone tap me on the shoulder. I looked up, and it was a young slender woman with her head shaved bald and jeans hanging low on her hips.

"Yo, ma, you wanna dance?"

I looked up into the most amazing brown eyes I'd seen in a long time. Her lashes were naturally long and incredibly thick. Mascara had nothing to do with it. I would give anything to have eyes like that. I don't know how long I stared at her before I finally shook my head. "Nah, boo. I'm strictly dickly."

The look she gave me rang loud and clear. She could do anything a man could do, only better. "Yo, don't knock it till you try it."

I smiled. "Not knocking it. I just prefer my dick to be attached, not strapped on."

"A'ight, ma. If you change your mind, you know where to find me." With a nod of her head, she turned on the soles of her Air Force Ones.

I watched her walk away and had to admit she had a hell of a swagger that made my nipples tighten. Damn, had it been that long since I had some?

I raised my hand and quickly ordered another drink. Yep, Tristan was right. I needed some dick—quick!

2

Trinette

"Trinette, open the got-damn door!"

All I wanted was a tennis bracelet. Instead, I had some knucklehead banging on my bathroom door, trippin' about a photograph he shouldn't have found in the first place. I don't know what it is, but once you give a brotha some, he seems to lose his damn mind.

The evening had started off perfect. I had made a fabulous dinner of a tossed salad and Cheeseburger Macaroni Hamburger Helper. Afterward, we moved up to my bedroom, where I gave Cory a massage. The entire time I was rubbing oil all over him, I was thinking about the beautiful one-carat diamond and ruby bracelet I saw at Jared that looked gorgeous on my arm. Ready to get down to business, I flipped Cory onto his back and rode him as if he were a mechanical bull. Ms. Netta got mad skills, and I had the brotha speaking in tongues. I just knew that by the time I was finished with him there was no way he was going to deny me my bracelet. But before I could even begin hinting about jewelry, that idiot came and then had the nerve to fall asleep. I was so pissed off, I decided to treat myself to a hot bubble bath before I put his ass out, and had barely put my big toe in the water when Cory slammed his fist against the door, scaring the shit out of me. Now all I wanted was for him to get the hell out of my house.

"Cory, I ain't in the mood," I warned.

"I want an answer," he demanded.

"Take your nosy ass home!"

"Yo, I ain't going nowhere till you tell me the truth!"

Damn! After reaching for my washcloth, I mopped beads of sweat from my forehead. The lukewarm water did nothing to cool my raging temper. "I already told you the truth," I mumbled.

"Then why you got this mothafucka's picture in your drawer?"

What the hell was he doing in my drawer? Didn't his mama teach him, if you go looking for trouble, you're sure to find it? Besides, it was my house. If he wasn't gone by the time I finished my bath, as soon as I dried off, I was putting his ass out.

When it comes to men, I know when to cut my losses. Well, I was there. I was tired of Cory's bullshit and his crooked dick. "I already told you. I forgot it was in there."

He snorted rudely. "You must think I'm stupid or something. I know you're still fucking him. Now open this door before I knock it down!"

Leaning forward, I turned the faucet on, adding more hot water to the tub while also trying to drown out his nagging voice. This is what I got for inviting his ass to my house. For once, I should have listened to Nikki.

Why is it after you give a brotha some coochie they think they own you? I ain't never been able to figure that shit out. There was no ring on my finger. Well . . . at least not this week. He wasn't paying my bills, yet Cory had the audacity to go through my personal belongings looking for some shit to trip about. A photograph he had no business finding in the first place.

Sinking lower into the water, I allowed my mind to wander back eight years, to the day I met Leon Montgomery. The first man I ever loved and the man I later married. He was also the man whose photograph Cory found in my drawer.

"Trinette, you hear me talking to you!" Cory banged on the door again and broke through my thoughts.

I shook my head while wondering how the hell I ended up with a psycho. I guess I had to take part of the blame. I should have been honest and told Cory I was married. My bad. I screwed up. I just didn't think that bit of information was important, considering we'd only been seeing each other two weeks and I didn't expect it to last much longer. It couldn't. There was nothing he or any other man could do for me but give me their money, buy me nice things, and lick Ms. Netta's coochie. Plain and simple. *Hmmm.* I guess this meant I wouldn't be getting that bracelet.

I don't know why I went out with Cory in the first place. It wasn't like he was my type. He's a pretty boy with gray eyes and wavy hair. I don't do pretty boys, because they spend more time in front of the mirror than I do. And I definitely can't have that. However, when I first spotted him at the gym, all I could do was stare as he used the equipment. I wasn't staring because he had muscles on top of muscles. I was staring because I had seen his face in the newspaper two months before after he had won the Missouri Lottery. $100k. While I watched, I wondered what it would take for me to get his attention. An idea finally hit me. I moved over to the deltoid machine and purposely faked ignorance. Sure enough, Cory came to my aid. It took everything I had not to run my tongue across his massive biceps. Then after a few minutes of proper instruction, he asked me out. Cory was shorter than my usual sponsors, but since his pockets were fat, I was more than willing to make an exception.

Big mistake.

"Trinette!"

I turned the water off because with him banging on the door and hollering like some damn fool, relaxing was totally out of the question. I climbed out and reached for a towel.

"Boo, why you lying to me? Huh? I want an answer!"

His whining was quickly wearing my nerves. I dried off and reached for my robe, hanging on the back of the bathroom door. "Lie to you about what?" I asked as I swung the door open. Would you believe the fool had the nerve to have tears in his eyes?

I rolled my eyes and moved over to my dresser drawer that was still sitting wide open. A colorful array of Victoria's Secret garments had been thrown every which way. Organization has never been one of my strengths, but that was beside the point.

Cory flung the photo back into the drawer. "I can't believe this shit! Everything I've done for you and this is how you treat me."

"Hold up. Everything like what?" Because he had yet to spend any *real* money on me. I reached for the remote and turned the television off. I wanted to make sure I didn't miss a single word of what he was about to say.

"I just made breakfast for you last weekend."

I laughed as I closed the drawer and moved to take a seat on the end of my queen-size bed. "Since when is popping two Eggo waffles into the toaster considered cooking?"

His brow bunched as he spoke. "It's the thought that counts. Besides, last week we went out to dinner and a movie."

"Oooh! Big spender. You took me to Steak 'n Shake with a coupon, and the movie was a matinee." Now, I don't have a problem with cutting corners. Lord knows my broke ass does when I don't have a choice. What pissed me off was we dropped by Walmart on the way so he could stuff my purse with candy and soda. He better recognize. Ms. Netta is used to being wined and dined by a man. I didn't mind giving a brother a little coochie for monetary gain. Hell, usually at this point in the relationship, brothas are passing hundred dollar bills my way to support my insatiable shopping habit, but not this broke joke. The money stopped coming my way after the first week. I'm not gonna front. Cory bought me a pair of diamond earrings, took me on a shopping spree in Chicago the weekend before, and even gave me two thousand dollars when I lied and told him my car was about to be repossessed. But for the past several days, all he wanted to do is lie in my bed and watch television. Uh-uh, as far as I was concerned, we still had thousands of dollars to spend. Or at least that's what I thought before I picked up his pants and tossed them at him, then noticed a crumpled piece of paper on the floor. He was still going on and on about finding Leon's picture and demanding to know who the dude was when I reached down and picked the piece of paper up and stared at it.

-131.48

What the hell? It couldn't be right. There was no way in hell Cory's account was negative in less than three months. But Wachovia Bank was the name on the debit card he had been swiping all over town the past two weeks. Or at least until the previous Thursday when we'd gone to get gas and he'd acted like the strip on the back of the card was bad. It was then that I wondered why. His fake ass was broke. I couldn't believe I let him play me like that.

Cory tried to speak, but I held up a hand, silencing him. "You know what, Cory? There's a lotta things I will tolerate, but never someone going through my personal belongings. So listen to what I am about to say. It's over between us. Now leave!"

He was pacing back and forth across the length of my small room. His chest was heaving and his hands were balled by his sides. He looked hurt. A muscle twitched at his dimpled cheek. His eyes were glassy. I wished I could feel sorry for him, but he'd used up all his chances. Besides, his behavior was starting to scare me.

I rose from the bed. "Cory, I'm not gonna ask you again."

"I ain't going nowhere till you tell me who that motha-fucka is!"

He moved all up in my face like he was about to beat a sis-tah down. I met him eye to eye. I'm no punk, but I'm no fool either. My heart was beating rapidly against my ribs. I took a step back just to be on the safe side. "Whoever he is, he obvi-ously has more money than you have, Mr. Lottery Winner." I balled up the ATM receipt and tossed it at his head. He picked it up, uncrumpled it, and stared down at it. Busted! The em-barrassed look on his face was priceless.

"You need to leave."

He moved toward me. "I said I ain't going nowhere."

"Now, listen to what I'm about to say. Koolaid's only a phone call away. So the choice is yours. Either get out or get put out," I said, with a combination of anger and fear marking my every word. Not that I needed my brother's help. With a quick left hook, I was almost certain I could get in a few good licks. However, since he knew my brother by reputation, the threat sounded much more effective.

Cory stared at me for a long moment like he was contem-plating his next move, then he reached out and tried to hold me in his arms. "Why you doin' me like this? I thought you were feelin' me, boo."

"That was before I discovered your ass was broke." I jumped out of his reach, moved around my bed for the phone, and made a show of punching numbers. "I'm calling Koolaid." I was really calling time and temperature, but he didn't need to know that.

"A'ight, I'll go, but this discussion ain't over," he replied, his eyes flashing with anger. "You still ain't told me who that nigga is in the photo."

I punched END on my cordless but continued to hold it in my hand just in case I needed to clock the fool upside his head. "We don't have shit else to talk about, and the man in the photo is none of your business."

He gave me a look of disbelief. "Oh, so it's like that?"

"Yeah, it's like that."

"Fuck you, then, you gold-digging bitch!"

See, this is what I was talking about. Take a deep breath, Netta. Any other time, I would have kicked a brotha in his nuts for calling me a bitch, but since he was getting the hell out of my house, I allowed the comment to slide.

While I kept an eye on him, Cory quickly slipped into a sweatshirt lying at the end of the bed. As soon as his Jordans were back on his feet, he made a show of grabbing everything he'd left at my house over the last two weeks, which wasn't hard to do, considering I kept most of it in a small box next to the door. Cory had gotten too comfortable. I'd been telling him to take his shit back home to his mama, because I wasn't about to be washing some negro's stinky-ass draws.

Cory grabbed the box, then took his time walking to the door as if I might change my mind. Halfway down the hall, he paused and looked me directly in the eyes. "Once I walk out that door, I ain't ever steppin' up in here again."

"You promise," I mumbled, then stepping around him, I went to the door and swung it open. "Have a nice night."

Suddenly Cory wasn't the tough guy anymore. Tears were running down his face, and thick white spit was in the corners of his mouth. "Why you doin' me like this?" he whispered.

My stomach did a nosedive. Damn, I hate to see a man cry. I almost felt sorry for him. "Because I told you I wasn't looking for a serious relationship. Obviously you forgot the rules since you decided to go rummaging through my stuff."

"Yeah, a'ight." He leaned forward and tried to kiss me. I quickly backed up. I'd be damned if he was going to touch me with that foul shit near his lips.

Cory shook his head like I was making a big mistake. "You a trip," he said as he stepped out of the door.

"No, you tripped!" I spat as I slammed the door and immediately locked it behind him. I then moved over to the window and watched out the corner of the blinds as he loaded the backseat of his orange Mitsubishi Eclipse. Bitch-ass car. I'd been teasing him since day one that he drove a gay-ass ride. I even refused to be caught dead riding in the passenger side, which meant most dates we rolled in my Benz.

I kept watching as he climbed behind the wheel. There was no way I was taking my eye off him. I had learned long ago to never turn your back on a brotha after you kicked him to the curb. I made that mistake once and had sugar put in my tank.

I waited until Cory had reached the corner, then sighed with relief as I made my way up to my bedroom. Once there I collapsed on the bed and stared up at the ceiling, wondering if my husband and his money would ever be enough. So far, the answer was no.

Damn! I really wanted that bracelet.